RANGE 19:
The Mission Continues

RANGE 19:
The Mission Continues

BY
S. J. "SANDY" WHITE
WITH CONTRIBUTIONS BY
Y-MOE

iUniverse, Inc.
New York   Bloomington

RANGE 19: The Mission Continues

iUniverse books may be ordered through booksellers or by contacting:

iUniverse
1663 Liberty Drive
Bloomington, IN 47403
www.iuniverse.com
1-800-Authors (1-800-288-4677)

Because of the dynamic nature of the Internet, any Web addresses or links contained in this book may have changed since publication and may no longer be valid. The views expressed in this work are solely those of the author and do not necessarily reflect the views of the publisher, and the publisher hereby disclaims any responsibility for them.

ISBN: 978-1-4401-3932-1 (sc)
ISBN: 978-1-4401-3933-8 (ebk)

Printed in the United States of America

iUniverse rev. date: 05/12/2009

DEDICATION

This book is dedicated to my wife Gwen, who consistently maintained my sense of balance, attitude, patience, pride and promise. She is my inspiration and soul mate.

ACKNOWLEDGEMENTS

First, I would like to thank Y-Moe for the many contributions he made to the writing of this work. His experiences and technical knowledge gained while assigned to the unit on Fort Bragg, N.C. with the largest and best mess hall in the Army were invaluable. Secondly, I want to thank all of the soldiers, sailors, airmen, and marines serving in our armed forces today. As George Orwell said, you are the reason we can sleep peacefully at night, knowing you are there to protect us from those who would visit us.with.harm.in.mind.

PREFACE

From the first book, RANGE 19: A New Beginning, published by iuniverse.com over twelve years have passed, and with time comes change.

The RANGE 19 team flourished under Simon Arpslot; affectionately known as 'Marplot, or simply The Plot'. His subtle leadership had combined with Colonel Timothy Michael 'Trademark' Slaughter's heavy hand to balance the team effort, and they survived with minor exceptions.

In the years since they had disposed of Microtech's CEO Michael Bailey for his crimes against the military, they had worked solely for the Chief Justice of the Supreme Court conducting what he characterized as 'sanitation missions'; but which were in effect kidnapping operations with the result being either complete disappearance or covert turnover to foreign authorities, as was the case of Julius Brown and his opium operation.

In recognition of said success, the Chief Justice had increased their budget and fought to get them the latest in high tech equipment that couldn't be traced to them; or to the Chief Justice or the court itself. He was very careful about that since they were still operating under the old

Clinton executive order and it's ten member Special Access Program (Clinton, Justice Nagey, and the eight members of RANGE 19). To the best of his knowledge, no one had briefed either of the Bushes about it's existence; and he hoped it could stay that way, particularly through the next administration regardless of who won the upcoming election.

After Slaughter and Sheila returned from their honeymoon they were surprised to find that they had their own bungalow attached to the hootch. The Plot had it built in a space at the side of the existing hootch's North end that was just large enough for a one bedroom, one bath, kitchen and lanai sitting area so they now had their own little domicile while still at the island itself. It was a wedding gift from their collective group: Master Sergeants retired Richard `Dyke' Dykestra and Roosevelt `Bunny' Buchanan, USAF Staff Sergeant retired Jesus Gonzales `Chico' Sirconi, an ex New York City detective by the name of Guido Lemke whom his wife had divorced because she refused to move to Florida; and the Peruvian witch doctor Ralph Leigh. That made eight.

From time to time, Slaughter, Dyke, and Bunny would travel back to Fort Bragg, N.C. ostensibly to attend a funeral or promotion ceremony, but really to visit "The Unit" and gather what intelligence information they could to prevent any unwanted intervention during their own operations. Slaughter's active duty status helped with much of that, but as time went by, many of his old friends had departed and younger faces met him with suspicion. Likewise, Dyke and Bunny found themselves tracking down old friends and operators who had retired and gone to work as body guards, heads of security for casinos in Las Vegas and elsewhere, or stayed at home with the wife for a change; which didn't last long for most.

There were two minor exceptions to the tranquility of the RANGE 19 team. The first was when their faithful dog Crud died. Although the dog had been raised by Slaughter, it seemed as if the whole crew had first rights in the bereavement of his passing. When Slaughter suggested he go to the pound and pick out a puppy, they all insisted on going with him and almost came to blows over the final selection; a two month old yellow haired chow mix with a big head and purple tongue that hung out of his mouth just like Crud's.

The second was when Robin and Dobbin Brain, aunt and nephew computer geniuses, had fought over Dobbin's desire to remain at the Hootch and work for the Plot and his medical company that he had founded while going through amputee rehabilitation at the Veterans Administration Hospital; which was now a multimillion dollar business making artificial skin, prosthetic arms and legs, and doing extensive research into biomechanical integration and tactile enhancement. Dobbin, at the time, had just turned 18 and had finished his four year science degree in computer programming and had simply said he was going to stay at the hootch. Robin was upset, but knew her nephew would not change his mind once it was made up. Both of these exceptions were considered and forgotten, except by Slaughter. He still missed Crud's horrendous crab farts, but Crud Junior was getting the hang of it and Slaughter felt sure he would be able to meet that challenge in the coming months.

Other than that, it had been a fast ten years for them all, but somehow stable. The Locklear girls still came to play scrabble and invent new meaning to the English language as well as Dyke and Guido's libido. Slaughter had taught Dobbin how to SCUBA dive and shoot a handgun. The shooting was mostly at the alligators that would wander close enough to get a shot at during daylight hours; but at night he could use a flashlight and and put the laser sight's red dot between their eyes with ease.

Sheila was content, to a point. She still had visions of a Pulitzer, but knew she'd never get it with the Plot's editorializing and as a U.S. Marshal. She'd decided already that she needed to shed that appointment, but hadn't told anyone yet.

Disgraced ex-Major Leopold Farnsworth had shed Doc Leigh's frog juice induced hypnotic suggestion that he was in love with Bill Clinton several years back; and was confined to the Bethesda mental ward as a patient undergoing post traumatic stress as a result of stitching his fingers together at his job as a seamstress, and then parading his bloody "handiwork" around the workshop. Once he was released he ran a newspaper and magazine stand in front of a porno store in old town D.C. until one day while he was cleaning up he found an old issue of Housekeeper magazine about Slaughter's marriage to one of their reporters. He immediately knew what was wrong all these years; he still wanted to kill the bastard. So he closed his bank account, which was considerable since he hadn't spent any money on anything other than necessities in ten years, and packed his bags and set off for Florida; again. This time he would not fail.

As always, this is a work of fiction, much of which is based on real people I've known and worked with. Many of them have bad language and a lack of political correctness; or a willingness to "pick up a turd by the clean end" as the winning definition states. Also, any work of fiction may contain exaggerations, embellishments, and outrageous content. I accept full responsibility for any and all of it. I did it for fun. If it offends the reader, that's too bad.

CONTENTS

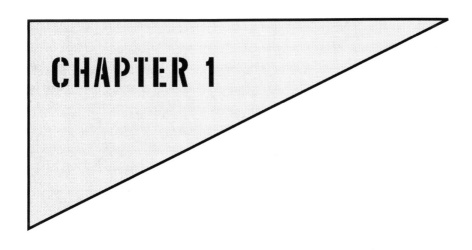

CHAPTER 1

THE CHIEF JUSTICE OF THE SUPREME COURT was not happy. In fact, he was seriously considering closing down the whole RANGE 19 operation; but he knew that would be very risky at this point, mainly due to the high potential of it becoming public knowledge. The Supreme Court had no constitutional authority to execute covert justice on its own, and that's exactly what Chief Justice Nagy had chartered RANGE 19 to do; without any paper trails leading back to him or the supreme court. High level bad guys and gals would just disappear in such a way that all their ill gotten gains would be available for distribution to those victimized and collaterally damaged, one way or another. That's what he liked most about the arrangement. He had been convinced that all of this was possible and necessary by one of his closest advisors and friends since he was the Attorney General of California, Simon Arpslot, more affectionately known only by his closest friends as Marplot; or, simply the "Plot".

He and the Plot had justified and obtained executive order approval from a highly conservative Attorney General who had president Clinton's confidence; and he had slipped the executive order in with other documents needing the president's signature. The order had gotten limited funding, Justice department appointments as U.S. Marshals for the entire RANGE 19 team, recall to active duty in the rank of Colonel for one Timothy Michael "Trademark" Slaughter, and even a U. S. Marshal's appointment for Slaughter's new wife and RANGE 19 Public Affairs Officer Sheila Hobgood. And it was all classified within a Special Access Program (SAP) so as to carefully control the flow of information. Not even the FBI or CIA knew anything about the executive order. Guido Lempke was the only additional SAP billet approved by the appointing authority, Colonel Slaughter, which included an appointment as a U.S. Marshal. Guido laughed at that and said he could get through more doors with his New York City gold detective shield and ID than any U.S. Marshal's badge.

And now, after ten years in what was supposed to be a Thai prison, Julius Brown had escaped from his palace jailhouse in Thailand and was at his new palace in South America at Rio De Janeiro, making opium tonnage move as if nothing but his long desired divorce had happened. He had managed to pigeon hole a hundred million dollars in an offshore account which he could access with a phone call, and the RANGE 19 intelligence had failed to pick up on that little bit of information thus allowing the current situation in which Chief Justice Nagy was very unhappy with. And he couldn't discuss any of it with his peers on the court. They had all made it plainly clear they didn't want any part of his scheme; but at the same time had supported him in concept with their silence about it. The idea being that the U.S. needed an architecture by which to deal with very powerful people in such a way as to either prevent any public knowledge of the extent of evil they had committed, or without going through years of litigation and expense when the evil was self evident; or both. So Chief Justice Nagy picked up the telephone and dialed a number from memory, and told the person on the other end to have the connection to the "Hootch" at RANGE 19 activated by the time he got there. "There" was a converted coat room from earlier days which he had converted to his own secure briefing room and was only three doors down the hall from his own office.

Seated at his "control room" chair, Chief Nagey stared at a blank four foot by five foot TV screen waiting for Simon Arpslot "The Plot" to show up. As the minutes ticked by he became more and more infuriated and began tapping his fingers on the armrest causing the TV screen to flash photos and images of all sorts of places and things around the world.

"I wish you wouldn't do that sir, I'm trying to get the feed in from South America.", his trusted young technician said quietly. Then, "Here it is now sir."

"Sorry to keep you waiting Mr. Chief Justice, but we were having trouble transferring your signal from the Hootch to where we are in Rio." Marplot said. His big bald head took up most of the screen, but in the background the Chief Justice could see mountains and the tops of buildings, and even a commercial airplane taking off from some distant airport. He continued with, "We're transmitting via satellite relay from the roof of our hotel using the suitcase module appropriated from the U.S. consulate in Rio. We've been able to track Mr. Brown to a villa he owns on the top of a small mountain overlooking the ocean."

At this point Slaughter burst into the screen stating flatly, "He's got about 30 local militia as hired guards and electronic security, but I believe we can get in and get him out without any trouble. We'll need an airplane with a ramp; preferably a CASA, and an oxygen console with six untraceable ram air parachute systems - - -"

"Stop.", the Chief Justice roared. "Who do you think I am, K Mart, Wal Mart, or maybe the Defense Supply Agency and the U.S. Air Force? All this shit is your idea in the first place; you handle it Slaughter. That's why you're a Colonel. Put Marplot back on."

Once the Plot was back in view the Chief Justice smoothly asked, " And just how did Mr. slippery assed Brown wind up in Rio in the first place? I thought you had everything under wraps in Thailand Plot.", the Chief Justice fumed; then, "Aw forget it. I know what happened. Your RANGE 19 intelligence lacks depth. I'm sending Elmore to Rio to help you. You should've known a big time drug dealer would know how to hide, move, and invest money, don't you think?"

"You're right Mr. Chief Justice, and I know who Elmore is. He'll be a big help. Will he be billeted in the SAP or made privy to the executive order and will you brief him prior to his arrival?", the plot asked.

"No, no, and no. Mr. Elmore will be told nothing about the SAP or executive order, and you can brief him when he gets there. All I'm going to do is financially retain his services to help you. It's up to you to decide what you want to tell him about the mission to get Mr. Brown's money and make him disappear. And no, I'm not sending him to spy on your operation for me. You'll know when it's time to shut things down before I do anything to make that happen.", Chief Justice Nagey said sharply.

"I thank you for that Mr. Chief Justice, your magnificence.", the Plot said with all the sincerity he could muster.

"Blow it out your ass Plot. Tell me what went wrong."

"My contacts in the Cayman Islands didn't know Julius Brown. He went by James Julius; deposited certificates of demand, and they didn't make the connection until it was too late. I'm working on a better infrastructure within the offshore banking cartels. That may need some funding and I've got some ideas on how to set up accounts in all the banks to do a little hacking - - -"

"I don't need to know about the details. You just get Mr. James Julius Brown out of the visible future, and figure out a way to get all of his drug money transferred to the RANGE 19 accounts you're establishing in the islands without anything coming back to haunt us. Got that Arpslot?", as the Chief Justice of the U.S. Supreme Court slammed his phone down in his armrest, forgetting that the TV cameras and screens were still operating.

"Yes sir, your orneriness!" the Plot said with a smile and pushed the right button to sign off all transmission before that James Earl Jones baritone could make any response.

The Chief Justice sat quietly for a moment thinking of his friend and confidant in Rio De Janeiro, Brazil and all that he and the RANGE 19 team had accomplished in the past twelve years; all the people they had exposed or made go away, and all the evil undone at minimal or no cost to the taxpayer. And he wondered just how long they would remain untouched by some bureaucratic entity snooping through dusty records. They had already "stood down" two times due to outside interest in "Who or what" RANGE 19 was until Dade County Sheriff Terry Baugh had gone public stating that it was a shooting range for his department that was also a cooperative effort with the state of Florida Department of Wildlife during the existing alligator population problem. That seemed to allay any local fears of a Nazi skinhead group running the place; and the cover had not been challenged again.

Then his thoughts turned to that reporter for Housekeeper magazine; and oh by the way, Slaughter's wife. Her monthly articles on "What's New in Crime" had become the bedrock for the magazines hugely increased circulation and had set the standard for exposing the mighty and powerful. Sheila Hoobgood had kept her maiden name and it was now recognized in 90% of the households in America as well as abroad. The Chief Justice was concerned about her fame becoming a liability. He would have to speak with Slaughter about any further need for a "Public Affairs Officer"; especially one appointed as.a.U.S.. Marshal.

Slaughter, on the other hand, couldn't be happier with his lot. At first he wasn't sure about married life, but he found out quickly that it suited him just fine. Sheila had found her way into his heart. He would do anything for her, up to a point. Lately she had indicated a dislike for carrying a gun and badge as a U.S. Marshal when her real function was to write articles for her magazine, limited in scope and detail as they must be. That little tidbit was what ate at her the most, but there wasn't much Slaughter could do about that, except coo in her ear in bed about how much good she was doing for public knowledge - - - and his hunger for her body. That usually redirected the efforts to his favor, but he could still sense something needed to be done to cut her loose. He knew it was the Pulitzer prize, but not how much it really meant to her. The real issue for her was the quandary of being offered very high paying jobs at prestigious magazines and newspapers, which would require her to relocate from the Hootch; and the knowledge that any of the several articles she had already published could have been expanded to Pulitzer level. She simply had to figure out a way to take advantage of where she was at to be able to exploit a RANGE 19 mission without any compromise.

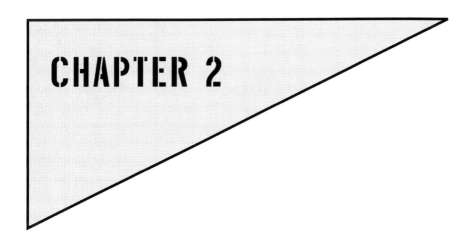

CHAPTER 2

FARNSWORTH TOOK THE BUS. IT WOULD GIVE him time to plan and get accustomed to having people around him that were considered "normal". After two years in the mental ward at Bethesda he knew two things to be true. One, there is no such thing as "normal"; and, two, psychiatric wards and psychiatrists were "not normal". They both operated from the premise that their own existence was the only solution to self actualization and, of course, gainful employment. His new hero was the big Indian in "One Flew Over the Coocoo's Nest". But that was all really yesterday's stuff. He managed to convince his "sweetpea" shrink that his internalized, misdirected attention caused him to revisit his self destructive behavior as strictly an isolated, attention seeking thing, and that he could handle outside life without that need anymore. But the humiliation of what had happened to him because of what that squat Peruvian had done to him would never be forgotten. He was a West Point graduate at the top of his class with a bright future in the Army until that damned Slaughter had pressed charges against him for sexual assault and gotten him thrown out in disgrace. Now he felt violated by some witch doctor's spell he had endured, and been ridiculed for; over a U. S. president no less. His brain had been severely messed with and both Slaughter and that bow legged "smiley faced" Peruvian would pay with their lives.

Leopold Farnsworth knew he had to calm down. The woman sitting next to him was clutching her purse under her chin and looking at him like his expression was as enraged as he felt. He had to get a grip, so he turned his head to look out of his window at the passing telephone poles. He was thankful he had taken the window seat and could ignore the woman's obvious apprehension of his displayed emotions for awhile. Then, after a few moments, he turned to her and introduced himself as Major, retired, U.S. Army Leopold Farnsworth III, headed to Key West, Florida on vacation and had she been there before; and did she know a good place to stay with a beach front view? The woman said "No, and no.", and turned away to look out of the other side's windows. Farnsworth leaned over and whispered in her left ear, "Well fuck you and the horse you rode in on bitch." She grabbed her bags and moved to an empty seat in the rear of the bus.

Farnsworth, for some hidden reason, felt much better knowing he could pull up the middle armrest and curl up once it turned dark and he felt like taking a nap. A brilliant move on his part. And as the telephone poles streaked by his window, he analyzed the threats he would face in getting to Slaughter and the Hootch. The surveillance stuff at the dock he already knew about and could deal with. Getting to the Hootch complex was his first objective; but, he was only one person who could do so much. Maybe he needed to rethink how he could place firepower on the Hootch without actually having to get on the little island. Air strike! He would hire a plane and bomb the place. Or just learn how to fly and do it himself; maybe an ultra light would be enough to do the job. He was already an expert with the Army's T-10 static line parachute. Yeah! HooAhh!! That was the ticket. He would get ultra light qualified by the manufacturer and buy himself a "bomber". He only weighed 127 lbs. He figured he could carry another 100 lbs of dynamite sticks, or homegrown bottles of high octane gas and hankies, or even one big duffle bag of fertilizer and fuel oil topped off with about six M80 firecrackers as a detonator. Ahh, the possibilities were endless.

Farnsworth pulled up the armrest in the middle of the two seats and curled his five foot nine inch 127 pounds up into a fetal position as the sun was setting and shadows were flashing past the windows. He closed his eyes and began to review his priorities and decided he had to kill the witch doctor first. That meant he had to catch him either before or after he was headed to or from the island. He figured he'd just shoot him in the head at the dock and be done with it. The alligators would take care of the rest. It was Slaughter he wanted to torture, but blowing up the Hootch at the island with a firebomb would be satisfaction enough. He just hoped the $28,450 he had in his bag would be enough to cover all the bills to accomplish his mission. This one would take more time and planning. He would have to be smart and patient. He wasn't really thinking about getting away with it or going to jail; or even what he would do after it was all over. He was focused, and sleep came easily now with visions of Slaughter cooking on a spit with the natives of Peru dancing around him.

At the bus station in Jacksonville, Florida Farnsworth was able to take a shower, shit, shave, and change clothes due to the three hour layover. While doing that, he noticed for the first time in years how long he had let his hair grow. Then he remembered the way the frog juice had changed the way he had seen himself as a woman and not a man. Well, so much for that crap. He went straight to a barber shop and got a "high and tight"; then thought that might have been too drastic since it reminded him of being a plebe at West Point again, so he bought a John Deere hat for $1.50 at the flea market next to the bus stop. That was better. He even decided to grow a Wild Bill Hickock mustache and goatee as well.

At the Orlando, Florida bus stop he was robbed in the "men's" room by two "salt and pepper" faggots. The black guy with an ice pick and the white guy with the switchblade. They took all his money and even his remaining bus ticket to cash in. They made him strip and took all of his clothes, even his socks and shoes. They had tied his hands behind his back and around the base of the commode and stuffed his underwear in his mouth and taped over it with 90 mile an hour tape. They had used his belt to tie his ankles together. All he could do was groan as loudly as he could, but that wasn't very loud. It seemed like an eternity before a crowd of men came into the place to relieve themselves, all talking about something or another, before one of them heard his unintelligible pleas and looked over the top of the stall door.

The cops showed in short order, and were obviously amused; but were polite and provided him with a set of coveralls they had on hand to crawl into suspicious places to protect their uniforms. Farnsworth looked like a starved "Grapes of Wrath" farmer when he told the cops that he was veteran of the gulf war they felt the need to dig into the Police Department's discretionary fund, which was mostly a very large amount of confiscated drug money, and get Farnsworth back on the road with $1000 in his pocket.

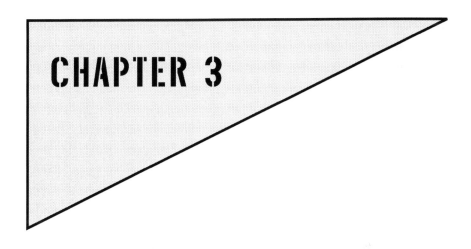

CHAPTER 3

FARNSWORTH WAS VERY GRATEFUL, BUT SITTING ON the bus to Miami next to a woman with more jewelry on her than Tiffany's had in its showroom he felt like dirt. And she talked and talked; mostly about her late husband, God rest his soul, who had treated her like a queen all of her married life. It was nauseating, but Farnsworth kept thinking about how much he could get in a pawn shop for just one of the rings on her fingers; or the necklace, my God the necklace would bring ten grand at least. It had all three stone groups. There was a huge diamond, at least two or three carats, and a matching ruby and emerald on each side, like yesterday's ruby, today's diamond, and tomorrow's emerald.

He looked at her for the length of time it took her to respond and he said, "That's the most beautiful necklace I've ever seen. It's got the three main stones arranged as if it were yesterday's ruby, today's diamond, and tomorrow's emerald."

"Oh my God!", the woman exclaimed. "That's exactly what my late husband said when he gave it to me on our 25th wedding anniversary. How perceptive you are. What's your name, if you don't mind me asking?" she swooned, wafting expensive perfume his way.

"I apologize madam. My name is Leopold Farnsworth the third. He had almost said "the turd", consciously avoiding his classmates' overuse of the difference. West Point class of 83'. I'm on my way to the everglades to study the environmental impact of local vegetable farming for the government.", he said and smiled as if he were in charge of all vegetable outcome in Florida.

When they arrived at the Miami bus terminal the driver found Mrs. Betsy Dowd, wife of machine tool mogul Donald Dowd, dead in her seat. It was determined later that she died of natural causes according to the medical examiner; and nobody on the bus could remember what the skinny farmer in the John Deere hat who was sitting next to her looked like.

Well now. Farnsworth had a pocket full of jewelry worth a bunch of money, but he knew he needed a fence to turn it into cash, which he desperately needed. He figured the best place of all to find a fence would be in the biggest pawn shop he could find. There were plenty of them on both sides of the streets in between the bars just looking both ways from the main entrance to the bus stop. He decided to try the place across the street and down a block named "The Prince of Pawn". If he acted fast, he thought, it would take weeks for the cops to finally figure out her jewelry was missing, and even longer for them to canvas all the pawn shops near the bus station.

He had to think of a reason for pawning so much expensive jewelry at once, but couldn't come up with anything reasonable; anything that wouldn't be out of the ordinary. So he decided he'd just try and pawn a ring that was actually worth maybe, five thousand dollars. He would then see where the conversation led.

Farnsworth walked straight up to the guy behind the counter and asked to speak to the owner, only to get, "The boss is busy. What've you got?"

Farnsworth didn't want to attract any unnecessary attention, so he simply said, "Something very expensive that I want your boss to see, or I'm gone."

The guy at the counter looked like he had been there before, many times, and shrugged his shoulders saying, "Yeah, yeah, yeah. All you Hank's are alike. Just a minute and I'll see if he wants to see you."

Big Bill Bogart was already looking through the one way mirror at the skinny guy in the John Deere hat wondering what the hell he had; or if he was another undercover asshole trying to make a bust on his fencing operation. Half the Miami cops on the beat in his area already knew they could count on Big Bill to give them what he could; small time of course. The big time stuff, well that was a different story altogether. He would have to go out front and see just what this clod hopper had to offer and tighten up his rope if he smelled of city hall.

"OK buddy, whatcha got? I'm a busy man. Don't waste my time.", Big Bill Bogart demanded while casting a 300 pound shadow over ex Major Leopold Farnsworth III.

"It's an heirloom from my grandmother. My grandfather gave it to her in 1926 and it's worth at least $12,000. I just need the money now so I can pay off the farm mortgage.", Farnsworth softly said.

"It ain't worth no $12,000 to me, I can tell you that buster.", Big Bill said. "But I might could go $3500 as he looked at the stone through his jeweler's loupe squeezed in his right eye.

"That's crazy. That is a five carat diamond stone; fine cut and flawless quality. I've got to get $12,000 to pay off that mortgage or I'll lose my farm.", Farnsworth pleaded.

"Sorry buddy. The most I could go would be four grand, period. Got anything else?" Big Bill asked with a smile that indicated he knew there was more. He'd seen these types before a hundred times.

"Even if I did have some more of my inheritance in jewelry, how do I even know you have that much money?", Farnsworth asked.

At that point, the guy behind the counter leveled a M1911 .45caliber automatic at his gut and said, "That's a bad question in this place buddy."

"Put it down Smiley. Mr. John Deere here, is just curious as to our ability to - - - negotiate. Right Mr. Deere?", Big Bill asked with a big smile on his face.

"Uh, yeah. That's right. You said $4000 for the ring. Here's a necklace worth ten times that much. Find me my twelve grand and both the ring and the necklace are yours. If not, then I'm outta here.", Farnsworth yelled.

"Whoa. Slow down partner. I can see you've got a dilemma with this kind of stuff as an inheritance; but I'll tell you what I'll do. You need to listen carefully to this my friend, because if you don't, and you blunder around trying to fence this stuff yourself, you'll wind up in jail. I'll give you $9,990.00 for the ring and the necklace so that a $10,000 number does not attract the attention of the IRS from either one of us. Got it?" Big Bill asked with a huge smile on his face.

Farnsworth still had more rings and bracelets in his pockets, but he couldn't resist Big Bill's logic and offer. He accepted a shoe box full of fives, tens, twentys, fiftys, and hundreds that took over 10 minutes to count out, and then quickly left headed to the street.

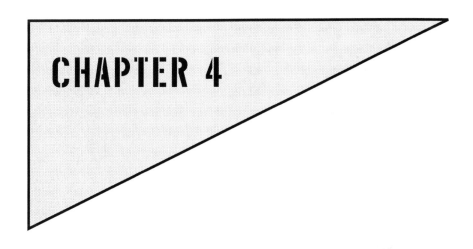

CHAPTER 4

S<small>ITTING UNDER A PATIO AWNING IN CUSHIONED</small> chairs on the rooftop of the El Presidente hotel in Rio, Slaughter and Marplot looked at each other and simultaneously said, "He's pissed."

Then Slaughter looked out over the roof at the landscape and asked, "Where in hell are we gonna get a CASA, oxygen console, and untraceable ram air parachute systems to infiltrate this turd's compound on top of a mountain; especially with these winds the way they are? And what about weapons? We may have to make this whole thing look like a kidnapping or robbery, ya know."

The Plot looked at him for a moment, and then said, "I've changed my mind. We walk."

"You gotta be shittin me Plot. That mountain he lives on has to be over 10,000' high; it'll take days to get there, and probably even longer to get him out that way.", Slaughter growled.

The Plot looked thoughtful for a moment, and then said, "I think I have the beginnings of a plan that will allow us to use a helicopter to get most of the way up the mountain to a staging area, and then back down the same way. I need to get a bag full of cash and talk to someone first. How about you getting a decent map we can work from, but don't go after anything our government has produced. Try the internet or the local drug store for a Michelin map; and we should expect to do a recon of the staging area once we select it. I'll be back in a few hours.", he said as he made his way to the door on the roof that led to a stairwell down to the elevator.

Elmore. That name brought back memories, not only of him, but of a red headed female pilot named Jill Slatterly who was recuperating in the VA hospital during the same time he was there. Elmore visited her regularly until one day he just stopped showing up. She had been shot down in her Blackhawk helicopter during Desert Storm and had broken her back in the crash. She had fully recovered and he had gotten a letter from her saying she was back in the air flying for an outfit that supported everything from Special Forces training and parachute testing at the Airborne Board at Fort Bragg, to actual in country operations in Afganistan. And if he ever saw Elmore again he should tell him to eat shit and die, thank you very much.

At the time Elmore was visiting her in the VA hospital, he was retired from the Army and working for the Defense Intelligence Agency (DIA) as a liaison officer to the Central Intelligence Agency (CIA), and was in a three month training exchange program. When that ended, he had to leave for a very sensitive overseas assignment he couldn't discuss with anyone.

It was a strange coincidence when they met. Marplot and "Slats", as she preferred to be called by her old call sign, sat alone together at the cafeteria in the hospital as they had been doing since she could walk while wearing a back brace, and she had joined him at the only table with two other empty seats. Then Elmore was standing there and had asked if he could join them. They said `certainly' and introduced themselves. Elmore just said, "I'm Elmore." Slats asked, "Elmore what?" Elmore said,

"Just Elmore". Slats broke out laughing and asked, "Is that like John NMI, no middle initial, Jones, or is your first name really `Just'; maybe short for `Justin'?

Without cracking a smile he replied, "No. My mother was a hot blooded Latino and my father was an Irishman with big feet. The night I was conceived, as my mother tells it, she yelled out 'El MORE, El MORE'. I don't like being called 'El' anything. So it's just Elmore if you please - - - Slats. And how did you come by that handle, anyway?"

Elmore's story tickled Slats and started her laughing so hard she slapped the table and sent a cup of coffee onto Elmore's lap, an incident that only made them all laugh even harder. When Slats finally stopped laughing she wiped the tears from her eyes and stuttered out, "From flight school. Fixed wing transition to dual engine jets that had slats in addition to flaps. Kept forgetting to put out the slats. Last name didn't help either. Scuse me. I gotta use the restroom.", and started laughing again all the way to the bathroom drawing strange looks from all those nearby.

"Jesus Marplot. I didn't think it was that funny", he said as he blotted his trousers and watched Slats walk away; but when he looked at Plot's purple face he couldn't help himself and started a muffled yuking.

Marplot had liked Elmore the instant they met and couldn't help but reply with, "You've got to be the biggest bull shitter ever conceived in daylight." And they both started laughing out loud. Over the next ten minutes it took Slats to compose herself and return, the Plot and Elmore had exchanged histories that were mostly truthful. Over the next three months they all became good friends. Elmore helped the Plot with some of his medical enterprises through some of his contacts who could help make electromechanical things do marvelous tricks with prosthetics.

Then one day Elmore, without saying good bye, just shook the Plot's hand and left. During his visits each time he had left Slats, he had given her a hug, and the first time he tried to leave without one, she called him back to get one. When he left the final time, he gave her the usual hug, took two steps away; and, then he turned around and gave her another one somewhat longer before he turned his back and left.

She knew that the Plot and Elmore had shared some of their

history with one another and often questioned the Plot about Elmore's background. When he stopped showing up she badgered him about what he did and who he worked for until the day she was discharged, but he couldn't tell her anything that would make any difference. Now he had to find her, somehow.

Back in his room he picked up his cell phone and autodialed a number to his contact at the VA. After the preambles he asked, "Can you get me Jill Slatterly's address and phone number?" His contact told him he owed him one, big time, and said he'd call him back with what he needed.

Slats was still in bed. She was hung over and didn't much care for the loud ringing in her ears that was coming from somewhere across the room. It would stop as the voice mail picked up and then started again almost immediately, so she finally got out of bed and went to find it. As she shuffle-stumbled toward the ringing she noticed she was naked and stopped for a moment to look for a robe and looked at herself in the full length mirror on her bathroom door. Not bad for 42 she thought. She put her hands on her hips and inhaled to fill her lungs to bursting. "Still trim and in shape", she thought, as a shiver went through her, making her nipples stick out suddenly, like popped circuit breakers. That damned phone kept ringing! She saw it, and grabbed it and demanded, "What?"

"Slats? This is Simon. Remember me?", he questioned, not sure it was her since he hadn't heard her voice in over 12 years.

"Plot. Is that you, you sorry sack of shit?", she almost yelled happily.

"It's me, my dear. How have you been?", he asked.

She climbed back in bed with the phone and told him how she'd landed the flying job; some of the good and some of the not so good, and how she missed their cafeteria times. Then she abruptly asked, "Have you heard anything out of that no good shit head Elmore?"

"Oddly enough, that's one of the reasons I'm calling. We've got a mission in Rio, where I'm calling from by the way, and we need a pilot whom we can count on. Elmore is part of the team, but he wanted me to call you first since he's not here yet. He wants to know if you can meet him at the Los Angeles (LAX) International terminal by tomorrow at noon.", the Plot toned as if nothing had ever happened between the two of them.

"Can you believe the balls on that SOB? He runs off without a word or even a postcard and now you are telling me he expects me to drop everything and fly from good old Smithfield, N.C. to Los Angeles. To just drop everything, fly all damned night cramped like a cabbage in a crate with no telling how many layovers just to meet his sorry ass? Now just why would I want to do that? Plot, you tell that sorry son-of-a-bitch to put it where the sun doesn't shine. I've got a nice cushy job right here with plenty of time off to get drunk and go naked. He can piss up a rope", she hollered into the phone.

"I know exactly how you feel dear. I'm asking you to put all that aside right now. This would be a personal favor to me. Trust me, we are perfectly legal and I assure you it's imperative that we have someone I can trust implicitly", the Plot soothed. I can't explain much here but trust me; it will all be clear as soon as you arrive. It's important and worthwhile and you would kick yourself in the ass later if you missed it.

The Plots words soothed Slat's initial attitude and woke her curiosity. In fact, a need to know what it was all about started to gnaw at her, to break down her initial resistance. She weakened," Well, I've got plenty of vacation time built up, and since it's a personal favor to you, I guess I can help you", she said, amazed at how easily she gave up.

"Excellent pardner, excellent".

Then before she could change her mind or ask any other questions he jumped in with, "Listen, I've made all of your arrangements: you leave from Raleigh, N. C. direct to LAX and then on to Rio, and return of course, all first class. There will be an envelope waiting for you at the Delta ticket counter that contains a new passport and $5000 expense money. I'll meet you both at the Rio airport when you arrive. I'm looking forward to seeing you again", he closed.

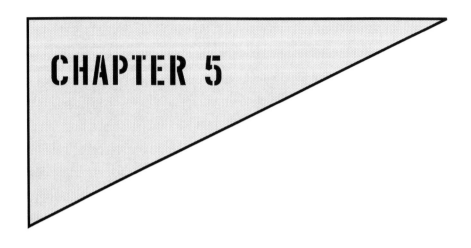

CHAPTER 5

Elmore spotted Slats as she entered the baggage area to reclaim her bags. He trailed her from a discreet distance as she move through the terminal to find the Crown Club. He didn't know how she would react when he met her but his optimism stuck a big grin on his face.

Although he'd been watching for her arrival he almost didn't recognize her. She stood more erect than she had when they first met and she was wearing a back brace. Instead of stiff uncertain steps, she walked with a long athletic stride. She had lost weight and was more attractive than he expected. Perky might describe her now, but not cheerleader perky: more just healthy perky. Her hair was hard to describe, more coppery flame than red or blond. Still, he was enough of a realist to avoid assuming Slats would welcome any boy-girl attention from him after the way he disappeared from her life. This would have to be business like, a professional approach.

It didn't work.

She spotted his reflection in the mirror-like finish off the wall behind the receptionist at the counter before he could try any approach. She spun around to face him, growling hoarsely, "Back up you son of a bitch so I can't kick you in the balls like you deserve."

The well coiffed pneumatic wanna-be-actress working at the Crown

Club counter had risen to greet her. She stood slack jawed with shock at the exchange. She recognized Slats from the photo she had been provided with when she approached, and had already retrieved her tickets for her follow on flight and the tan manila envelope from the lock box.

She had started with," Welcome to Los Angeles Ms. Slattery. Here are your tickets and an envelope for you," when she was rendered mute by the developing situation.

Slats spun back around to face the young woman; snatched the two envelopes from her hands, only nodding a 'thank you', and started back toward Elmore. He instinctively backed up keeping one knee slanted protectively across his groin and staying out of kicking distance. He circled around to back into the clubs lobby where he backed into a chair and sat down with a plop. He looked up to see her standing in front of him; hands on hips and chin thrust forward. Obviously working hard to maintain composure she asked in an even tone, "Can you please explain why you deserted us, no, can that! Why you deserted ME the way you did? Why there was never a dammed word out of you for over 12 years? "In a low voice cracking with emotion and on the verge of tears she whispered, " Can you just possibly do that little thing?"

"I was kidnapped and just escaped?", he pleaded with raised eyebrows. No joy there, he thought, dumb jokes would certainly not work. Her expression hadn't softened a millimeter.

Deciding some truth was the best approach he just said, "No Slats, I couldn't tell you why I couldn't say goodbye. I couldn't do it then and can't now or ever. Does that explain anything?"

She stood silent for a moment sorting out what he was trying to explain. The truth of the situation was coming clear now. Her experience with special operations briefings and plans had exposed her to new aspects of how the world worked. Her time flying both "White" and "Black" SOF units operationally had also exposed her to other organizations and how they and the intelligence community had to work. She had come to understand that there were those that worked deep in the world of intelligence and espionage and how the job controlled their lives.

For the first time since they met that night, she really looked at him. He had lost some weight and a little hair, and sported a new scar that split his right eyebrow and continued into the cheek below. She also noticed that his eyes were glassy. Suddenly she realized that he had missed her as much as she had missed him. In the same instant she realized he was one of those dumb asses that let the mission invade and overwhelm any personal life they might have had, and that it made him leave her the way he did. His cold departure had not been by choice, but on orders.

She thought, maybe, just maybe, the SOB had cared too much, too much to say a real goodbye. Impulsively she closed the distance between them wanting to jump into his arms with a, "You are such an asshole!" Unfortunately he thought she was launching an attack on his nether regions. In his frantic attempt to avoid traumatic castration he tried

to jump to his right to escape her, and the chairs clutches. His effort to escape was to little avail, his feet tangled, and he slipped and fell over the side of the chair. The only visible effect of his exertion was to overturn an end table; spill someone's coffee and pastry and break a very nice lamp. Elmore only succeeded in making himself look foolish and drawing the attention of everyone in the lounge.

At least a dozen people sitting nearby saw and heard the entire exchange. As soon as Slats was able to go to her knees and grab the semi-supine Elmore, she threw her arms around the man and alternated jabbering and kissing. As the two seemed to be reconciled, the spectators started clapping, and Elmore, his clinical eye never totally turned off, noticed a couple of the women crying like it was a marriage proposal, or even worse, he thought mournfully, a funeral. Oh shit!

When they finally unclenched and were sitting shoulder to shoulder on the floor, she asked, "Do you know what's going on in Rio?"

"Some, but not all, " he said looking around." I'll tell you what I can after we get on the plane, OK?"

Elmore had prearranged their seating such that they sat in the last row in first class with him in the aisle seat. They were just getting settled when the flight attendant came to offer them either orange juice or champagne. Having no interest in either juice or wine, Slats asked, "Would you happen to have four little bottles of Chivas scotch and two cups of ice?"

Elmore just looked at her, somewhat astonished. She said, "What? I'm a pilot on a plane that someone I don't know is flying. That makes me nervous." Elmore shook his head and said, "I'd like a Coors if you've got one."

After the first two bottles of Chivas were gone and they had reached cruise altitude, Slats turned to Elmore and demanded, "OK. Tell me what's going on."

"Well.", he started, "All I know is that the Plot wants me to help with their intel on an international drug smuggler living in Rio, and he wants you to do some helicopter work." "What's the guy's name?", she asked.

"Julius Brown. The Plot's RANGE 19 team caught up with him in Thailand and turned him over to the local authorities, but apparently he bought his way out with money he had stashed away and is now back in business. This time, they want to make sure he's out of business for good", Elmore said.

"RANGE 19 team? Never heard of them. Who do they work for anyway?", she asked with a frown on her face

Elmore had a strong hunch that they worked for someone very, very high up in the government; maybe even directly for someone like the Head of the NSC or the Attorney General himself, but he just said, "I think they have a connection to the Drug Enforcement Administration (DEA) or the US Marshals, but I'm not sure. I do know that some of them, including Marplot, have U.S. Marshal badges and documentation, but of course that could be a cover."

"So we're working for some guys, but we don't really know who they work for or exactly how legal this is. They want us to help in what is essentially a snatch and bury mission, right? What's the plan? You big guys with big guns grab Brownie and I fly out over the ocean and we wrap him in twenty yards of one inch steel cable and chuck him out from 5000 feet?" she blurted, halfway through her second glass of ice and sixth ounce of scotch. Her immediate response to the idea was clear, "I don't think so. But I will wait and see what the Plot's got in mind before I jump to conclusions or jump ship, OK?", she said quietly.

Slats was quiet for a bit leaning back in her fully reclined seat with her feet up on the foot rest. The Scotch was working on her and she was visibly relaxed. Just as she seemed to be asleep she slurred, "Speakin of conclusions. How bout you telling me straight out whether're not you're in love wif me."

Without another word she let her head fall on his shoulder and passed out. At five foot five and 112 pounds she obviously didn't need much to drink to get a buzz, but after the red eye from Raleigh, N.C. to LAX and little if anything to eat, she was wasted on the six she'd had in the hour and a half they'd been on the plane. Elmore turned his head to look down at her and got a face full of her hair. It smelled really good, and when she moved to adjust her head he instinctively pulled up the armrest and put his arm around her shoulder. She more or less threw her right arm around his waist and was out like a light.

Elmore adjusted his seat after a few moments and leaned his head back thinking he could close his eyes and her question would go away. It didn't. But his eyes did close and he fell into a deep sleep as only a veteran soldier knew how.

Sometime later he was awakened by her movement. She had slid her butt closer and had lowered her right hand down to his upper thigh. She had also snuggled her face into his neck with her lips just behind his ear and quietly asked, "Are you awake?" Without moving a muscle Elmore said, "No; and neither are you." He then unfastened his seatbelt and stood up. He opened the overhead bin above them and found a blanket and sat back down. He took the blanket and wrapped it around her, and at the same time repositioned her head on his shoulder with his arm around her and said, "Go back to sleep. It's a long flight and you can use the rest. I'll wake you when they serve us some food. OK?". Slats said, "Sure.", and pulled the blanket over his right leg and then let her right hand slide back to his upper thigh underneath it; which made Elmore give out an almost inaudible moan and Slats smiled impishly while her eyes were still closed. Elmore couldn't tell whether she was still asleep or not, but the affect it was having on him was becoming more and more evident. Fortunately, the product of the affect was moving down under his other leg. He just hoped nothing would require him to stand up quickly.

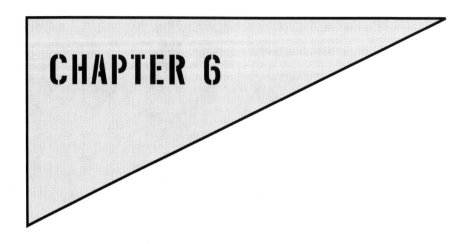

CHAPTER 6

TRUE TO HIS WORD THE PLOT MET them outside of customs at the airport in Rio and helped them get their bags loaded in the black Land Rover he had rented for the occasion. Conversation was minimal until all were in the car when he asked, "So. How was the flight my friends?"

Slats just stared at him as if he had a seven toed foot growing out of his forehead and finally said, "It was a long one Marplot, and what's in that brown envelope is just enough to get me back home without staying here one more minute. I want to know what is going on. Who is who and who is working for who. I want details of what I'm expected to do and how much I'm going to get out of it, and I want them now.", she flatly stated after they were in the Land Rover and moving; Elmore in the front and she in the back.

Elmore looked over at the Plot and when he looked back Elmore just shrugged his shoulders and said, "I'm more than a little curious myself dude. I remember the little bit you've already told me, but I still don't see how it's all going to come together. And what kind of intelligence information do you need me to ferret out of the Cayman island banking industry? Its gonna take a bag of bucks to get access there."

"Ladies first, of course", Simon Arpslot, the Plot said and continued with, I've

managed to lease, with an option to buy, a UH-1N helicopter recently out of the Bell Corpus Christi depot maintenance facility in Texas. It is currently sitting over there at the private terminal across the main runway. You can just see it sticking out of the side of the hangar on the right. It's the only helicopter there."

"Holy shit Marplot. That damned thing is older than I am. Just how long has it been out of depot maintenance? How many total hours are on it? Are both engines original?", Slats blasted, the professional aviator in her showing.

"I checked all of that Slats; as well as rotor blade replacements, magna fluxing inspections for cracks, tail rotor balancing, skid paint, muffler belts, transmission lights and piss tubes, er cups." the Plot rattled off. Then said, "But I'll leave the final decision of its flight worthiness to meet our requirements to you. As far as your compensation is concerned, you'll certainly still get whatever Smithfield is paying you now, plus $1000.00 a day you are with us, if that's agreeable."

All Slats could do was grunt a, "That'll be fine, so far. But I still want to know what that means in the way of flying risks and expectations."

"All in good time, my dear; but nothing out of the extreme flight envelopes you're already dealing with, I'm sure.

That comment made her nervous, but she didn't say anything.

"As for you Mr. Elmore, I need you to backtrack Julius Brown's money trail as far back as possible. We need to know how he hid his money. We want to find out how he got access to it, and finally, we need to know how he used that money to finance his escape from prison and got out of Thailand. We need to be better prepared for things like this in the future. I'm sorry to tell you that the only thing we know is that the money was hidden in one or more bank accounts, at least one of which is still in the Caymans. You may have to go to Thailand and the Cayman islands right away while the information is still fresh.", the Plot said.

"And do I get $1000.00 a day plus expenses like she does", Elmore asked?

"Yes. Enough on that subject", the Plot said flatly. You don't even know this, but you're a millionaire already. All you need do is sell the Arpslot Surgical and Prosthetic Supply Company's stock I signed over to you after your help with the prosthetic engineering division. Stock which totaled 10,000 shares when I signed it over to you after you helped me get my legs working the way I wanted. I started that company from scratch. You were just a friend who became a stockholder. That stock is worth $248.50 a share as of today's market. What do you think about that big guy? Think you can find your own money", the Plot laughed?

"What the hell", Slats said loudly? The Plot gave a second's glance in the review mirror to gauge her expression. He quickly put his eyes back on the road as they had entered heavy bicycle and moped traffic as well as vintage cars spewing thick exhaust; and said, "Not to worry dear. Your stock as an objective observer and mental therapist is probably worth the same as his; you are a millionaire as well. When we get settled in at the hotel I will give you both your broker's name, address, phone number and each of your account and PIN numbers so you can pick up the phone in your room and see just how rich you are.

At this, Slats just sat there with her mouth agape. As she recalled their sessions at the hospital cafeteria, they seemed to be mostly about the Plot's positive influence over her physical and mental recovery, not much with anything she had done for him. If it was true or not the idea was wonderful. On impulse she leaned forward and threw her arms around their necks and squeezing hard, said, "I love you assholes. This whole thing is a dream to me."

Both the Plot and Elmore twisted their heads toward hers to give her a peck on each cheek, but didn't say anything. They were just now pulling into the valet parking area of the El Presidente hotel. Elmore jumped out to open her door while the Plot had the bellman put their luggage on one of those huge flat bed transporters. The kind with the two inch diameter polished brass arches that one bell hop could push into the elevator, and therefore get the entire tip. In the well appointed room on the 22'd floor, the Plot gave the bell hop a $5.00 tip, which was about 100 Escuda on the exchange, but `the right' tipping rate for such things as only the Plot would already know.

The room had an entertainment section with a wide screen TV showing a NASCAR race; a wet bar, a sectional couch, end tables, and two reclining chairs. Two bar stools stood at the wet bar, and the view out of the patio windows gave an expansive look at lower tiered buildings fronting the beach and a glassy azure Caribbean sea stretching to the horizon. "This is beautiful Plot. Is this your room", Slats asked?

"No Slats. It's Elmore's and yours. I want it that way so that we can avoid unwanted attention. There are two bedrooms, and you are registered at the front desk as Mr. and Mrs. Elmore; and yes, Elmore, I've checked. You've never been to Brazil, much less Rio, so unless someone's following you or monitoring your credit cards for some reason, you are both without trails. Now I've got some work to do, so I'll leave you guys to unpack and knock off the road dust however you choose. The rest of us are in room 532 sleeping on the floor without daily expenses and huge pay per day. It's 4:15PM now. How about we meet in the dining room at 7:00PM for dinner? Unless you two are too tired and just want room service. If that's the case, we can meet at 7:00AM for breakfast. Decision time", Marplot toned evenly.

"Breakfast", they both said at once and laughed at their own thoughts.

"Fine. See you at 7. By the way, that briefcase on the coffee table over there in front of the couch contains all the information we have so far. Please try and find time to examine the contents so we can discuss a plan after breakfast. OK", the Plot said?

With that he left knowing these two people were meant for each other, but that neither one of them knew it yet. Like Slaughter and Sheila he thought; and that made him smile.

He also knew that they were perfect for what had to be done concerning Julius Brown and his drug enterprise. She could fly anything rotary that made noise and beat the air into submission, and Elmore was as sly as the best pit boss in Las Vegas. He could spot things nobody else would ever see, and he was smart enough to be really clever without any demonstrations for the sake of ego. Both good team players; Marplot just hoped they wouldn't get into too much playing and forget why the real reason they were here.

The moment Marplot left the suite Elmore went over to Slats and wrapped his arms around her and said, "Do you know what you were doing to me on that damned plane?"

"You betcha dude, she said with mischief in her eye, adding. "And I know what to do in one of those big beds we've got too", she added, as she led him toward the bedroom closest to them; the one on the left with the view of the ocean.

"Oh shit", was all Elmore could exclaim as he meekly followed the willowy figure ahead of him!

Afterwards, neither Slats nor Elmore could speak as they gasped for air and coughed. When they had both caught their breath they again spoke at once with, "Did you ---? Yeah, did you? Well, I couldn't tell for all the other sounds, could you", Elmore panted out?

They lay silently for a few minutes, one hunger appeased, when another kind of hunger surfaced.

"Why don't you look at the room service menu and pick something big and juicy, something medium rare, for me and whatever you want while I jump in the shower." she murmured in his ear.

"Good idea," Elmore agreed, "but I don't need a menu, and it won't take two minutes and then I'll join you. We'll do rub a dub dub, two folks in a tub".

Elmore picked up the cordless phone, got room service, and gave his order. He ordered two thick Porterhouse steaks burnt on the outside and red in the middle, two baked potatoes with the works, whatever veggies they recommended, and a bottle of Meridian Merlot 1981. One mission accomplished he threw the portable phone on the bed and padded barefoot towards the shower. They were still making love in the shower when the phone rang. They couldn't hear that one or the one by the commode in the bathroom. For that matter, anyone with their ear to the bathroom door would've barely heard the phone ringing over all the groaning and moaning going on, and they would have probably thought that someone was getting a lot more than one of El Presidente's massages. But it was just the hotel's room service manager wanting to verify their order and see if they would like desert. He would be thoroughly upset if they had decided to leave without calling to cancel their order. But he would not worry about it further. He would put it on their bill regardless.

The couple was sitting on bar stools, in the thick terry cloth robes that came with the room, and sipping an aperitif when dinner arrived. Dinner entered the room on a table with rollers pushed by a room service attendant. The table was covered with starched linen and had just about everything imaginable on it, including a lit candle and small vase with fresh flowers. Steam was coming up out of the vent in the top of each metal cover on the plates and sizzling sounds gave notice of what was inside. Elmore quickly signed the check adding a 20% tip while the service waiter was seating Slats in her chair. The table was set up in front of the big window by the wet bar, the window with the ocean view. They sat facing each other so both could enjoy the view, but they spent most of their time looking at each other.

The waiter left and they dug in with `Ummm's and Ahhh's' and slurpy sounds, and "delicious". After the edge of their hunger was blunted some, conversation began and they talked about this and that as if nothing had happened between them at all. Conversation focused on bringing each up to date on the past. Where they had been and what they had been doing and had either of them gotten hitched, divorced, or otherwise involved. The answers were all in the negative so both smiled and seemed to enjoy a few moments of silence; a silence Elmore sensed wouldn't last unattended with the peculiar look Slats had on her face.

"You gonna tell me you love me or not", she demanded staring him down.

Surprising even himself, Elmore didn't hesitate a second, "Of course I love you Slat's. I only hope you know what that means to me and with what I have to do for a living. With who I work for, and my inability to answer most of your questions sometimes."

She stuck out her steak knife at him with a scowl on her face and growled, "Only one rule hotshot; and it applies to both of us. There'll be no one else in the equation, just you and me in the sack. I understand all the rest of your secret squirrel shit." Then without skipping a beat she asked. "Want some more wine? We can go outside on the patio and watch the sun go down. Maybe, if the conditions are just right, we'll get to see the remnants of the legendary green flash way off to our right. Ever seen one?"

Elmore reached over and picked up her left hand and said, "You amaze me woman. Can you really understand what you're getting into with me? You'll never get to know all there is to know about me, or even where I'm at or what I'm doing. Do you really think you can live with that?"

She smiled at him and said, "As long as you can remember rule number one. It's called trust, dip shit. Now answer my last question. Have you ever seen the green flash?"

"No. I have not. Exactly what is it anyway?", he asked.

She beamed and said, "Well, at the precise moment the bottom of the globe of the setting sun hit's the ocean's horizon, if the atmospheric conditions are just right, there will be a green flash of light all across the horizon in the West, which we can't see from here, but will be able to see the last of it by looking South West. The islanders in the Pacific believe that when this happens, we can make one wish that will come true; but we cannot reveal what that wish is, ever."

Elmore raised one eyebrow and said, "I'm not one for superstition, but it sounds like you need to have a standing wish beforehand. And, it better be a good one since the flash doesn't occur very often if it's dependent on perfect atmospheric conditions. Did you notice the smog in the air over Rio when we were driving in?"

"Make a wish asshole," she ordered. We've only got about three minutes by my estimation. I've already made mine".

"OK. I'll play along. You know you're a hopeless romantic. You know that", Elmore smiled at her. It wasn't a question.

"All pilots are. ask me how many types and kinds of aircraft I'm rated in `Buckwheat', and I'll tell you which ones I can remember. Ask me how many times I've crashed and healed to fly again and I'll tell you the ones I remember the most. Ask me how many thunderheads I've had to fly through with shit flying all over the inside of the aircraft due to turbulence and I'll tell you about the worst windshield cracks and blowouts. Have you ever heard the expression, "The sky, even more hazardous than the sea, is least unforgiving of even the slightest mistake.?", Slats rattled off. Then, "Have you made the damned wish yet?"

"No. I'm still crashing in an airplane. I do have something in mind though", he said.

"God I do love you Elmore. You can take such a view of things so threatening and shake them off like finishing a healthy piss. Do they teach that kind of thinking to you in spook school", Slats asked? Then she continued with, "OK, it's getting close. Let's see if we're lucky with the bottom of that big beautiful orb of fire."

In spite of the smog and against all odds, there was indeed a green flash that evening. Elmore sat motionless, mesmerized by the event. Slats response was to leap up from her chair and do her version of river dance in the space between the chairs. She danced and whooped and hollered adding, "Yes, oh yeah. You bet!"

Elmore wondered if he really would get a bigger dick.

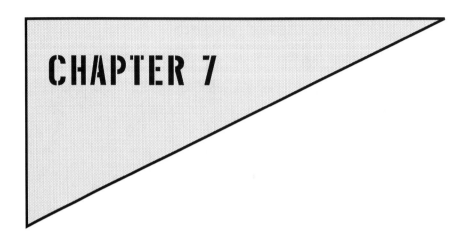

CHAPTER 7

EVENTS WERE UNDER OBSERVATION AT THE HOOTCH, a complex setting on a small island just outside the everglades swamp and the Tamiami highway. Dyke, Chico, Guido, Bunny and the two Cuban house maids, Maria and Rosa were watching nervously as Crud Jr. circled the grave of Crud Sr. after eating the crab cakes the women had made for him a few hours ago. Both of the women had been with "Mr. Simon" from the time he'd built the Hootch and with his help, had become U.S. citizens. Both women had mourned the passing of Crud Sr. and were anxious to see how Crud Jr. would fit in.

With a final turn, he stopped and squatted in the ungainly unflattering position dogs use to take a crap. Crud Jr. let loose with half crap and half fart that immediately filled the air with as obnoxious a stench as one could imagine.

The women covered their noses and mouths and emitted loud groans, but the men all clapped and cheered at the event, all the while breathing through their mouths. All of them were SCUBA divers used to isolating the mouth from the nose, so that was no problem. They couldn't wait to relay all the details of Crud Jr's latest accomplishment to the rest of the RANGE 19 crew.

At that same moment, Leopold Farnsworth III was sitting in the backseat of a taxi passing the big RANGE 19 mailbox. Every molecule of his being was focused into thinking about how he could blow up the Hootch and kill Slaughter in the process. He needed to be patient, he knew. He had to get settled in and plan for the duration of the mission. It would take time and planning to make it all happen, so he leaned back in his seat and closed his eyes to imagine Slaughter's blood and body parts flying in all directions.

At the highway intersection where the Motel 6 was located, there was a combination bar and restaurant on the same corner as the motel. A combination auto parts store and service station sat on the opposite corner. The general store he remembered from his first trip was on the other corner to the left side. A huge woman named appropriately Large Marge, ran the general store. At least that's what he remembered the local sheriff calling her. And what was the fucking sheriff's name? Oh yeah, he remembered. It was Terry Baugh, who, from all indicators, had all of his in-bred relatives working for him. He wondered if they were still around.

Directly across the highway from the motel was a large building with lots of tables in front and a large parking area on the side. When he looked up at the sign on the building it said "Bingo". There was a smaller sign underneath proclaiming bingo was played every weekend starting at 7:00PM. The sign draped over the center table declared, "Flea Market every weekend 6:30AM till 7:00PM. Farnsworth thought that this must be the place to be on weekends.

He went inside to the registration desk to get a room and asked the pimple faced young man behind the counter, "Does this place have a name?"

"Yeah mister. It's a Motel 6. There's even a big sign out front says so.", he curtly replied. Farnsworth had to bite his tongue at the little shit's smart assed reply, but calmly asked, "No, I mean the community here."

"Well now, that'd be `Crossroads', since we got the only intersection of highways within 28 miles. Kinda makes sense doesn't it? You wanna room for the night? It'll be $39.50. Cash or credit card?", he asked.

"How much by the week? I've got business with people at a place nearby and I'm not sure how long it will take.", Farnsworth asked.

"Don't got no weekly rate. Nobody ever stayed that long before. But if you stay more than one night you get a coffee maker and the mixins.", he said as he reached under the counter and pulled out a coffee maker and a bag full of "mixins". Then, "Who's yer business with? I know everybody a hundred miles from here. Maybe I can be of some help to ya."

Farnsworth thought for a moment about this, then smiled and thinking `intelligence information`, said, "I'm negotiating the purchase of some property that the RANGE 19 folks down the road own. Do you know Mr. Arpslot?"

"The Plot? Sure everybody knows him. He's a character; AND a genius. Did you know that", the kid asked?

"No I didn't. Tell me more", Farnsworth urged, seeing no reason to miss an opportunity to learn about the enemy and to exploit this bumpkin .

"Well, when my sister got her arm burnt real bad pumpin gas across the street, the Plot had her flown to Texas where they put artificial skin on her and you can't tell the difference tween it and what her other arm's skin looks like. He's somthin I tell ya. Didn't even charge us nuthin. Said it helped his research lab with learnin how to make the stuff. By the way, my names Murf Holiday, and if you're a friend of the Plot's, you're a friend of mine. I'm givin you a room with a color TV and cable that works; and no jokes about my first name, OK?", the kid said as he smiled at him and looked down at the registration card to see a Mr. Jonathan Smith on the card.

"No car", the kid asked?

"No, I took a taxi here from the airport. I planned to rent a car while I was here. Do you know of anything", Farnsworth asked?

The kid looked sheepishly at Farnsworth and then said, "There ain't no rental car agency out here, but I can let you use my truck if you fill it up when you're done."

"Deal my friend. Where's it at", Farnsworth asked?

"Well, it's across the street getting some work done. Shouldn't cost ya more than $200.00 to get it tomorrow morning around 9:00AM. Oh yeah. I don't drive it at night so I didn't have them fix the headlights so I hope you can get your business done without having to drive at nightime. It's a special kinda 4X4 I use to sneak up on gators and such, if ya know what I mean.", the kid stammered.

"Anyway, it's available if'n ya want it. Just tell Mickey you're paying the transmission bill and need the truck right away. Mickey'll snatch the money and give you the keys without a word. Then he'll come over and ask me what the hell it's all about, me turnin over my prized 54' Chevy truck to some - - - never mind.", the kid said; then asked, "You want it or not?"

Farnsworth figured he'd probably need the truck for the entire week or at least most of a week at minimum and he didn't want to lose this kid's trust. He might be a big help when the time came to pull things together, so he smiled at him and said, "Sounds like a deal Murf. You can call me `Johnny Moneybags`; just between us of course". The name made Murf go into a fit of "yuking" the likes of which Farnsworth had never heard. He wondered if his Mom and Dad had been close relatives.Farnsworth asked for the room toward the end and it wasn't half bad. He was surprised, but there was still that incessant smell of sulfur in the water that he despised. But he forgot about that as soon as he thought of his good fortune to run into a bigmouthed kid who could definitely help him with his quest.

The first thing he did was lay out everything he had in his bags for a quick inventory. The clothing was minimal, but enough to get by with around here; two pairs of levis and four non-descript short sleeved shirts without any `tourist' patterns, loafer style boat shoes and tennis shoes, and a John Deere hat that with some sweat stains would fit in perfectly with this crowd.

His briefcase held the money; a legal pad, and both a mechanical pencil and a ball point pen. He counted his money; $9945.00 still in the shoebox. He'd have to break it all down before he started to buy things. He couldn't just hand over a handful of hundreds for a $200.00 transmission fix for example. He'd use a fifty, seven twenty's, and a ten. Then he looked at the remaining jewelry. He had five diamond rings and three diamond bracelets; a pearl necklace, and a diamond and gold Rolex watch. Not much he could do with this stuff here in Crossville, but it was satisfying to know he had resources he could use. He also had his PPK 9mm pistol; the one he shot the tip of his left toe off with the first time he'd attempted to shoot Slaughter. Sheriff Baugh had sent it back to him once he had obtained an affidavit from a D.C. lawyer threatening legal action if it wasn't returned as he had not committed any crime with the weapon. The small pistol laying next to all the stolen jewelry pretty much confirmed that he was a criminal. He certainly didn't feel much like an honorable West Point graduate with a bright future, after stealing all that jewelry from that old woman on the bus, but what choice did he have, he asked himself?

He felt some hunger so he put everything away and cleaned up to go eat. He decided he would try out the local restaurant. As soon as he got outside his motel room door he remembered the John Deere hat. He thought it was an essential part of his cover if he was going to front himself as a man interested in buying farm land. He went back in his room, put it on and checked his reflection in the bathroom mirror. All he needed now, he thought, was a set of those artificial buck teeth and he'd fit right in.

CHAPTER 8

MARPLOT WAS THE FIRST ONE TO WAKE up. He followed his morning routine by starting a pot of coffee at the wet bar and then hitting the shower while it perked. He was using the bedroom next to the patio; the one that had the ocean view. He chose it only because he was the first one to arrive. Slaughter and Sheila arrived two days later, and even though he offered it to them they both said no.

As soon as he heard the shower running, Slaughter got up to take a leak; a part of his routine for the last ten days while they kept track of Julius Brown. Marplot finished his shower and without turning the water off, grabbed a towel and hollered, "It's yours." Slaughter said, "Thanks.", as usual, and stepped into the bathroom and into the shower. Sheila stayed in bed sleeping for another 30 minutes. She claimed it was the best part of her sleep; half awake and half asleep; the dream more vivid.

Always the same dream, of course. Her and Slaughter on a big sailboat going nowhere in particular, with the wind blowing them wherever it decided to take them. After her extra 30 minutes she rose to use the bathroom, officially beginning her day. Little nonsense from now until the cocktail hour, and "jolly good old sport" she thought, still frustrated at being expected to curtail her journalistic freedom.

Right! This whole drug smuggling thing and what they were doing was really beyond her. She knew what opiates were. Among the most powerful natural drugs, they could become dangerous street drugs or indispensable medical pain killers, the best known of which was morphine. Besides that, she didn't know much, but perhaps there was a political angle. She knew opium poppies were grown in a number of areas including Afghanistan, Pakistan, India, Burma/Myanmar, Thailand, Laos and other locales in Southwest Asia. Opiates made up a major part of the gross national product in many countries, especially Afghanistan. Where, she wondered, was the Pulitzer hiding in all of that? She would need to do more research and find an angle. An angle that wouldn't affect the RANGE 19 mission to stop Julius Brown and his operation.

Promptly at 7:00AM everyone was seated at a table in the hotel dining room and had made introductions. The specialty in Rio de Janeiro, for every meal was prize beef, mostly shipped in fresh from Argentina. Brazil had some home grown beef of its own, but it wasn't even close in taste or tenderness.

Before the waiter even left their table for the coffee Slaughter and Sheila both said, "We'll have the usual Juan." Marplot looked at Elmore and Slats to explain, "That's steak and eggs with potatoes and slices of tomato; and Juan already knows how they like the steaks. Next to having the poor animal still bellowing, they like it bloody red in the middle and burnt outside. I'll have my poached eggs with dry whole wheat toast, Juan", Marplot said. "We'll have the same as those two", Elmore and Slats chimed, as the Plot looked at them like it was, well, "a plot" against nature itself.

"Alright little ones, now that you've stuffed your faces with some poor animal's flesh let's get down to business.", the Plot said, pushing his plate back and leaning forward to fold his hands in front of him. "First, did you have a chance to look at the material in the briefcase?"

Elmore frowned and said, "Yeah, but I couldn't find anything I didn't already know about the hawala system of money lenders in the Islamic countries. The article on the American who was the former financial advisor and Chief of Staff to the Sultan of Brunei and is now the financial advisor to the monarchy in Thailand does give me a lead however. I'll run him to ground when I get over there. If he's also a hawala from his days with the Sultan, that could be the key to how Brown got his money moved around."

The Plot smiled and said, "Good idea. Now, we've got the helicopter back at the airport. Slats, you'll have to go check it out; and by that I mean a check flight to make sure the thing can land and take off loaded at 10,000' above ground level. We've pre positioned ammunition boxes, full of live ammunition by the way, in the hangar so we can load up the aircraft with a test weight of 3000 pounds. I think that should be more than enough to represent a five man team and one hostage", the Plot was going to continue, when Sheila interjected flatly, "And one woman with a camera". The Plot shot Slaughter a seriously questioning look. Slaughter just winked at him, a wink that offered little comfort to the Plot.

The Plot dropped that subject for the moment, he'd talk to Slaughter privately, and continued with, "I've managed to slip some money to the Commander of the guard troops in the Brazilian militia who are moonlighting as Brown's personal protection and security force. He has made four MP5s with sound suppressors, ammo, and C4 with caps and timers available; and he will call an emergency formation when we need to reduce his security; but Brown still has two hired mercenaries and one of them watches his back at all times. We may have to neutralize them". As the Plot said this last fact, he looked directly at Sheila and said, "That cannot be on camera." She scowled, but remained silent.

"We've picked out three different sites where Slats can put us in close enough so that we can infiltrate the place. It will take about 40-50 minutes hacking through the brush to reach the top of the mountain. Unfortunately, there's not a single place she can put both skids on the dirt. We'll have to either fast rope or just jump the last foot or two; I don't know, and we won't know until Slats reviews the places and picks one. OK by you Slats", he asked?

"My bet is I can get one side down and nobody will have to go down a rope or do any jumping, but I'll give them all a look with the bird fully loaded. Then we will see what that rust bucket you've shelled out two million for can do.", she said and then added, "But it's hot and humid here so density altitude will be a factor. With the other unknowns like winds, rain, and center of balance with a full load, we will have to do some good rehearsals. I'll need somebody to go up with the deadweight and move around in the back to see what kind of control movements I'll be up against. Sheila, can you and your camera come along and help me with that?"

Sheila's face blanched at the question but she was trapped. She didn't know what to say other than, "Fine, if it'll help." After all she was a U.S. Marshal and RANGE 19 plank holder; a founder of the team to fight evil - - - and I don't get a Pulitzer prize for "stupid" or, "I can't do that".

"I think maybe I'd better go along too, Plot. There're some things I want to look for at this guy's villa. We need to see how he gets his electrical power and what the road is like; and even if he's got any radar or other antennas there. Stuff we should know about before we blunder across the FEBA (forward edge of the battle area) if you know what I mean", Elmore said sarcastically. "And it's a good idea to have some current photos of what we find, as well as a public reason the helicopter is flying in the area in the first place, don't you think", he continued?

Slaughter smiled and said, "Brother Elmore is starting to earn his money already. I'm thinking that we can have the militia commanders we paid off let Brown know there will be a helicopter to look after his interests in security while the troops are unavailable; and for the mission, we stand off with the helicopter at altitude and watch for the militia guards to leave, and initiate our attack plan on the villa. If we can cut commercial power on call; locate and disable any generator or other backup power sources, it'll probably knock out whatever electronic security devices he has. We also need to find out if he's got any guard dogs besides the two human Dobermans", Slaughter added.

With breakfast finished, there was nothing left for Elmore, Slats and Sheila to do but go back to their rooms and get Sheila's video and still cameras and whatever else they needed and leave for the airport.

Marplot went to their room to call the Militia Commander about the helicopter coverage while the troops were assembled, and Slaughter went back to the roof and set up the satellite link to the Hootch and made arrangements for Dyke, Chico, and Bunny to leave for Rio immediately. They would use their U.S. Marshal credentials to get priority seating and weapons carrying authority.

Guido would fly to the Cayman Islands and snoop out what he could from the British authorities about James Julius until Elmore arrived to finalize arrangements for handling the funds hidden there. He would establish the channels to transfer Julius Brown's fund from his covered accounts to other sites where the funds would become more useful to the team and U.S. taxpayers.

Now it was time to find Doc Leigh and bring him to Rio as well. The Doc would work his magic to get the account numbers from Brown. He'd have to do so before Brown realized he was actually a human and not a 5 foot 4 inch tall 245 pound tabby cat. He hadn't changed at all in over ten years according to Plot's sources in Thailand, and at 65 you would've thought he'd be diabetic with a couple of heart attacks behind him; but not so.

"The only way to get in touch with Doc Leigh is by single side band HF radio and you know it. We don't have single side band Plot; and none of our high tech satellite hookups can cut it." Slaughter fumed.

The Plot calmly took the headset and punched in some numbers on the little keyboard and waited a few seconds before saying, "Yes. This is Simon Arpslot. May I please speak to your military attaché, Lieutenant

Colonel Pickett." Another few seconds longer and LTC Pickett came on the line and the Plot said, "Roger my man. Are you still happy and healthy chasing young ladies around the dirty streets and foul air in Lima?", and after a moment the Plot laughed and said, "I need a favor from you my friend. I need for you to get on your single side band radio and send a message to Doctor Bailey's Bald Head. Yes, it's Doc Leigh's nephew, but we really need Doc Leigh to come to Rio as soon as possible. I need confirmation on this one Roger, so call me back at this number as soon as you make contact", the Plot said and gave him their satellite phone number.

"We'll be standing by for the next hour or so, then again at 1:00PM local Rio time. Good to hear your voice again; and you know you can count on me for anything you need, right? Blue Skies to you as well, Plot out", the Plot said and put the phone back in it's cradle.

At 1:10PM Rio time the satellite phone gave off a low buzzing and the Plot picked it up and simply said, "Rio, how can I help you?"

"What you want Plot", a strange voice asked?

"To whom am I speaking?, the Plot asked, somewhat bewildered at the voice on the other end.

"I Doc Ralph's nephew Leantoo. He too tired to travel today, and he tell me to take care of whatever you want. What you want?", the young voice asked.

"Is he sick? Does he need any help?", the Plot asked nervously.

"No. He do womanhood ceremony last three nights to make 11 of our virgins woman and ready for marriage. Old record was 9 in four days. He big hero of village again. I remember him talking of you now. Thank you for Bailey's Bald Head. I fully qualified Peruvian Witch Doctor now. All training finished. I have my own bag of juices, bamboo injection slivers and knives now, but good tape is hard to find. You can help with that", he softly asked?

"Of course Leantoo.", but before the Plot could say anything else

"LEE AN TOO" came blasting back at him with, "Don't you know our speaking way? You one idiot"?

"No, I'm sorry about that Le An Too; but, and this is important, I need to know if Doc Leigh, Ralph, can come to Rio De Janeiro, Brazil right away; or, if he can't, can you do what he can? By that I mean, can you put a person to sleep to get them to reveal information they wouldn't otherwise talk about?", the Plot rattled on with more details wondering if the kid understood what he was asking for.

"Easy. Uncle Ralph, he made frog sweat smoke of this and marked my trip to do this in the sand for me. He give me money and tell me what to take. I make airplane seat from Lima tonight all the way there. I will spill the sacred bones to find you once I am on that soil." Le An Too said confidently, sounding as if he were going to hang up.

"No no Le An Too. I will pick you up at the airport when you arrive; but you must wear western clothing and you can't bring any metal knives or things like that in your bag. What airlines are you flying on, Pan Am", which is what the Plot expected?

"Yes. That one. But I don't know what time it sits there", he said.

"Never mind, I can find that out. Did your uncle tell you what I look like so you will recognize me at the airport?, the Plot hurriedly asked before the kid hung up in favor of his "smoke" and "sand trail".

"It is not important that I see you; it is more important that you see me. I am the one who is painted with the gifts. Not you", he said with such finality that the Plot could imagine himself in some ancient ritual where the anointed one pulled out all of his teeth with just his thumb and forefinger.

"Hey partner, you still there", LTC Roger Pickett asked?

"Yes; and thank God you're still on the line. Go catch that kid before he leaves and tell him to get his uncle on the way regardless of the number of virgins he has to convert, will you", the Plot hurriedly said?

"OK buddy. Force if necessary?

"Yes. Drag that bow legged Peruvian bastard away from his rutting and back to the Hootch as soon as you can."

"You got it; but I imagine you want him alive and functional, right"?

"Com on Roger. I need his talents and little leather bag; not some kid with his own ideas about societies needs", the Plot pleaded.

"OK. Out here", Pickett said, signing off.

CHAPTER 9

SHIELA HOBGOOD DID NOT LIKE IT. SHE was in the helicopter's rear, seated in the outward facing seat on the starboard (right hand) side, her big video camera on her shoulder and just a seatbelt around her waist to keep her from the great void outside. After she finally learned how to use the headset and intercom she screamed into it every time Slats made a right hand bank that forced her to look straight down at the ground. She had no trust in the quick release buckle holding the seat belt together; she was sure it was unsafe and would let her fall to splatter all over the landscape if anything went wrong. She had never flown in a helicopter before and she had no confidence in them. This was her first experience at what they did in the air, and it was not pleasant, comfortable, or conducive to even turning her camera on - much less using it professionally. She pleaded, "Slats, I'm begging you, is there any way you can slow this thing down, keep the wind from blowing in my face, and let me not bounce around so much; the video will not turn out very good with all this vibration and bouncing.", she stuttered with the helicopter's beating blades.

Elmore was laughing his ass off in the right hand pilot's seat, without activating the intercom of course, but Slats was watching with a knowing smile.

Slats pulled her cyclic intercom trigger and said, "Why don't you and Elmore trade places. I'll move out away from this mountain into smoother air and you can unbuckle, but first let's have Elmore get out of his seat and come back into the cargo compartment to get your camera and help you in case there's a wind gust or something, OK?"

In an amazing feat of fearless movement, Elmore managed to unbuckle a semi-panicked Sheila, guide her across the wide open cargo compartment and into the right hand pilots seat, while keeping control of the video camera.

After the exchange, Elmore found himself centered over the boxes of ammunition ballast in the cargo compartment so he could move to either side of the open cargo compartment to look at whatever he needed to see. Sheila Hobgood was more than happy to point her camera out of the small window access in her door, a door firmly closed and locked.

They flew over Julius Brown's villa at 12,500' AGL from each direction, standing off about one half of a mile. Sheila mounted a telephoto lens and motor drive on her still camera. She used it to expertly capture images of the entire fortress and other points or items of interest. Elmore captured similar data with her video camera, taking advantage of its image stabilization and zoom lens, the latter letting him go from a pan view to a detailed study of key targets.

Slats and Sheila thought the flight was done, but Elmore needed more and gave additional instructions, "No. I need you to drop down to about 500 feet over the top of the place and slow down to 60-70 knots, whatever is comfortable flight wise, and make a slow turn all the way around the place. Sheila, you can pull your camera in for this one. I'll be looking out the starboard side with my little bino's Slats, and I'll be looking at the roof for any antennas. I need a smooth ride for this pass because we can only do this once. Otherwise we'll attract the wrong kind of attention. Did you see Mr. Brown and his Doberman when they came out to look at us? Give a wave if they're still out and watching when we make the low pass."

Bigger than shit Elmore observed, Julius Brown had his own little satellite phone link capability. That would have to go at the same time as the generators. They learned there was no commercial power feeding the site. The diesel generators located behind the garage was the main power source; and there was surely a battery back up. Elmore thought for a moment, and then said abruptly, put me down somewhere close.

While they were loading the cases of ammunition for ballast he had discovered a case of C4, a can of non-electric blasting caps, and a bag with 30 day timers. He was also entering his "Get'er done, mode", which Slats immediately recognized, and responded with a, "No way Jose. And anyway, whatcha gonna set the timers for?"

"Never mind. Just set down less than a mile from the target and I'll put things in place for when we need to "set timers". I suspect it'll take me about an hour unless you put me out at the bottom of this big hill. I want to be able to take out his communications and security at the same time so we don't get caught up in an international incident, given he's paying the Brazilian brass for protection. We need to be swift on this one. In and out without anything left behind.", he said without feeling. No blood, just craft.

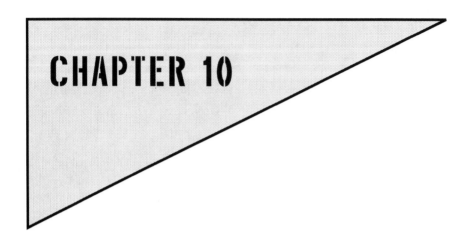

CHAPTER 10

FARNSWORTH DIDN'T HAVE FAR TO WALK TO the restaurant. It was almost an appendage of the Motel office, and as he passed by and looked at the door there was a sign hanging in the window that said, "Maniger next door". Sure enough, as he walked through the restaurant door he saw Murf sitting on one of the stools at the counter eating what appeared to be a bowl of chili. There were three guys sitting in a booth further down chatting up the waitress, and two teenagers were at the far end of the counter on stools working on fountain sodas with ice cream. Farnsworth decided to take a stool next to Murf and see if he could get some more information he needed.

"Mind if I join ya Murf?", he said as he slapped Murf on the back lightly; as if they were old buds already.

"Naw. Pull up a stump and have some chili. It's a mite charged with heat, but ain't that what chili's all about?", Murf said grinning through a mouthful.

Farnsworth looked at the blackboard posted beside the cash register at Murf's right and saw "Blueplate Specials" at the top; then "Pork Chops, gravy, rice, and corn $4.95, and Fried Bass, French fries, and corn $5.95, and Homemade Chili $2.50". When the waitress saw Farnsworth sit next to Murf she automatically assumed he was a friend of that idiot Murf and took her time getting back around the counter to them. She put on a flalse smile that confirmed poor dental hygiene and asked him what he'd like.

"I'm pretty hungry. How about the Pork Chops and a cup of coffee?", he asked.

"You got it. Coffee need cream?" she asked.

"Black is fine, thanks - - - Meg", he read from her nametag.

"Comin right up.", she said as she whirled and headed toward the cook's window to holler "Chops" and fill a coffee cup from the big coffee maker. Farnsworth imagined this was the only place for miles that had a coffee maker that big with a rack of cups next to it. As he turned back he noticed in the big mirror beside the coffee cup rack that there was a truck passing by with something strange in tow. He turned to look out the window to see that it was an airboat; very common here for use in the "River of Grass" as the Everglades used to be called years ago. This prompted him to ask, "Hey Murf, do you know of any ultra light airplane places around here? I've always thought it would be fun to fly around in one of those. A lot less expensive, and they don't require you to have an FAA pilot's license either.".

I know a guy who's got a two seater he gives rides to tourists for $20.00 on weekends durin' the day. He takes'em out over the 'glades and some of the mangrove islands to see gators and stuff. He makes enough to stay high or fired up when he aint flying.", Murf said, wiping chili and saltine fragments from his chin, and then continued with, "he's also got one for sale, I think; but it's only got one seat. I don't know what he wants for it now but it can't be much. It was wrecked won'st and after he got it fixed he decided to sell it. He aint had no takers and keeps dropping the price. Last I heard he wanted about three thousand for it! Can you imagine anyone spending good money for one of those things? That's enough money for a real good pickup", he stated firmly keeping his mind on his own priorities

Farnsworth couldn't believe his good luck. He smiled and said,

"You reckon you could take me to this guy's place after we eat? I'd make it worth your while; say ten bucks?"

"Naw, I can't leave the motel till 10:00PM and by that time Whitey'll be drunk as a shit house rat. But if you get my pickup tomorrow morning I can draw you a map on how to get to his place, and since it'll be a Saturday he should be full of coffee and halfway sober by 8:30 afore he starts givin rides.", Murf offered.

"Sounds good Murf. I can wait. Changing the subject he asked, "What's to do around here at night, anyway?", he asked.

"There's a bar with pool tables and dance floor about a mile up the Tamiami. Ya can't miss it. There'll be two dozen pickups parked alongside the road just before ya get to it. There's a Bluegrass band playin tonight, and I'm walkin down there myself after I get off work.", Murf said with a measure of excitement. Farnsworth cringed just thinking about what the place would be like. By ten o'clock everyone in the place would probably be snot slinging drunk and looking for a fight over who made the best tractor or pickup so he said, "Thanks Murf, but I'm not that big a walker, or runner either for that matter. Desert Storm shrapnel cured me of that.", he said.

He wasn't about to tell him the truth. That he shot the tip of his left toe off in a drunken rage with his own gun at the RANGE 19 mailbox over ten years ago. Then he thought about one of the scenarios he harbored in his fertile mine; the one where he killed everyone by blowing up the Hootch. His new train of thought brought a change in the subject, "Say Murf, do you know where I can get some dynamite sticks? If I buy some of the RANGE 19 property I'm going to need to build a pond. I would prefer to blow it and I'll need a couple of sticks to mix with some heavy fertilizer and fuel oil to do it."

Murf looked at him a little suspiciously and said, "Maybe, but it'll cost ya unless you want to get Sheriff Baugh's approval. That's required and he's the only one with the paperwork to authorize the purchase in Miami-Dade Municipal."

"Just for a couple of sticks?", Farnsworth asked, then justified it with, "I don't want to have to go through the hassle with filling out paperwork when all I want is just two or three sticks." Next thing I will have to hire a guy with a commercial license, a special vehicle and all that crap. It's a lot of bull shit to sift through for five minutes work!

Murf seemed to agree with it being a hassle and said,"I suspect they'll cost ya maybe $25.00 a piece that way. A box of 24 is $120.00 after paperwork, and I know a guy who's probably got some left from blowing stumps and such. We get a stick every now and again; for a little fishin, if ya know what I mean", Murf winked and smirked at him. Murf's eyes were a little red and glassy and there was a slight smell of burnt rags about him if you focused a bit.

"Ah, maybe my man has been testing the local agricultural byproducts this evening," thought Farnsworth.

"Murf, you're The Man! I'll give you $60.00 if you can get two sticks for me with a couple of caps and a few feet of fuse, and you keep them safe until I need them. Can I count on you dude," Farnsworth asked beaming his best good old boy smile at him.

"You're purty sure you're gonna get that land, huh?, Murf said as he eyed him.

"Well, if I don't, you aint out nuthin' are you? Hell, you got yourself two sticks of dynamite to fish with doncha?", Farnsworth said; then, didn't I tell ya to just call me Mr. Moneybags?" At which Murf went into another one of his yuking spasms.

The next morning Farnsworth crossed the street to bang on the garage door until Mikey finally opened up. He paid Mickey off and got Murf's pickup. He filled the nearly empty fuel tank and drove up the Tamiami highway following the dubious map Murf drew on a paper napkin the night before. Luckily the odometer worked so he was able to measure the 4.7 miles Murf had said to go before turning right on a gravel road. It was actually 4.9 miles but since it was the only right turn close to 4.7 he turned in and drove another mile until he saw the cleared field on his left. The next turn off was to the left next to a mailbox which proved to be Whitey's driveway. He turned into the drive and followed the dirt track a few yards to a small poorly maintained wood frame house sitting under a large magnolia tree.

He arrived before 8:15AM and as he came abreast of the house he saw a man exit the side porch of his house with a large mug in his hand and start walking toward a long, wide shed at the edge of the field behind the house. Farnsworth's presence finally pierced the man's consciousness; he stopped midway and stood staring blankly at the raggedy pick up until Farnsworth pulled up next to him with his driver's side window down and asked, "Howdy. You Whitey?"

"Yup. Whatcha doin in Murf's truck? Ya here for a ride? It's $20 bucks for 15 minutes. I take you up and we go up over the glades and then out over the coast till we get back here", Whitey said flatly. He was about six feet tall and weighed maybe 200 pounds, and he had on a well oiled John Deere hat pulled down to shade his bloodshot eyes.

"I'm borrowing it from Murf. I came to see you about the ultra light airplane you've got for sale. My name is Johnathan Smith, and I've always wanted to learn how to fly but never seemed to have time to learn how to fly a big plane. I figure I might be better off to get one of the ultra lights. Less money and problems, ya know? Do ya still have one for sale? Can I see it?", Farnsworth rattled off. He'd already thought through what he was going to say.

"Park over behind the hangar there." Whitey pointed, then said, "And come on around at thu other side an ya can have a look at what I've got for sale; and it's a firm $3500.00 cash. No check. Non negotiable."

After Farnsworth had walked around the little Rotex tail dragger with the pusher engine mounted behind the pilot he walked up to Whitey, who was leaning up against the hangar door with his arms folded over his chest and said, "Two things and you've got your $3500.00. First, I want to see you fly it and make some maneuvers so

I know its ok; and second, I want you to teach me how to fly in your two seater."

Whitey just looked at him expressionlessly for a moment and then asked, "You ever fly anything before?"

"I'm a qualified Military Free Fall parachutist and can fly a square parachute if that means anything", Farnsworth said.

"Just enough I hope. I reckon you got a deal.", Whitey said while slightly shaking his head back and forth.

He went to the back of the little Rotex plane. He easily lifted the tail and pushed it out of the hangar and guided it toward the open field. Without a word he got it and yanked the pull cord to start the engine, increased the RPM to start a slow taxi while checking the controls for effectiveness, and then with a larger increase in RPM the small plane seemed to jump into the air. Farnsworth watched him do rolls, split esses, and back loops for about 10 minutes and then he landed right in front of the hangar, threw his cowboy boot out and dug the heel into the soft turf and revved the engine slightly, effectively turning the little plane back around and ready for takeoff. He climbed out, walked over to Farnsworth with his arms crossed and asked, "You good for the $3500.00 - - -cash?"

"Sure. In fact I'll give you a $300.00 deposit right now.", Farnsworth said and peeled off a hundred dollar bill, nine twentys, and two tens.

"OK." Whitey said taking the money. "If you're satisfied with the demo, help me pull the two seater out of the hangar and we'll get your show on the road right now.", Whitey said as he uncrossed his arms and started toward the other side of the hangar.

At first, Farnsworth over controlled the responsive airplane by erratically jerking the overhead cyclic, and he had trouble remembering to use the pedals during wildly skidding turns; but after two and a half hours in a traffic pattern making takeoffs and landings Whitey told him to taxi the plane over to the hangar so he could fill the 10 gallon fuel tank. Once the tank was full he told Farnsworth to turn it around and take it up by himself; make five takeoffs and landings; and then bring it back to where it sat now. Then he said, "Ya might wanna keep in mind on yer first takeoff that I'll not be sittin next to ya with my 200 pounds. You'll have to use more rudder to offset the torque and she'll lift off quicker. And by the way. If ya break it, ya buy it." He then took up his pose at the hangar door with his arms over his chest.

Farnsworth's first takeoff was wobbly and it did pop off the ground faster than he expected, and he almost stalled it before he lowered the angle of attack and managed to recover some air speed. He calmed down and applied what Whitey had taught him and flew a halfway decent traffic pattern. His landing was rough and bouncy, leaving a lot to be desired, but he got it down and slowed to taxi speed. Since there were no brakes, he didn't bother with a full stop but rolled up the power and took off again; this time with more control than the last. When he had finished his fifth landing and taxied over to the hangar Whitey was clapping his hands and when he was close enough for Farnsworth to hear him, he said, "Not bad. Thought sure I'd be callin for an ambulance after that first takeoff tho. Now alls I need is the money, three thousand five hundred dollars."

Farnsworth, all smiles now, said, "I won't be able to get you the cash until Monday, and I'll need you to keep it in the hangar for me after I pay you. Will that be OK?"

"Monday's fine. How long ya gonna need to rent my hangar and field?", Whitey asked with a scowl on his face.

"Not more than two weeks at the most Whitey, and what say I give you another hundred for those two weeks rent and field use; and do I need a key for anything?", Farnsworth asked.

"That'll be fine. No key. As far as I know, you and I are the only ones around can fly em, anyway.", Whitey smiled for the first time, revealing his grandly rotten front tooth.

CHAPTER 11

SLATS DROPPED ELMORE ON A BARE OUTCROPPING on the same side of the hill as Mr. Brown's villa but nearly 1500 feet below. He stood on the skid on the approach and jumped the two feet to the rocks while the aircraft came to a hover. Slats slid the aircraft sideways out into clear air and looked to wave at him with a thumb's up, which he returned from a crouch, signaling everything was "OK". For the first time she noticed that he was wearing pale grey cargo pants and a tan vest; both with pockets bulging with God knows what stuff that could make things go boom. The plan was for him to take no longer than one hour during which Slats would orbit at a predetermined location at level altitude about a mile away. That was what the Militia Commander had told Mr. Brown they would be doing in the way of a familiarization flight even though the militia moonlighters were there. The purpose was for them to identify his villa and all pertinent landmarks and the road to be able to know if anything was out of place when the required roll call alert happened and the guard had to leave. The ruse seemed to be working since Mr. Brown and his two other body guards had apparently gone back inside the main house where they remained out of sight. The Plot was in contact with the Militia Commander, and nothing occurred to cause any alarm. mostly about how much money it would cost to bring in the militia and pay them their meager salary for active duty time and an appropriate bonus.

So Slats and Sheila did a little bonding for the hour until they went back in close to extract Elmore, who was nowhere to be seen. After searching fruitlessly for 30 minutes, Slats' nerves and bladder combined to make her ask Sheila to hold the stick while she "watered the foliage". Slats had reached down and turned up the friction on the cyclic so it took some level of strength to move it, but not much; and had looked over to Sheila and said on intercom, "Just hold it steady. Put your feet on the pedals. You can reach them now since Elmore pulled the seat forward before he got out. Just keep the tops of your feet on the pedals evenly. I'll take care of the collective power for 'up and down' stuff. OK?" When she saw that Sheila had her feet on the pedals and her right hand on the cyclic she said, "You have the controls. You'll repeat that back to me when you see that I have my feet on the pedals and hand on the cyclic. Got it?"

"I've got it, but I'm damned sure I don't know what the hell I'm doing with it.", an obviously frightened white knuckled Sheila stuttered.

While Slats unzipped her flight suit and attached her "cup" to the standard piss tube funnel at the center of her seat and began to relieve herself she said, just hold everything steady and it'll be fine."

She had turned over the controls to Sheila headed away from the little mountain and she was taking longer than she thought to relieve herself so she stepped on the intercom button on the floor so as not to disturb Sheila's hold on the cyclic and said, "OK Sheila, I want you to push in a little left pedal and just think about moving the cyclic to the left. Go ahead and do that, will you?"

The next thing Slats knew she was pissing on the floor and they were skidding to the left. She instinctively stuck her right foot out pushing the right pedal to straighten the aircraft and when she did her piss hit the cup at the top and splashed the front of her flight suit, whereupon she stopped pissing and hollered "Shit" loud enough to make Sheila look over.

"I have the controls.", Slats said into the intercom firmly.

Shelia kept hold of the cyclic and pulled the intercom transmit button and said, "I guess I pushed too hard, huh?", Then, "But I kind of liked trying to fly."

"We'll have to work on your touch some more. Later. Much later. Where's that asshole anyway?", Slats growled as the outcropping came into sight.

Elmore was just making his way back to the pickup point; about another 800 feet of downhill slope to negotiate and he'd be there. He'd taken more time than he had anticipated, but everything was in place to set the timers to blow not only the diesel generator and it's huge tank of fuel, but also the antenna and security feed lines and breaker box at the side of the main house. To top it all off, Elmore had slipped inside the garage and placed charges with caps and timers on the bottom of each of the three vehicles inside; a big Mercedes, a GMC van, and a Ford F250 Crew Cab truck. He'd done good and knew it. Now he just had to get back to the pickup point fast. He knew Slats must be low on fuel by now. It had been over an hour and a half since they'd dropped him off, and another half hour of flight time before that, at least. He tried to pick up his pace, but quickly found out he risked sliding on his ass and a very long fall if he wasn't careful.

Slats looked at the blinking "Fuel Low" light on the instrument panel. When it came on it was supposed to tell the pilot there was only 20 minutes of flight time left. She tapped it with her right forefinger and it went out, but then came back on again and she said, "Shit. I just hope to hell the damned thing is accurate and we've got 20 minutes of fuel left before the engines quit."

"What?", Sheila screamed without using intercom, and at that moment Slats saw Elmore sliding the last few feet to the outcropping and she immediately set up an approach that would allow him to jump inside the cargo compartment.

Once inside and hooked up to the intercom Elmore said, "Hi ladies."

Slats growled back at him, "You son of a bitch. You sorry son of a bitch. What in the hell took you so long? We're about out of fuel. MAYBE enough to FLY back to the airport."

"What's that smell?", Elmore asked. Then, "Did somebody piss their panties?"

CHAPTER 12

DYKE, BUNNY AND CHICO ALMOST MISSED THEIR flight out of Miami because of a suspicious Homeland security agent who wanted more than just their Ids and badges, but Marplot had prepared them for that. Each one of them had a card with a name and phone number on it that Dyke handed to the agent and asked that he call that person at the number given. It was the U.S. Attorney General's Chief Administrative Advisor in Washington, D.C. who immediately pulled up the agent's personnel information on his computer and discovered his middle name was "Humphrey" and said, "Agent middle name Humphrey you will expedite the boarding of my three U.S. Marshals or you will find yourself providing homeland security in Nome, Alaska. Do you understand?"

"Yes sir.", was all that Dyke, Bunny and Chico heard the agent reply. Then, "Please follow me.", in an obviously disappointed voice. The agent was no more than five foot two and about as wide, and Dyke's imposing six foot three 260 pound shadow following him closely was no doubt imposing to the authoritative little man. He had put on 30 pounds in the last ten years, but it was still solid beef. Bunny, on the other hand, at five foot nine had lost at least 30 pounds from his previous, and ten years younger 210. This was mostly due to his new vegetarian and workout diet. He was a leaner, meaner, fighting machine even if he was pushing 50 right along with Dyke. Chico hadn't changed a bit. He was still five nine like Bunny, but had kept his same weight at 165. Of course, he was almost 20 years younger than both Bunny and Dyke, and they often affectionately referred to him as the "Taco Kid" or just "Taco".

The Plot met them at the airport with the Land Rover and had made arrangements with the El Presidente hotel clerk to put them up in two rooms across from his. He briefed them up on what had transpired thus far while enroute to the hotel and dropped them off at the entrance with, "Now I've got to go back to the airport and pick up Doc Leigh. At least I hope it's him and not his nephew Lee An Too."

Both of them were waiting at the curb when Marplot arrived back at the airport. Doc Leigh with white shirt, Chinos, and brown loafers with no socks; and Lee An Too with painted face, three animal incisor teeth in his left ear, hair in a braided pony tail down his back tied off with a small bone, leather vest without a shirt, new levis, and no shoes. Doc Leigh had a suitcase and Lee An Too had a leather satchel slung over his shoulder and nothing else. Doc Leigh also had bloodshot eyes and the foulest look on his face the Plot had ever seen as he said, "Plot, one of these days I'm gonna juice you into a dung beetle for interrupting me like this. I wasn't done with my tribes virgins, and there's another I have to tend to as well. The only reason I came is because I've not yet acclimated Lee An Too in the cultural morays of your side of the world, and I was afraid for all of you pissing him off to the point where he would do something about it you wouldn't like very much."

"Such as turning us all into dung beetles?", the Plot replied dryly.

"No.", Lee An Too piped in, and then stated flatly, "I make you all inside out and you shit for rest of life; smell yourself to death. Yuk yuk yuk!"

"Quiet.", Doc Leigh snarled. Then asked, "OK Plot. What's to do?"

"We're going to snatch Julius Brown and once we've got him I need you to put him under and get some bank account numbers and PINs from him, as well as some information on his smuggling architecture; names, places, exchanges etc.", the Plot said.

"You waste my time. Why didn't you call for me after you had him already?", Doc sighed.

"Primarily because we're all staying in the El Presidente hotel close to the beach in Rio, and I wanted all of our assets in place before we tried to get him so we could plan it all together. For example, how do you think it would look if we just brought him through the front door of the hotel gagged and tied up; and how long will it take for you to get him to reveal his secrets?", the Plot replied sternly. Then, "We need to plan on a dusk to dark snatch, and finding a safe house to use while you do your work, don't you think?"

"OK, but it still seems to me like you could've found a safe house and snatched him by now; and you should remember it took an afternoon and all night to get Bailey's secrets.", Doc steamed back. He certainly was in a foul mood, but the Plot knew he would calm down after he'd eaten and had a good night's sleep. Doc was well over 60, but nobody really knew how old he really was. Even his military 201 file just said he was "Peruvian male over 18". Under the category "born", some smartass clerk had typed in "Yes" and then had to try and erase it for the new one which was substantiated by a notarized sheet of paper out of the American consulate in Lima, Peru. Doc Leigh was known as Lee An within his Peruvian tribe, but when he had enlisted for Special Forces to be a medic in 1960 the records clerk said he needed a last name first, and a first name last as a minimum, so Doc asked the clerk what his first name last was and the kid said "Ralph". So he told the clerk his name was Lee, NMI, Ralph, and after seven years as a medic on an A-Team, he went to medical school and became an MD on an Army loan; which he repaid by serving 24 years and retiring as a Lieutenant Colonel. He had been recalled to active duty twice after that to participate in classified operations with a high probability of casualties, and was consequently upgraded to the rank of Colonel for the rest of his retirement. Now he was a very short five foot two, fat 220 pound, cranky retired Colonel that was hungry and tired.

"Whatsay we get you two into your room and fed, and then I'll brief you on what we've got so far?", the Plot soothed. Two "grunts" came simultaneously from the Doc beside him and his nephew in the back.

CHAPTER 13

IN HIS ROOM FARNSWORTH CAREFULLY COUNTED OUT $3500.00. He used thirty two of the hundreds, but included fourteen twenty's, three fives, and five ones just like a bank might make change for someone. Besides that, it made the stack of money look more meaningful he thought. Then, almost forgetting the hangar rent and field use for two weeks he added another hundred dollar bill. Now he was down to $5512.00 cash in hand. He would still need to pay Murf $60.00 for the two sticks of dynamite and buy 100 pounds of fertilizer, and he would probably have to give Mickey some money for fuel oil. He was thinking about all of this while walking to the General Store and hoping that Large Marge either wasn't there or wouldn't recognize him.

She wasn't there, but an older gentleman was behind the counter reading a newspaper spread out in front of him. He looked up when Farnsworth's entry caused the little bell at the top of the door to ring, but immediately went back to reading his paper. It must've been the John Deere hat Farnsworth thought as he looked around and finally saw what he was looking for. He plucked a box of black plastic trash bags off a counter and then went further down the aisle to the back where there were Army surplus items scattered all over. Entrenching tools, fatigue pants and shirts, field jackets, and ah hah, a couple of duffle bags. He looked them over and took the one that appeared to be in the best shape and walked over and set them on the counter beside the old man's newspaper and asked, "How much for the duffel bag, and have you got some fertilizer?"

"Let's see.", the old man said as he rubbed his chin trying to remember how much he'd paid for the duffel bags, and then he remembered he'd given the guy $12.00 for the three of them. "The trash bags is $2.99 and the duffel bag is $12.00 making it $14.99, and I've got 50 and 100 pound bags of High Nitrogen fertilizer. Fifty pound bag is $21.99 and the 100 pound bag is $39.99.", he said.

"OK. I'll take the trash bags, duffel bag, and a 100 pound bag of the fertilizer.", Farnsworth drawled.

Surprising Farnsworth completely, the old man said, "Hear yer tryin to buy the highway frontage land down at RANGE 19. Whatca gonna do with it if'n ya don't mind me askin?"

Farnsworth thought quickly and said, "Well, the first thing I'm gonna do is a little irrigation by making a pond large enough to raise catfish in. I aim to raise em and sell em to grocery stores cleaned and packaged."

"Figured somthin like that. Want some advice?", the old man offered.

"Sure.", Farnsworth replied.

"Shrimp; raise shrimp. That's brackish water you'll be getting in yer pond, and I do believe you'll have trouble raisin either freshwater or saltwater catfish. Sides that, you'll get more money per pound of shrimp and they'll do right well in that kinda water.", the old man said with a grin; and then, "I like shrimp a lot better than catfish anyway. Expect some to come my way every now an then for the advice, eh? That'll be a total of $80.68 with tax.", the old man smiled.

They walked through the rear door to the store into a fenced in storage area where the fertilizer was kept and the old man helped Farnsworth stuff the fertilizer inside the duffel bag with the trash bag box on top and then get it over his shoulder so he could haul it back to his motel room. Things were working out nicely, Farnsworth thought. The fuel oil wouldn't be a problem. He could get Mickey to fill up two five gallon gas cans for him which he would keep in the back of Murf's pickup until time to line the duffel bags with two of the trash bags, pour in the fertilizer, and mix in the fuel oil. Then the final step of rigging the two sticks of dynamite with short fuzes and - - - shit, he thought. He'd have to figure out some way to rig the whole thing to the aircraft with a quick release without Whitey or anyone else seeing him do it. He didn't have much doubt that the little ultra light airplane would lift him and the duffel bag, but he'd have to figure out where to put it on the plane without it interfering with flying it. Damn. Always something.

Farnsworth got the duffel bag into his motel room and stretched out on the bed to catch his breath. He didn't realize just how much 100 pounds was these days and thought to himself, maybe that was too much anyway considering the problem with carrying it on the little plane. He knew a quarter pound of C4 with a 50-50 mix of fuel oil and fertilizer in a 55 gallon drum would blow a hole in the ground about six to eight feet deep and clear an eight inch tree that was 10 feet away, but he really didn't know what a duffel bag would do. Anyway, he figured he could rig it to the plane on the night he planned to drop it on the Hootch and Slaughter, but he'd have to go out and fly some more tomorrow and take a closer look at the undercarriage and sides to see how and where he could attach it to the plane. Since tomorrow was Sunday there would be little else to do but that and find out what Whitey drank from Murf so he could take him a bottle. Then he would seal the deal Monday afternoon.

The next morning Murf woke him up by banging on his door at 7:30AM asking if he wanted grits and eggs, and oh by the way, the RANGE 19 Hootch maids had told Large Marge that Mr. Simon and everyone was gone for the next week or so.

Farnsworth quickly got dressed and went to the restaurant with Murf to get grits, eggs, and a full repeat. Son of a bitch. He'd have to cool his heels; but on the other hand it would give him time to work out every last detail.

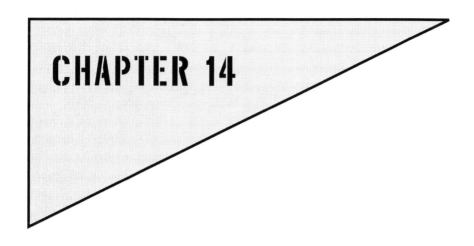

CHAPTER 14

THERE WERE TEN PEOPLE INCLUDING MARPLOT CROWDED into his hotel room, all listening to him relate details of what had transpired thus far into the plan to snatch Julius Brown.

When it appeared he had covered everything Lee An Too piped in with, "I take skull and gall bladder."

Everyone looked at him except Doc Leigh who simply stated, "I assume we are not going to try and confine him somewhere; and feed and water him for the remainder of his life. What's the plan of disposal?"

Marplot raised his hands and said, "Let's leave this subject for the time being and concentrate on getting him under wraps first, shall we?" He had no intentions of discussing this in front of everyone present so he asked, "Slats, are you comfortable with the helicopter and the flying end of the mission?" To which she simply gave a thumbs up so Marplot continued with, "Elmore. How about you? Are you satisfied we can disable his security and communications, and get in and get out without any problems?"

"I believe I've done everything I can. The C4, blasting caps, timers, weapons and ammo you got from the Brazilian Militia Commander appears aged, but healthy enough to do the job; and I've placed redundant charges in case any one of them fails. I do believe we need to completely immobilize the target and strap him to a stretcher to get him down the side of the mountain and into the aircraft just like he was a casualty; and, I believe we should conduct a rehearsal in two parts. The first being the infiltration, neutralization of the body guards, immobilization of the subject and any hired servants; and the second being the downhill recovery to the pick up area and loading on the helicopter. We'll need to ballast for one of the snatch team who will ride in the stretcher and thrash about in case Brown becomes conscious. We'll need to ballast however much weight we need to meet the 245 pounds Brown weighs as well.", Elmore said.

Slats said, "I think I know a spot on that next mountain South of Brown's where we can do the up and down stuff, but somebody else is gonna have to find a house to clear."

Marplot said, "I anticipated this requirement and have already rented a safe house outside the city and away from prying eyes. It's also where we'll be taking Brown for the Doc to do his thing to get all the numbers out of him. Since today is Sunday, I suggest we plan on doing all of our rehearsing tomorrow and plan the snatch for the following evening around 10PM. I'll have the Militia Commander call his alert at 9PM which will give them an hour to all get gone. Once we have the Bank names, PINs and account numbers, Elmore will be on his way."

Sheila immediately piped up and said, "I believe I need to go with Elmore as well since following the money trail would be a large part of the article on how the international drug smuggling operation worked."

Although Slaughter had worked with Elmore on and off years ago, he wasn't sure about his amorous proclivities and blurted out, "I'm not so sure I like that idea Sheila. It could get nasty if Brown has his own people there looking out for his interests."

"Ah hah! That's why I have a gun that you taught me how to shoot things with; and I've even got an ID and badge to prove I can even wear it on my hip if I want.", she facetiously replied.

That's that damned Pulitzer talking again, Slaughter thought and angrily said, "Well I can change that right now if you think I'm just blowing sunshine up your ass."

"Oh boy." Elmore whispered and thought, I'm not getting in the middle of this one.

Marplot quickly said, "Alright, lets not ruin our planning before we're even finished. I agree that Sheila should go with Elmore; but I also agree that she should not go with her U.S. Marshal's status. It would attract too much attention from customs and alert anyone that might be interested in finding out what she's there for. She will go on a different flight with different reservations and meet up with Elmore on location as if a single tourist. How's that?"

"FINE", Slaughter and Sheila both said at once and scowled at each other.

"Now.", Marplot continued. "Elmore, you are booked into the Hyatt where Guido will be staying and can meet with him at the bar or something; however you want to work it. Sheila, you should stay there as well to make things easier to coordinate, but not arrive until a day after Elmore to give him and Guido a chance to find out what they can. Elmore, you will be carrying a cashiers check for $1,500,000 U.S. dollars which I have already paid taxes on, and you will open a business account in the name of Arpslot Enterprises LLC, a Limited Liability Company at this address in the Cayman Islands.", and he handed Elmore a business card with the company name, address, and local phone and fax numbers embossed in gold.

"Exactly what kind of business is it?", Elmore asked.

"Financial Consulting and Personal Wealth Management", Marplot smiled and said; and then continued with, "We may even wind up making money once we find out more about, hold on to your hat, financial management. Heh heh."

CHAPTER 15

THE LITTLE RED AIRPLANE FARNSWORTH WAS GOING to buy from Whitey sat motionless in the low ceiling hangar as he looked at it searching for a way to rig the duffel bag of explosives. The only place besides his lap would be at the very front of the little plane's front tubing, but the area was way too small and the weight that far forward would be a problem getting the thing off the ground and controlling it in flight even if it would leave the ground. He simply had to come up with something smaller. He might have to resort to Molotov cocktails and just throwing the sticks of dynamite themselves making several passes over the little island and it's Hootch. As he sat looking at the plane Whitey came staggering around the corner and slurred, "Thought it mite be you Smitz. Havin second thoughts are ya?"

"Naw. I'm just admiring it some.", Farnsworth replied and stood up to face Whitey. At that point Whitey offered Farnsworth an open quart canning jar which was filled three fourths of the way to the top with a clear liquid, and it had a peeled peach resting on the bottom. Farnsworth took it and asked, "Lightnin?"

"Best in the `Glades' if I do say so myself. Take a swig an tell me whatcha think.", Whitey said with a knowing smirk on his face.

Farnsworth wasn't fooled. If he had learned anything at Ft Bragg and the surrounding area, it was that moonshine, or "sploe" as it was known in some quarters, was best tested lightly before supping deeply. He knew better than to take a big swallow, so he took a small taste. Still, it made him gag a little and he could feel it burn all the way down to his stomach. He took a big breath and said, "Oh yeah. That's the real McCoy."

"Ya jus sipped. Ya need t' have a real swig t' givit proper preciation.", Mickey rumbled behind a destructive flow of rancid breath. Not to be intimidated, Farnsworth took a large swallow and then could only exhale all the air in his lungs as he cleared his throat with a loud, "Augggh".

"Thas better.", Whitey smiled benignly and with his lips pressed together, retrieved the jar from Farnsworth anticipating his turn. He had himself two large swallows and wiping his left forearm across his mouth saying, "Damn thas good. Wan another bite?" Farnsworth declined the offer by reminding Whitey that he had to drive back to the Motel and didn't want to get arrested for drunk driving. As he started to head toward the pickup Whitey said, "Yeah. Ole sheriff Baugh can be a hardun on that. Gets re'lected ever year on his recerd of cunvictions fer DUI. Been in office o'r 16 year now. Say, aren't ya curious bout where I git this stuff?"

"I figure ya made it yursef Whitey. Probly got you a still in the 'glades somwheres, and an airboat too. I'm not as dum as I look.", Farnsworth said noticing the slight squint Whitey had put on his face at Farnsworth's suspicion. Then immediately said, "But it ain't no business o' mine. Rekon I could have anuther pull?"

"I lik u boy. Tomorra I want ya to meet a frienda mine might be able to hep ya with whatcher doin; an I kno it ain't blowin no pond to rais catfish er shrimps. Yu're here to either caus sum grief to the folks at Range 19 or yur undercover DEA lookin fur sumpin else. Don't think it's me cause if'n that wus it, you'd of already dun put the bracelets on my raggedy ass. Ennyway, this guy I know, Rob; he's got lots o' former military experience flyin helicopters an livs jus down the road. He owns the auto parts and repair shop at Crossroads. Mickey works fer im.", Whitey slurred on as he passed the quart mason fruit jar to Farnsworth, who took a manly slug. He was feeling pretty cocky, yet disturbed that Whitey had read him so easily. He needed to come up with something fast, but couldn't. Still, things were falling into place one way or another but it seemed out of his control, so to give himself some time to think he asked, "What's Rob's story anyway?".

Whitey took another deep pull from the jar and seemed to go away for a bit. Shortly he came back, looked at Farnsworth for a moment, then said, "He's got a buncha medals and got shot up pretty bad. Friends shot down and murdered. Had lotsa operations an medcal treetment. Fer a while there his hed wus all fuked up causa what he'd seen down in South Amerika durin some drug bustin operations. Seems sum lil kid came around the corner of a building he was suppos to be gardin an opened up on the helicopter with an AK, so they kilt him. Seems he sees that kid gittin kilt over n' over in his sleep, but he hanls it purty well now, even with suma thu other shit he did fur the guvmen't still botherin him. He wuz gonna buy lil red there, but his wife nixed it. I figure she figured he'd jus fly it off into the sunset an not come back."

"Sounds like PTSD to me.", Farnsworth said, and then continued with, "Whitey, I'm not undercover anything; I ain't no kinda FED and I really am here to meet with the owner of the land alongside the highway at Range 19; Simon Arpslot's his name I believe, if the Dade records are correct. There's about 28 acres and the water table is supposed to be more than 28 inches below ground; perfect for a long filtrated pond in which to raise something to sell - froglegs, shrimp, minnow bait, you name it. Thas my plan anyway." Farnsworth sincerely pled his case.

"Yeah, yeah, yeah. Yer fullashit. They ain't nuttin wifin 100 miles that'd wan any tha. No market. Been here almost fifty year an tha dog don bark much less hunt. Yer up t'sumpin else, but I don givashit as

long as ya cum thru wif tha dough fer the plane. An what's a PTSD?",
Whitey stammered.

"It's Post Traumatic Stress Disorder Whitey. It's a psych term for
bad memories that keep botherin ya over an over; like a long sliver
stuck in your foot that even after ya pull the sonovabitch out ya gotta
wait for the rest of it to get pushed out by yer body; but in this case
it's the brain's gotta do the pushin, unnerstan?. Whitey looked at him
with glazed over eyes and a cocked head, then shrugged his shoulders
and said, "Guess so."

That over with, Farnsworth said, "I'll be here tomorra bout 10AM
after I git to thu bank an back. Closest one is back toward Miami
bout 15 miles, so I shud makit by 10.", Farnsworth stuttered. He was
definitely feeling the peach, but felt sure if he drove carefully he'd make
it back to the motel without any problem.

Once he got on the highway he realized he had no headlights and
had to creep along at 30 miles an hour with the parking lights barely
illuminating the edge of the road. Cars and trucks coming at him
from the other direction all honked loudly at him and flashed their
headlights. This was really dumb. He could get caught by the cops
from either direction; so, at the first driveway he pulled over, turned
off the parking lights, and shut off the engine. Then he curled up in the
front seat and went to sleep. The moonshine took over and he was able
to ignore the mosquitoes for the night.

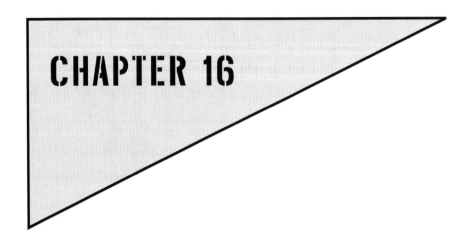

CHAPTER 16

THE NIGHT BEFORE THE SNATCH ON JULIUS Brown was to take place Sheila demanded a meeting with Slaughter, and Marplot in Marplot's room, isolated with no probability of interruptions; meaning cell phones off and the hotel phone unplugged. She had done this immediately after the big gathering to finalize details. She simply grabbed both by the arm and saying, "We need to talk, alone, here, as soon we can get rid of the others."

"OK Sheila, what's up?" Slaughter asked knowing full well 'what was up'. It was that damned Pulitzer shit again, and her feelings of being professionally and artistically thwarted in her opportunities to get it.

"Here's the deal you two. You got me into this RANGE 19 secret squirrel shit such that my true journalistic talents, however meager they may be, are hamstrung by your blackouts and restrictions on what I can put to print - - - and I can't accept that anymore. I can't take the way this badge and gun albatross around my neck limits anything I try to write. I want out of the U.S. Marshal business, and I want freedom to write. Don't get me wrong. I truly appreciate the opportunities I've been given and the insight I have into so many things now, but I can no longer accept all the internal censorship and redacting to everything I create."

For several minutes there was nothing but silence and two somber faces looking at her. Then, Marplot said, "I understand. You have all this sensational information and the skills to write about it. You want to publish this stuff and you want the recognition and kudos that should accompany it. You still harbor the dreams of a Pulitzer prize, don't you? That's a fair assumption, right Slaughter?".

"Yeah, I suppose that's it Plot. But I don't think giving up her U.S. Marshal status is mutually exclusive to any recognition she may get from the media squirts that judge these things.", he blurted out.

"They are not `MEDIA SQUIRTS'. They are distinguished journalists. Journalists that have been selected by their peers to decide what awards are given. And the U.S. Marshal shit is a joke. Slaughter, all you trained me to do is shoot a gun. I'm no lawyer, and I don't even know the elements of probable cause for a search warrant." Sheila immediately reacted.

"That's not why you need the credentials Sheila. The status gives you clearance through airline security and customs; it makes it easier for you to move about and provides some other protections, that's all - besides having something to protect yourself with just in case." Slaughter said as he moved closer to her to put his arm around her shoulder. She looked up at him and then said, "Alright, alright. But I want more literary freedom with this case. I want to collect exclusive information on how drug money moves around the globe and why it's so hard for the authorities to track it; why it's so hard to step in and do something about it."

"I kind of like that idea. But I still have to retain overall editorial authority to make sure nothing goes public that would harm the RANGE 19 program in any way. Will that work for you Sheila?" the Plot asked softly.

Sheila looked at Slaughter who was smiling broadly and she knew immediately that her journalistic status had already been discussed between the two of them. She would have to quit underestimating these guys, so instead of being pissed, she smiled and gave each of them a hug saying, "Thank you. In different ways, I love you both very much."

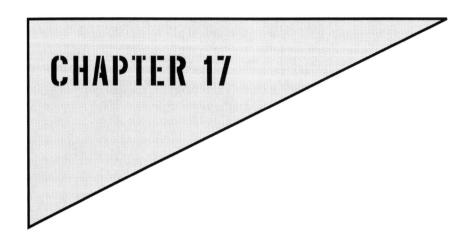

CHAPTER 17

GUIDO CHECKED IN AT THE MARRIOTT HOTEL in the Caymans and as soon as possible took a tour of the business district where he identified no less than nine banks, all with shiny brass lettering or plaques on marble bases advertising their presence. Some even had marble steps leading to huge tall entrance doors with lavishly attired doormen and valet parking attendants. The banks seemed to have congregated on the inland side of the island's main thoroughfare while the other side hosted the beach front hotels and tourist shops, but there was one large four story building that was identified solely by plain metal numbers in the facade. He ventured inside the lobby to find a desk in the middle with an attractive young black woman attendant who watched him walk over to the directory on the wall. It didn't take him a moment to spot "James Julius Enterprises, Inc. and turn smiling at her, prompting her to ask immediately , "May I help you, sir?"

"I'm here to see Mr. Julius. Do you know if he's in his office?", he asked.

"If you give me your name I will call and tell them you are on your way up.", she chimed.

"If you would please, just ask if I might speak with Mr. Julius, or make an appointment if he is not available. My name is Guido Lempke from the New York Police Department.", Guido said and smiled as if he knew something she didn't. All part of the game he'd played many times before.

"Of course sir." she said promptly but with a hint of uncertainty. Following a short soto voce conversation on the phone she said, "I'm very sorry sir. Mr. James is not on the island at present and there is no itinerary showing his return time or date. Could anyone else help you?" she formally asked.

"Well I don't know. Is there a Vice President or Senior Financial Officer who's here? All I need is some information on a client of theirs if someone could help me.", Guido played along.

"Let me find out for you sir." the receptionist said flatly; and then, "Tammy, Mr. James' Personal Secretary can help you. You can take the elevator to your right and the office is all the way down the hall on the right."

"Thank you very much Susan." he said as he read her nametag and turned toward the elevators. This was too easy, he thought. He would run by Mr. James' personal secretary a list of known big time drug dealers in New York City to see if her eyes gave him any connections and if there were none he would try and woo her for a drink and dinner; play it cool. He still had some level of charm and grey hair just over the ears with dark black hair above; and he was in good shape. We'll just have to see he thought as he pushed the button for the 4th floor. It was a short ride up but a longer walk along the corridor to the main doors of James Julius Enterprises. When he walked in he was greeted by a tall blond who spoke with a French accent saying, "Mr. Lempke. How may we help you?"

Guido didn't immediately respond to her question, but rather walked toward the huge left hand window to admire the ocean view and said, "Wow, what a beautiful view."

"Yes, everyone who comes to this office does the same thing. For me, it's the same thing everyday, no?" He laughed at her comment, giving him a chance to show off his new dental implants and addictive smile.

Then, "Tammy, I'm sure the young lady downstairs has already told you I'm a cop from New York and I am investigating some people who may have business with your office. I'm also on a boondoggle goose chase called a paid vacation. You follow me?" he asked with a raised eyebrow.

She looked at him strangely and asked, "Boondoggle? I'm not sure I understand."

"I'm on official business looking into a smuggling operation as a part of a team that hasn't arrived yet, so I'm also on vacation and I'm looking for someone to show me around and have fun with. I don't know a soul on this island except you and the young lady downstairs. Can you help me? " he pleaded trying on his best "bad boy looking for a good time" expression.

"By that, do you mean a referral to an escort service?" she coyly asked.

"No!" he replied laughing merrily. "I meant you. That is if you're unattached and not too busy. And I really do need some financial advice about what to do with my retirement funds.", Guido beamed.

Apparently his approach worked. She looked him over with a cocked head and seemed to be judging the pros and cons of his approach. After several long moments she seemed to reach a decision, she gave him a radiant smile and said, "Sure. I can put the phone on transfer to my cell phone in case anything comes up. Shall we go?" He noticed that as they left the office she stuck a sign on the inside of the door that said, "Call local 415-4150 for official business." and then locked the door behind them asking, "Where would you like to start? My time is your time for the next six hours until I have to return to the office to close out the day's receipts and transfers; and you must feed me a very expensive lunch."

Receipts and transfers. Guido would have to dig into that area, carefully of course. He was very attracted to this woman, even though she was two inches taller than his 5 foot 10 inches. She had to be at least six feet tall and with her chignon and spike heels she seemed to tower over him. She had a silky stride in spite of the three inch spiked heels which most definitely did something for her breastworks and posture. He automatically stood up straighter and squared his shoulders as they entered the elevator. In the parking garage she led him to a shiny black 81 Mercedes 380SL that already had the convertible top down. The black leather interior was spotless and smelled of a mixture of rosewater and saddle soap.

"It's a mixture of rosewater and saddle soap", she said as she noticed his sniff at getting in the car.

"This model Mercedes has been my favorite ever since they started making them. It's got the most classic lines and shape ever made." Guido said while rubbing the leather dash softly and passing an appreciative eye over the dashboard, steering wheel, and her legs. He was admiring her legs when she decided to start her own investigation by asking if he were married or had any children; or maybe he was gay, no?

"NO, no and no.", he snapped, and then said, "I was married, but found out I was married to my wife's mother and it didn't work. So I'm divorced. How about you? As beautiful a woman as you are you must have a dozen men on the string, or are you gay and it's a string of women?"

She laughed a wonderful, throaty laugh that was as contagious as anything could get and made him laugh as well.

"No no no. I prefer men to pamper me, not women.", she said, and then laughed again. Her teeth were very white and even except for a small gap between the two front teeth that reminded him of a model from the 80s. Her tan was genuine as shown by the tiny wrinkles by her eyes.

"Well, let me pamper you today. Show me the sights of the island, call the best restaurant on the island and make a reservation for lunch;

and then maybe we could rent a boat and see the island from the ocean view. What do you think?", he bubbled.

"I think I know the restaurant, and I own my own small motor sailer. Did you bring a bathing suit? We can go snorkeling at a wonderful place I know ", she enthused, getting into the idea of stolen time off.

"No I didn't bring one. I haven't been swimming in years. I'm not sure about any snorkeling." he scowled.

"She laughed again, only this time with a glint of mischief in her eye. "We will buy you one and I will teach you how to snorkel, yes?", she said smiling that beautiful smile of hers. Who could resist.

Tammy was short for Tammarah Guido found out. He also found out she drove the beautiful little sports car like she stole it. There were bicycles, three wheeled cabbies, and pedestrian tourists scrambling for safety as she blared on the little car's horn, challenging them for space and right of way, but Guido was too enthralled with her beauty to say a word about her driving.

It only took about an hour and a half to drive around the main parts of the island.

Soon they were back near the business district and shops where she suddenly pulled into a vacant parking space on the street adjacent to a large dry goods store. She hopped out of the car and with Guido in tow skipped into the store.

"What size are you?", she abruptly asked him while holding up a very loud bathing suit in the half leg boxer style. It must've had every color on Monet's palate imprinted on it and he wrinkled his nose and said, "I'm a 34 inch waist and might do better in something that didn't scream loud noises at the fish, don't you think?"

She laughed that wonderful laugh again, which started him up again. She turned back to the suits on display and quickly picked five of various patterns, all brightly colored. She held them up in front of him on display and demanded, "You pick."

They all screamed at his sense of style but he realized he had to pick one. He took one that was predominately New York City Cop blue but all were constructed in a style similar to the suit she had originally picked out. Then he saw racks of Bermuda shorts and other plain colored shorts and, carrying his blue swim trunks he walked over to that area. It only took him a moment to spot a pair of tennis shorts, size 34, and he held them up for her approval. She wrinkled her nose and wagging a disapproving forefinger said, "No no no. We are going snorkeling; not making an old James Bond movie. I must be able to see you better under water, and the longer suit legs will help protect you from any coral you may bump into." So he shrugged his shoulders in resignation and put the tennis shorts back only to look up and see her paying for the bathing suit with her Platinum credit card at the cashier's counter.

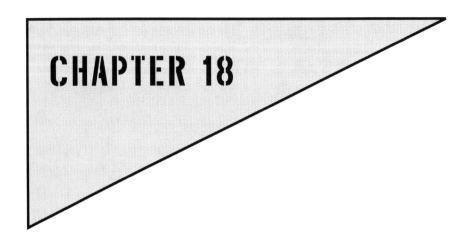

CHAPTER 18

THE PLOT WAS ON THE PHONE WITH the Commander of the Militia, so the operational team of Slaughter, Elmore, Dyke, Bunny, Chico, and Sheila could only hear his side of the conversation. Slats was at the airport pre flighting the helicopter. She would take off in 30 minutes, arrive at the old farm house in 15 minutes, leaving 15 minutes to get to the landing zone on the side of the mountain.

"Can you call for them in one hour and explain to Mr. Brown that the helicopter surveillance will begin right away?", Marplot asked, then, "Excellent. If all goes well I will have a nice bonus for you my friend; and please remember, you know nothing of Mr. Brown's whereabouts or activities. I'm sure General Emelios would not want to hear of his militia alert force hiring themselves out as bodyguards for foreigners, eh? Yes, yes. I believe you my friend. So long for now, I must go."

"Last check for equipment.", Slaughter said with a slightly raised voice.

They were all wearing dark shirts and pants with black Kevlar armored vests with integrated combat pouches and kits and sturdy rubber soled black boots - nothing shiny except Bunny's eyes, but all of their eyes would be the only thing shiny once they pulled down their wool balaclavas and had their black nomex gloves on. Each operator carried "flash bang" grenades, smoke grenades, C4 gas grenades, M26 fragmentation grenades, gas masks, MP5SD 9mm submachine guns with built in suppressors and telescoping stocks, and seven loaded magazines of 30 rounds each as well as a 9mm Glock pistol and three 15 round magazines. Each also wore a headset with a voice activated microphone linked to a small VHF radio that provided encrypted voice communication. The radios were mounted on the side of the vest. Some had knives mounted according to personal preference; and all of them had a small, powerful flashlight stored in a vest pocket with another mounted on their MP5SD. Even Elmore, who would do most of the running around setting fuzes and timers, was carrying the same load of gear as everyone else. He would carry out his tasks while Chico provided security and he did his work; the rest would remain hidden about 100 yards behind to await Elmore's call. Then they would make the assault on the main building and Bunny would peel off to cover the servants quarters. That was the plan at least.

Slats was concerned about the weather. A thunderhead was building rapidly a short distance to the South, the direction from which the winds were coming, and that meant a thunderstorm might move in about the time they were scheduled to finish the job. As she settled the helicopter down in the cleared area in front of the farmhouse and sat at flight idle waiting for the men to board she noted the time on the console clock and compared it with her GMT Rolex. Even though it was a man's model, she wouldn't wear anything else while flying; and the timepieces were in synch.

"Hey beautiful. Give a poor GI a lift?", Elmore said as he slid into the right side pilot's seat. Slats would normally occupy that seat as it gave the pilot access to the more critical circuit breakers and overhead switches, but she was more comfortable flying from the left seat as the aircraft commander, and it gave her a better view of the LZ when she had to slide in to discharge the team.

Before she answered Elmore, she twisted around to check the

personnel in the rear. She saw that everyone was buckled in and that Slaughter was wearing the crew chief's headset, not saying anything, but sticking his fist out with his thumb up. Looking out the front windshield she saw Sheila with her hands on her hips shouting something into Marplot's face. Her camera equipment was all on the floor of the porch and Marplot grabbed her by the arm and all but drug her back inside the farmhouse. "Obviously, Sheila is not coming.", Slats observed matter of factly.

"No, she's not. She's got all the footage and still photos she could possibly need to write her article. She doesn't need video of a bloody commando raid with explosions and the snatching of a fat man. Besides, she's got to take a round about route to the Cayman Islands and catch up with Guido to cover the money angle with him and Elmore once we're done here.", Slaughter's voice stuttered in synch with the slow moving rotor blades.

"Well, if this is it, then we're off to Disneyworld.", she said as she lifted the helicopter to a hover, turned it around, and then pulled in more power and lowered the nose to go through translational lift and increase airspeed.

"Oh by the way. See that big thunderhead off to the right? We may be in for some nasty weather depending on how long you guys take.", She said over intercom, which only Elmore and Slaughter could hear; and when she looked at Elmore she saw him look back at Slaughter and shrugging his shoulders as if to say "it don't mean nothing - we got a job to do". "Just thought I'd mention it.", she said dryly. "Oh yeah, Doc Leigh and Lee An Too are up on the satellite telephone, that's number 5 on your overhead dial, newly installed by me in case you're wondering; and he said he'd like a call when we're about 5 minutes.", she said.

At the LZ she slid the helicopter into position avoiding strikes on the surrounding trees, held the aircraft at a hover about a foot above the flat rock. She was surprised at how smoothly they all moved and how fast they exited, especially Elmore who had to get out of the pilot's seat and maneuver his body and equipment back between the two pilot seats and then cross the cargo compartment to hop out onto the flat rock. His weight moving that much from right to left did cause her to dip the aircraft a little, but not enough to create a problem as he was the last one out.

She climbed vertically 50' to clear the trees and smoothly peeled up and off to the right, continuing in a wide climbing turn until the aircraft was 1500 feet above the top of the mountain and the villa. She leveled off and took up an orbit to appear that the aircraft was watching over Mr. Brown's privacy. Apparently the cover story concerning the militia and helicopter security was working when the elusive Mr. Brown came out onto his veranda during her second pass and waved at the helicopter before abruptly turning around and going back inside. Slats didn't see a bodyguard, but assumed he was probably just inside the doorway.

"OK." said Elmore, " I'll lead the way up to a spot I found about 100 yards short of the alarm tripwire fence that circles the perimeter. If you hit it an alarm will sound but its pretty simple, just do not touch it and you're clear. I've put fatigue cloth on the wire so you can see it. Just step over it and move directly to the back of the machine shed housing the primary diesel generator. That's where I'll be. We'll start the show by blowing the control box in the shed. It controls all the security cameras, the motion detectors protecting close approaches to the main residence, and the perimeter tripwire alarm; and then I will cut the fuel flow to the generator. Then he took a few seconds to review the key aspects of the operations from that point.

"Five seconds after you guys execute the assault on the main house and servants quarters, I will make things go "boom". If you meet anyone outside that is unarmed, take them down without killing them if possible; if they are armed and present a threat, take'em out -- neutralize any threat you encounter. And don't' forget. This is a burglary. Take rings, watches, and billfolds from the bodyguards and any jewelry Brown has in his bedroom or elsewhere. Don't take anything from the servants, and don't speak any English. Slaughter, do you have anything?", Elmore asked.

"Yeah, I do. Even though we've all got commo, don't use it unless absolutely necessary, and use secure mode only. The DEA listens in 24/7, and they've got NSA assets on call which means we can't underestimate their capabilities to monitor or exploit radio communications, so it's emergencies only. Elmore, you don't know our codes so don't use your radio for anything but calling for one of us you can see. Remember, just like we rehearsed, our call signs are the first letter of our names. Bunny is "Bravo", Dyke is "Delta" etc. Once you and Chico have blown everything up but the buildings, how about covering just outside the front door for us?", Slaughter asked. "No problem; but Chico and I can keep visual between us so I will cover the front for you and Chico will do the same for Bunny?", Elmore suggested.

"Better idea, thanks.", Slaughter smiled and said.

According to plan, the main security circuit box and generator all went "Boom" just as Slaughter and Dyke entered the main house. They literally ran over Julius Brown on entry, spinning him around till he fell into his bodyguard. Apparently he was on his way back outside; to look at the helicopter. He was carrying a large pair of binoculars that went flying only to shatter the lens on impact.

His bodyguard, walking ten feet behind him, was pretty good. He quickly recovered from his initial surprise, and skipped to one side to clear his client's rolling bulk, but his attempt to draw his weapon from his shoulder holster was stopped in mid-draw. Dyke's suppressed MP5SD spat three phitt, phitt, phitt's; the first round struck the bodyguard's left eye; the following two struck an inch apart in the center of his forehead.

Already dead on his feet, the man's knees buckled, his corpse dropped into a boneless heap. Julius Brown was screaming "Juan, Juan, hurry Juan." as he struggled to get his bulk off the floor. Slaughter's kick struck the side of his head just an inch behind the left ear. He was out like a light.

Juan's loyalty had already evaporated. Juan did not know what was happening but he heard the crack of the charge in the shed. Adding Brown's panicked screaming was all it took to dilute his loyalty.

When Dyke reached the entrance to the back bedroom he gave a quick peek before entering. A peek was enough; Juan was in the middle of skipping out via the back bedroom window. Dyke ran into the room, moved to one side of the doorway and gave the entire room a quick visual sweep keeping his weapon in the center of his vision during the sweep.. With his submachine gun at the high ready he remained set to immediately engage any threat he might encounter. In this case, during the time he took to clear the room, Juan dropped below the window. Chagrined, Dyke ran to a point just inside the window. He looked around the edge of the window in time to see Juan jump to his feet and with pistol in hand, start running to the woods at the edge of the facility. Dyke raised the weapon, put the red dot in his optical sight on the back of the running man's head and shot him twice. He crawled out the window without taking his eyes off of the prone bodyguard, dropped down to the ground and walked to the body. The entrance and exit wounds told him the man was dead but he felt his neck for a pulse to be absolutely sure.

Following the plan, he retrieved the man's wristwatch, wallet, and the thick money clip he found inside Juan's left front pocket. He also picked up the Browning 9mm automatic lying on the ground near the body and heaved it as far as he could down the side of the mountain. He listened till the noise from the pistol crashing through the trees ceased; then went back into the house through the window he'd exited and cleared the rest of the house until he arrived back in the main entryway where Slaughter and Elmore were dealing with a gagged and flex tied Mr. Brown. They were trying to get the still groggy man onto his unrestrained feet. Slaughter had talked Elmore into trying to get him down the side of the mountain without using the stretcher. It would take all four of them to haul him down on the stretcher. With weather closing in they needed to be faster and the terrain proved to be rougher and the rocks looser than the recon indicated. It would be easy to injure their own people on the rough terrain. Better if he could stumble along himself. If not, then they would just roll the fat fart like a hoop if need be.

Bunny and Chico were watching a woman and small child as they hurriedly walked down the dusty road that led to the base of the mountain, the road to their village. They had decided to let them go once Chico found out that there were no others at the villa. Their bloodshed would only cause unwanted visibility and local concern, and there was no tactical necessity to harm them anyway. They had seen or heard nothing worthwhile.

As the member of the team assembled at the objective rally point, the slanting sun was suddenly blocked by thick clouds. Wind direction changed and a humid cool breeze swept the hacienda. The evening turned dark and chilly. Slaughter realized the weather was rapidly deteriorating and Slats' concerns were becoming reality.. Without a word everyone realized they had to haul ass to the pickup point, or be blocked by a violent storm. Then they would have to execute Plan B and no one was sure what that was!

After another quick head count to confirm all were present, Slaughter explained last minute adjustments to their plan, they grabbed Brown and started to the extraction point.

Even though it was easier going down than up, all were exhausted from having to keep the uncoordinated Brown upright, on his feet, and uninjured. They had all but ripped the obese man's clothes off from efforts to protect him from rolling to his death while traversing some of the sheer stretches of the route to the extraction point. Even rotating the duty to grab him so he could keep his balance or to stop him from slipping on loose rock everyone of the team was whipped.

A totally exhausted and mentally shattered Brown collapsed into a pile of human suet as soon as they arrived at the rock and Slaughter finally called a halt. Brown plopped his broad ass down and cradled his head in his fettered hands. All the while he took deep convulsive and gasping breaths. He squeezed his eyes tightly closed as if the situation and these terrifying men could be kept away so long as his eyes were closed.

Slats was on the ball. As soon as the attack began she descended to a holding point about a mile away from the PZ on the side away from the approaching weather. Once there, she flew a tight orbit until the group was about to reach the flat rock. A quick code word on the radio and she turned inbound just as the first fat raindrops began to splatter on the Perspex windshield. It would be a close thing, she had to make the pickup before the rapidly closing thunderstorm arrived and the violent winds and limited visibility made a pickup impossibly dangerous.

CHAPTER 19

GUIDO AND TAMMY HAD AN EXCEPTIONALLY GOOD lunch at Romero's, a boutique restaurant with an ocean view. The restaurant was located between two of the banks and was well known to tourists and the employees of these banks.

A pleasant host greeted Tammy as a valued customer and smoothly led them through the crowded tables to an excellent table on the patio, a table under a colorful umbrella and shaded by flowery plants. The table offered them a degree of privacy from other diners and traffic noise. Guido's new bathing suit was in the shopping bag next to his chair and seemed to want his attention. After a waiter provided menus and took drink orders, he opened the bag to look inside. Even in the shadows the colors were startlingly bright; he just shook his head ruefully, and quipped, "I don't have to get ear rings or pierced nipples to wear it do I?"

She laughed that contagious laugh and answered, "No, but a diamond in your right nostril might go well." which sent both laughing and led to comments on a variety of subjects till they ended in a happy discussion about the menu. Tammy finally selected Conch salad with the house white wine and all but insisted that he try the blackend Mahi Mahi with black beans and rice. Guido really wanted of all things, a steak, but in the end he ordered the Mahi Mahi and also selected the house white wine. For some reason he wanted to make this woman happy.

The wine was served and did not disappoint; it proved to be properly chilled and had a crisp clean flavor, fruity but not overpowering. The food followed quickly and proved to be delicious prompting Guido to say so, twice, then adding, "No. It wasn't delicious, it was fantastic; especially with you to share it with, Tammy." As he lay his folded napkin on the table alongside his empty plate and sat back in his chair, she beamed her radiant smile and suggested that they head straight to her boat in the marina. Guido agreed and after signing for the meal, they headed out. On the way to the car Guido paused to ask, "Is there a place I can change into my suit?"

"Of course.", she smiled and continued entering the car, "The same place I'm going to change; on the bow of the boat. I'm three quarters French and one quarter Italian, and we believe nudity to be a form of communication as well as other things; perfectly natural. I do hope you're not one of those shy introverted puritans. It'll ruin the whole experience.", she grinned and winked at him.

Tammy proved to be an expert at handling her boat; all Guido had to do was follow her instructions and keep out of the way. Soon she had the engine started, and after Guido had released the bow and stern lines and hopped back on board, they backed out of the slip and were soon motoring out of the marina and into the channel heading for open water.

They enjoyed the smooth water and warm sun as they motored around the island until Tammy guided the vessel to her spot and it was securely anchored. As soon as the anchor was fast on the bottom he learned that she wasn't kidding about undressing. She walked to the bow where she removed and folded her business blouse and skirt and stood there wearing just sheer blue high cut French style panties. Guido quickly looked all around for other boats and people, but there were none close; and they were too far from shore for anyone to see without high powered optics. She fixed him with a quizzical eye and asked, "You thought I was kidding, didn't you? Well I wasn't. Are you coming or not?", as she said the last she slipped out of her panties and reached into a small bag she had carried to the bow. She plucked out a white string bikini and started to put it on.

Guido sat back in his seat and said, "Wait a minute, please. Let me enjoy the view." And she did. She turned and posed for him as if modeling a new outfit. Even at 5 foot nine she was perfectly proportioned; a flat belly lay beneath breasts neither too big or too small, and she had an ass to cry for. All Guido could do was say, "Beautiful, absolutely beautiful."

At that comment, she turned to face him with hands on hips and challenged, "OK buddy. Your turn."

Guido had slipped his trousers when her back was turned during a pose. Still wearing his shirt and boxer shorts, he stood and walked to the bow, pulling the shirt over his head as he did so. Before leaving the boat's cockpit he threw the new swimming suit forward and as he reached the bow area he reached down to pick it up but she grabbed it first. She took it with her back to the seat he had just left saying, "Oh no you don't. Now you can pose for me. Get to it."

This had to be the most exciting and erotic woman Guido had ever met; and her effect on him was becoming evident. With his hands on his hips and "Spike" sticking straight out the opening in his boxers he went into a slow poleless pole dance. He danced to music in his head, music that strangely featured the Red Army Chorus singing revolutionary marching music. Focusing on this decidedly non-erotic music he began taking off his underwear. When his shorts were freed he draped them on the head of his penis. He followed that act by gyrating his butt in a circular motion and twirling them around until they slipped off and sailed on the wind into the water. Tammy's happy contagious laugh became almost a cackle of delight as tears ran down her cheeks. Guido laughed too but not as heartily. while donning his new bathing suit he wondered if he could retrieve his underwear while learning to snorkel. He watched them drift on the current as they sank out of sight.

"Not to worry. We may find them. And if we don't, no one is hurt. Now come down here beside me and do what I do.", she said between giggles. She handed him a mask with a snorkel attached to the left side of the head strap while she held her mask by the face plate. She looked at his and he was holding it exactly like she was, so she said, "Now spit in it and rub the spit around the glass. Then we'll take them over the side to wash them out with salt water. That will keep them from fogging up.", she explained. Both of them leaned over the side to wash out the masks. "Now put on your face mask like this.", she said and demonstrated the procedure. Guido followed suit and placed his mask on his face. Sounding like she had a bad cold, she then said, "OK. Lets get the swim fins and sit on the edge of the boat and put them on. When that's done, we put the snorkel mouthpiece in our mouth and flop backwards into the water holding our breath. After we go under, we come back up with our heads tilted back, and when our heads and snorkel are out of the water we blow out our air and that will clear the snorkel of any water in it's bottom. Got it?", she asked.

He nodded, they flopped, and he damn near gagged to death because he didn't keep his head tilted back and the snorkel was so full of water he couldn't blow it all out. So when he inhaled he got some water in his lungs and went into a coughing spasm.

Tammy pushed his butt so he could get his arms over the gunwale of the boat and cough up whatever salt water was left. When he was breathing normally again, she asked, "Do you know what you did wrong?" "Yeah. I forgot to keep my head tilted back and the damned snorkel filled up with too much water for me to blow out.", he said, and continued with, "I'm going back down. I think I saw my underwear on the bottom."

"Oh no you're not.", she said as she swam over to him and put her arms around his neck while slowly `finning' the water below to keep their heads above water. He, in turn, wrapped his left arm around her back and placed his right hand on her left buttock and gently pulled her in close to him; real close such that she could tell Spike was at it again. She pushed him away from her laughing and said, "We can wait a little while for that, yes?"

"A little while seems like an eternity to me right now, but yes. I guess I'll go after my underwear now.", he grunted.

"OK, but there are two more important things you need to know. First, when you go deeper you will feel pressure in your ears. In order to equalize that pressure you must squeeze your nose and blow like you want to blow your nose. You will do this every time you feel the pressure in your ears. You will hear the squeal and feel the pressure equalize.", she said.

"The second thing is getting rid of any water that may seep inside your mask. To do this, you must tilt your head back and barely crack the seal of your facemask at the bottom and at the same time blow a little air into your mask through your nose. If it's just a little bit of water in your mask, don't worry about it. Do you think you can do these things, yes?", she smiled and said.

He nodded and she continued, "If you think you can reach it, it's about 40 feet to the bottom here: but, it's the top of a coral head. The real bottom is about 100 feet. Lets just hope your underwear isn't on the real bottom because I don't have any weight belts or dive gear with me. When you decide to try, take a few deep breaths first, then point your arms and head toward the bottom and haul your real bottom up in the air and straighten your legs, then pull with your arms until your fins are in the water and you can kick your way down with your arms at your sides.", She said.

She was a good teacher. He made it to the bottom, but his lungs felt as if they were bursting. He kicked over to where his drawers were snagged on a piece of yellow looking coral. Before she could get to him he grabbed the coral with his left hand and broke it off to free his underwear, then he tossed it aside with his thumb and first two fingers and kicked hard to get back to the surface. By the time he broke the surface his thumb and two fingers were on fire.

Tammy surfaced along side and ordered, "Quick, get in the boat. Take off your fins one at a time and throw them inside, then your face mask and snorkel so that you can get a leg over and pull yourself in." When both were in the boat she grabbed his wrist and held it over the side of the boat and poured white vinegar over his now swollen and inflamed thumb and fingers. She kept slowly pouring vinegar over the hand and watched the redness and swelling subside. Guido's expression let her know the burning was becoming more tolerable. At first he had felt like screaming at the pain, but was able to hold his response to some tight jawed grunts, no crying out loud, that would certainly undermine his macho veneer.

Watching the set of his jaw loosen she said, "You must have a high pain threshold. That was fire coral you grabbed through your shorts. When you broke off that piece with your bare skin the nasty little critters that call the stuff home stung you. Guess I forgot to tell you not to touch anything down there. I'm very sorry about this."

She cut a towel into strips; soaked one with the vinegar and wrapped it around his thumb and fingers saying, "We're going back to my place to complete the treatment. And don't bother trying to put your clothes back on after being in salt water. We'll hose ourselves down with fresh water at the dock, then go to my place for some meat tenderizer. That's the next half of the treatment for fire coral stings. Works for jellyfish stings too.", she added.

By the time they parked next to her isolated beach house the pain was reduced and the swelling had subsided to the point that he could freely move his fingers. He reported as much as they entered the front door, but Tammy only replied with a follow me gesture. He followed her through a very feminine bedroom to a large well equipped bathroom. She said, "I suggest we take a shower before applying the meat tenderizer. We need to get all the residual salt out of our hair and off our skin with good old soap and hot water. I'm sorry but we will have to shower together, my water heater is too small for both of us to have hot water if we do it separately. Besides you might need some help.

"Then she said as means of explanation," I set the dishwasher to 2:00PM so I'm sure the hot water is down." He gulped and said cheerily, "Fine with me."

As soon as they were in the shower together Tammy adjusted the water and both started to shower, but Guido's hands were still stiff and swollen. He could not keep a grip on the soap. The two kept bumping heads when they bent to retrieve it. Finally, Tammy told him to leave it to her, and she grabbed a container of body wash from a shelf and poured it into a mesh sponge. Working up a good foam she scrubbed his fingers and thumb thoroughly. His hand finished, she soaped her own body and then turned back to Guido. She washed his body from the head and worked down, spinning him around to make sure she got all sides; and, working below the waist caused the expected reaction. She washed his butt and lower back seeming oblivious to the rising expectations on the opposite side. Squatting on her hams Asian style she spun him till he faced her. Tammy batted his growing erection from side to side with the sponge, then looked slyly up at him with an enigmatic smile on her lips, dropping the sponge to the shower floor. She let the shower rinse them both free of suds. Apparently satisfied that the soap was gone she demonstrated the genetic skills passed down by her forbearers, soon bringing Guido to a near critical sensation. His reaction was to pull her standing upright so he could better address the lovely body sharing the space.

They made love in the shower until the cold water made them cut things short. It wasn't too late for Guido and Tammy however. Without drying they guided each other straight to her bed where they very slowly finished what had started in the shower.

CHAPTER 20

SLATS SAW SEVERAL HUGE RAINDROPS HIT THE windshield and immediately turned on the wipers as she maneuvered closer to the outcropping rock. She saw that it took all four of them to lift the nearly comatose Mr. Brown up and into the cargo opening of the helicopter. As soon as his body hit the floor she hollered, "Shit. How much does that asshole weigh?". But nobody else was on the intercom to answer her as she fought to keep the helicopter level and steady against the growing wind gusts. When they were all aboard she found the torque guage pegged at the edge of the red, so she beeped up both engines a notch using two sliding buttons on the collective power control that let her increase the engine revolutions to 110% and then announced to the boys in back, "It's gonna be a rough flight through this thunderstorm. Everybody get buckled in good and tight. The good news is that we'll be descending all the way so I'll be able to reduce power and airspeed to minimize the bouncing around we'll be getting. I just hope this bucket stays in one piece."

Slaughter and Elmore just looked at each other and shrugged their shoulders. They had both been in much worse situations where the "bucket" did not stay in one piece and was full of holes. Slats saw them shrug their shoulders, realizing that they were resigned to their fate, a fate they had put in her hands. She just shook her head at their blind trust in her skills; then thought "what the hell, I'll break them of taking me for granted!". Without ceremony she told Elmore, "Hold the controls for me a minute Elmore, I need to adjust my seat cushion." Without waiting for a reply she released her hold on the controls as soon as she felt his hands on the cyclic and collective she added, "You've got the controls."

The helicopter went immediately out of trim, the passengers thrown this way and that by the unpredictable winds and Elmore's over controlling. She knew Elmore had a commercial multi-engine fixed wing ticket and was instrument rated, but he had no helicopter flight training so she was not surprised at his struggles. His problems seemed to be getting worse as the rain increased and the light show presented by the storm gained magnitude.

In spite of the hazardous conditions, professionally she wanted to teach all present a lesson, personally she was enjoying his discomfort. She also was enjoying the play of the lightening on everyone's faces. Their overall confidence was being shaken by conditions outside their control and she was struck by the way their features took on a blue cast in the flashes of lightening. As Elmore fought the controls and conditions she heard Slaughter say on intercom, "What the hell are you playing at Slats. Brown is puking his guts up all over me back here. Get this son of a bitch under control and out of this shit"

"OK. OK. I have the controls", Slats said with a smirk on her face and glanced over to see Elmore giving her the "nasty one fingered salute" and silently saying really bad stuff about her lineage and how many feet her mother had. It gave her a warm feeling all over!

She had guided the overloaded chopper down and away from the hill mass and accompanying turbulence. As she lost altitude conditions smoothed and the rain and wind diminished as they escaped the storm track, and she made the "inbound" call to Doc Leigh. Soon they were scooting along at 80 knots and 1000 feet above the ground. Shortly, the old farmhouse came into sight about a mile to their front. Slats started her landing checklist and executed a low straight in approach to the same cleared area as before.

Her final approach and landing were flawless. As soon as the team felt the rotor blades begin to slow and the airframe settle solidly on the ground, the four of them grabbed an appendage apiece and half carried, half dragged Brown onto the porch. They could not fit through the doorway carrying him, so they stood him on his feet and leaned him against the wall next to the door until he quit dry heaving and could totter inside by himself. They guided him to a room with a single bed just barely wide enough for him to lay upon without spilling over. There was only the heavy two inch thick bedroom door and a rather large upper vent window near the low ceiling, which wasn't much over six feet high. Slaughter had coated the entire surface area of the window with thallium without telling anyone but the Plot. Even a very small amount of the highly lethal material getting into the bloodstream would cause initial nausea, sore throat, diarrhea, loss of consciousness, and death within about eight to twelve hours; faster with exertion and no fluids.

They removed Brown's restraints after Doc Leigh and Lee An Too had administered the frog juice extract. The immediate affects were to put Brown into a state of semi consciousness and he started to babble about chocolate moose and strawberry pie. Then Doc said, "It'll take porky here longer to get completely affected due to his body weight; maybe another five or ten minutes. Give me the list of questions you want him to answer and everyone except Lee An Too will remain silent!" the last was an order given to make it clear to all present that he was in charge.

After six minutes Doc pulled back one of Brown's eyelids and looked closely at his pupil. It was completely dilated and did not constrict to light. Satisfied, he began the questions with, "What bank do you have an account with?"

Brown slurred, "Banks, banks?"

"Do you have accounts in different banks?", Doc asked as Lee An Too began a whispering chant in Brown's opposite ear.

"I like banks. I like banks like The Bank of Brunei; the International Bank of Thailand, the International Bank of the Caymans, and the First National Bank of Brazil.", Brown slowly rattled off. "Give me your personal identification number and account number for the National Bank of Thailand.", Doc said authoritatively. "8304" is my PIN number for all of my accounts. The account number for my bank in the Caymans is 113223JB.", he muttered.

They continued in this manner until they had other access codes for any safety deposit boxes and required disposition data for three of the financial institutions Brown was using. The last was the International Bank of Thailand.

As Doc continued, Elmore discovered a flash drive on a small gold chain strung around his neck in the shape of a gold Budda. He carefully unlatched the chain and put it and the Budda in his pocket for a later review of it's contents, which were probably encrypted. That should exercise Plot's genius and might provide additional information for use later.

"How did you get out of the prison in Bangkok?", Lee An Too whispered into his ear. Slaughter saw that they were "dog and pony-ing" him like "good cop; bad cop". It took a moment for Brown's muddled mind to focus on a different subject, but then he said, "Hawaladar. Financial advisor to the Thai monarchy is a hawaladar for the Bank of Brunei and paid my fine to the monarchy.".

"And the National Bank of Thailand?", Doc continued.

"None. All transactions with that bank are done through the hawaladar in person.", Brown said more clearly and distinctly.

"How do you get your money here in Rio?", Lee An Too whispered in his ear again.

"His answers were short and ungrammatical. "Sat phone. International Bank of the Caymans. Electronic transfer to First National Bank of Brazil. Why uh, why don't you know this?", Brown asked as if he wondered why he was talking to himself.

"He's coming around. We better hurry. Two more questions at

best.", Doc said rapidly while nodding at Lee An Too and taking two foot long bamboo tubes out of his leather bag. Both he and Lee An Too placed one end of each tube to their mouths to speak into Brown's ear for further questions. This would change the voice pattern dramatically and help to keep Brown confused.

What's your name?", Brown asked, still befuddled and somewhat groggy but realizing there was more than one voice in his head. Doc pulled an eyelid back and noted that his pupils, while uneven and unfocused were beginning to react to light normally. Quickly he asked, "Who is the Hawalada in Thailand?".

"Thomas Grey. We already know that; he is the financial advisor to the monarchy. What is going on. Oh God, my head!", Brown moaned and tried to sit up. At that point Lee An Too dipped the very sharply pointed tip of a bamboo sliver into his

leather gouda bag and then pricked the carotid artery in Brown's neck while whispering a chant in his ear. Brown went silent immediately and he was snoring loudly in seconds. Lee An Too stood up smiling and said, "He sleep for two, maybe three hours now; then he want head to be someplace else."

"I'm not sure I understand all this Hawala shit.", Slaughter blurted as they prepared to leave without Brown.

Elmore looked at the assembled team inquiringly. They all either cocked their head or shrugged their shoulders so he said, "Hawala, is also known as hundi. It's an informal transfer of value system. It is based on performance and honor among a huge network of money brokers working primarily in the Islamic countries, but also in some adjoining countries like Thailand. I suspect that this Thomas Grey is connected with the Hawala network and advised the Thai Monarchy to levy a significant fine on Brown, release him quietly, and let him collect a handling fee. I also suspect this guy is formally connected with the International Bank of Thailand as well as the Hawaladar network. He probably even handled Brown's profits from the raw morphine he was moving through northern

Thailand, for a fee of course. His banking credentials would have made it easy to legitimately establish other accounts starting with the Caymans since their banks are the most liberal, yet secretive as well. Of course, we can't forget abut the trading families in the Pashtun mafia. They provide oversight and linkage with financial institutions all over the world. I wouldn't want to be the one to try and penetrate that bunch."

Slats was spooling up the helicopter and pumping her right fist up and down signaling them to hurry up. With all on board and buckled up she lifted off rapidly, immediately taking a heading for the airport tapping the fuel gauge, which made the needle wiggle and finally settle just right of the red, meaning they had about 30 minutes of flying time left. She was glad she had shut the engines down while they did whatever they did with Brown. She had nixed a suggested requirement for 55 gallon drums of extra fuel being pre positioned at the farm house as not being necessary; now she was right on the margin of error. Noticing how well the helicopter lifted off she looked to see Julius Brown was not aboard, prompting her to ask, "What did you do with Brown?", over the intercom.

Elmore looked to Slaughter, so he answered with, "We left him untied and sound asleep snoring in his little bed with the door to his room locked and blocked. When he wakes up I suspect he'll pull the bed over under the big ventilation window and squeeze through it to reach the outside world. He'll probably get all scratched and scraped up dragging his fat ass through the vent, but I believe he'll make it. With no ID, no cell or satellite phone, no money in his pocket, I think old Julius will have a hard time making it out alive."

Elmore immediately reacted with, "That's horseshit Slaughter. That's about the weakest assumption I've heard lately. He should've been eliminated so he can't cause any trouble down the road and you damn well know it."

"Let's talk about it later.", Slaughter said as he looked Elmore in the eye and winked.

That wink told Elmore all he needed to know. Brown was a dead man walking, if he was still able to walk at all.

They landed at the airport and quickly got out of their tactical gear and changed into the clothes the Plot had dry cleaned for them for the flight back to Miami. Slats got the deposit for the helicopter back after the owner had inspected it carefully and pocketed a small bonus, and then got the owner to secure a passenger van and give them all a ride over to the departing flight entrance at the international terminal. The crew went directly to the bar. Each would depart individually and take different seats to Miami with the exception of Elmore; who, if the Plot had it figured right, would take Slats to the Caymans with him.

Elmore sat next to Slats and ordered a liter bottle of water for each of them along with a Mojito chaser. First they needed to hydrate; then they could relax over a civilized drink. They sucked down the water and started to sip at the Mojito while they enjoyed the air-conditioned air and felt their bodies refresh as they sucked up the liquid. As they mentally decompressed from the operation he leaned over and put his lips close to her ear and asked, "Hey girl, wanta come visit the Cayman Islands with me?"

She still had ten days left on her leave from Smithfield Aviation, and knew some of the others still had jobs to do. Elmore's invitation solved her logistical uncertainty about what to do with the next ten days and her emotional uncertainly concerning his feelings. Her reply was to grab him around the neck and kiss him hard on the mouth saying, "I thought you'd never ask."

The rest of them smiled at the exchange; Slaughter was surprised to feel a pang of jealousy lurking behind his happiness for the couple, coping with the fact that he was headed for Thailand without his wife, who would probably wind up in Pakistan or Afghanistan with very little in the way of creature comforts.

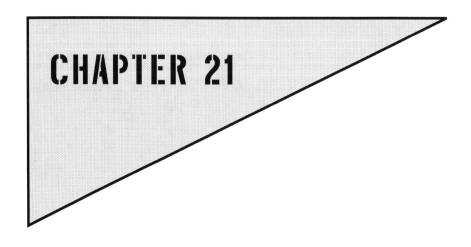

CHAPTER 21

Sheila Hobgood started pouting when the Plot told her she could not be participating in the final events of Brown's snatch. Now she was still pouting but had added the silent treatment. She was getting even angrier as he seemed impervious to her attitude.

Driving the Land Rover to the airport, he reached over to hold her left arm and said sternly, "Sheila damn it, you know all too well that you've got far more footage and photos than you will ever need for your article on Brown's villa in Rio after his escape from Thailand. The real road to a Pulitzer will be to reveal how he moved his money around; how he bought his escape from prison and how he financed his flight to Rio so he could continue his operation. Interpol, U.S. and British authorities should have prevented him from doing any of those things. The combined law enforcement agencies of the free world failed. If you can find out what they couldn't.........well, let's just say you'd be high on my list of Pulitzer candidates."

As they weaved through the congestion and dark clouds of exhaust belching from fully laden trucks and busses, Sheila answered her cell phone. After a quick exchange, she handed it to Marplot saying, "It's Slaughter for you.

The one sided conversation went, "That's great. Yes, I'll brief the boss when I get to the Hootch. By the time I get there you may know something further about our subject's disposition. Try and call me from the plane if you have anything pertinent. Yes, the payoff has already been made, including the use of the farmhouse; along with specific instructions to have one of his training exercises burn the place to the ground. No, he wasn't very happy, but he's a rich man now and I've got enough on him to make him very uncomfortably poor if he talks. No, nothing from our resources in the island yet. We're just about there now. Thanks. You have a good flight as well.", Marplot closed and handed the phone to Sheila saying, he wants to talk to you again, but no names or places please.

"I already miss you, you lug nut. No, I'm not pissed anymore. I got a "reality check" and I really understand.." She grinned at the latest news about the helicopter pilot taking the trip to the islands, then turned her head away from Marplot and softly said, "I can't wait either. Love you too." Then she looked at the Plot and said, "I really meant what I said about the "reality check" Plot. Thanks for bringing me down to earth."

The big video camera would fit in the overhead bin of the aircraft and the rest of their luggage was stowed in carry on bags so they went straight to security. Once again, Marplot had to have the eager beaver customs officer make the call upstairs so they could get through with their handguns. The badges and Identification cards didn't seem to mean much in Brazil where anyone could get about any kind of document they wanted if

they knew the right people and had the money. Finally, with profuse but obviously insincere apologies the local officials passed them through security. Once on the departure side they went directly to the counter at their departure gate.

The harried ticket agent assigned them seats when they presented their "open" tickets; and it was a good thing they were 45 minutes early. They got the last two adjoining seats available in first class. All the seats in "Cabbage Class" were filled with sunburned tourists and there were only a few single seats left unoccupied in first class.

It was 5:45PM when the landing gear retracted and the flaps squealed while retracting into the wings.

It would be midnight when they arrived in Miami; one in the morning in Washington D.C. From Miami international, the Jet Ranger he ordered would take another 40 minutes to reach the Hootch. He would use another ten minutes to review his notes and set up the secure link to Chief Justice Nagey. "Zero one fifty in the AM ", Marplot said out loud, smiling at the thought of waking the old curmudgeon to give him his report.

"Huh? What did you say?", Sheila leaned over and asked.

"Oh I was just thinking out loud. Want something to drink before they serve us dinner?", he smiled and asked as he motioned to the attractive blond flight attendant.

"What would you care for?", she politely asked as she leaned forward to take their request.

"Ladies first.", Marplot said, and Sheila ordered two scotches and a large glass of ice.

"I'll have a white wine if you please; and can you bring us a dinner menu?", he asked

"Certainly. I'll be right back with your drinks.", she replied.

"Tell me what you know about the hawala system of money transfer that Elmore is supposed to be chasing down.", Sheila asked.

"Well, all I really know for sure is that it goes back hundreds of years to the early money brokers along the Mid East, South West and Eastern Asian trade routes. Transactions were made based on promises in good faith and honor, and the commodity may have been gold, silver, jewelry, spices.....you name it. No paperwork was signed, only amounts were recorded by the lender and buyer. As banks evolved with international trade, and currency was developed, the currency was treated as a hawala just as if it were a bag of rice, or a brick of gold, and there was still no paperwork until letters of credit were invented. The money brokers would then affiliate themselves with a local bank, or start one themselves, and could then cross the lines between formal banking and finance and the hawala system. It depended on who they were servicing with their money. And that's about as much as I know. That and the fact that the authorities are having big trouble identifying and tracking terrorist funding as well as monies associated with drug smuggling.", the Plot quietly told her.

"Hell, even when they do find the funding trail they can't get convictions in court because there's no documentation behind the money transfers. The money brokers won't talk; it's their business and honor at stake. Even if you caught the money lender and his client exchanging the cash, what would you charge them with?", he asked. Then, "No, I think the best approach is to get video and/or stills of the poppies in the fields; harvesting the sap, processing the opium or morphine base and follow one shipment all the way through the various stages till it really reaches the user. You need to ferret out the money transfers along the way with a narrative that explains the good and the bad from an international and human affects standpoint. Just like a CNN check.", the Plot said as he smiled at her.

"Good grief. You're not asking for much, are you?", Sheila balked.

"Not really. You'll be going to Pakistan with Elmore, and he already knows his way around that country. He also has friends among the old intelligence veterans who live there, and among some of their Army's Special Forces and Border Patrol Police: ones he can trust", the Plot mused. He'd thought about sending Slaughter and Dyke or Bunny with Elmore, but figured he'd wait to see how things developed.

After they had reached cruising altitude drinks were served, and they were each given a card with three choices of entrée's; fillet of sole, baked chicken breast, or beef tenderloin. The vegetables included a choice of asparagus, green peas, or a salad; and also a choice of rice parfait or baked potato. As Sheila looked over the menu the stewardess explained, "Ordinarily you would have been served right away in first class while still on the ground, but there was a late loading of beverages and meals, but we would still able to make our take off time. That's why cabin service was a little late catching up. We're very sorry." Marplot smiled and gave a wave of dismissal at the apology.

Sheila poured both of her scotches into the tall glass and started swishing the scotch around inside to chill it before enjoying a large sip. When she was about halfway through the drink the stewardess came back to their row and said, "Mr. Keystone is on the line for you Mr. Arpslot", as she pulled the phone from the back of the seat in front of him. ("Keystone" was Slaughter's code name for open phone line conversations.) Before the stewardess left, Sheila raised questioning eyebrows to the attendant and made a circling motion over her nearly empty glass with her other hand's forefinger pointed down; the Brazilian stewardess smiled her understanding of the international signal for "pour us another round."

As in the Land Rover, she only got one side of the conversation, but she was able to understand most of it from the comments Marplot made into the phone, "You're absolutely certain our subject has offered up everything we need? Your equally certain he left the arena and wont be back (meaning he provided all his account numbers and access information and was dead)? Good, to know."

"Did Slats get my deposit back in U.S. currency (that was for the helicopter)? OK, fine. And the excess equipment we locked in that metal locker in the hangar for the site supervisor? Oh!"

"Well he'll be pissed about that. Was there a reason for keeping it and the clips? Pakistan?. Sheila's credentials? Can't he get whatever he needs over there? OK, never mind. How about the fruit from the trees (meaning all watches and other jewelry, but not cash)? Did it rot in the ground? That's too bad, but it was too ripe to eat anyway. What about liquid assets (meaning money)? Hmmmm. That's a lot. Call LTC Pickett in Lima and find out who's the U.S. Military Atache' in our consulate in Rio, and if he can be trusted to accept the cash and wire transfer it from the International Bank of Brazil to the account Guido sets up for us. Our cover is that we are U.S Marshals who came to Rio with an FBI and DEA extradition warrant for Mr. Julius Brown who has disappeared; but we have recovered the money he had hidden in his villa and need it in the account where his other liquid assets from his smuggling operation are deposited. If Pickett doesn't have a high degree of confidence in doing it this way, ask him to see if he can manage a trip to Rio to dig it up from the ruins of an old farmhouse and handle it from Lima. And tell him to let us know one way or the other; or if he's got a better idea.", the Plot said rapidly; his frustration showing.

"No, nothing else: you? Sure. I don't mind that at all. If what you say about the nephew is fact, I suspect the Doc will be going back home and will turn him over to us to do the suspended animation work. You all did a good job. Anything else? Sure.", he said as he handed the phone to Sheila who immediately said, "You knew I'd be going to the Islands, didn't you. Yes you did, too. I know, I know. I'll call you when I get settled into the Marriott there. Luv ya, bye."

"I think I got most of your one sided conversation, but tell me anyway.", she demanded.

"Julius Brown gave up his PIN numbers, access codes and account numbers. He probably scratched himself up crawling out the vent window where he either inhaled or introduced a toxic substance into his person. Then he likely tried to keep his 245 pounds at a brisk trot in a frantic search for assistance until said substance kicked in and he collapsed in the dirt. That would be where some farmer found his body and reported it to the Commandante. He would mention it at the airport as he was recovering his equipment and supplies.

"Elmore kept one of the suppressed MP5s with seven loaded magazines, which the Commandante did not like at all, but couldn't do much about it. Elmore wants it in Thailand and plans to use a ranking customs officer, one who owes him a big one by the way, to help him get it into the country. They buried all of the jewelry they took off of Brown and the body guards, but there was over $720,000 in U.S. currency they couldn't leave behind. I told Slaughter to contact LTC Pickett in Lima, Peru to find out if our Military attaché in Rio would be able to get it wire transferred to our Cayman account. Doc Leigh is going back home; says Lee An Too is even better at tribal witch doctoring than he is, and he still has a number of young women in his tribe who must be introduced to womanhood. Lee An Too is coming to the Hootch so we can familiarize him with RANGE 19 operation and the lay of the land.", he finally said.

The stewardess returned with two little bottles of scotch and a tall glass of ice and asked, "Are you two ready to order dinner yet?"

"Yes, we are.", Marplot said gesturing to Sheila that she should order and an accompanying look on his face that said, "Whether or not you're hungry, you will order."

"I'll have the baked chicken breasts with asparagus and rice", she said with droopy eyes. She was on the verge of exhaustion and the scotch was taking its toll. The Plot wanted her to get something inside her besides more scotch; scotch that would likely end up in his lap if she didn't.

"I'll have rare tenderloin, asparagus and I'd like sour cream and chives on the side for the potato.", he said and smiled up at her.

"I'll be right back with your meals.", she said, beginning to eye Sheila a bit warily.

Sheila went to sleep immediately after working her way through most of her meal, resting her head on Marplot's shoulder. She hardly moved, sleeping straight through until just after the breakfast was served. Passing on the coffee and food she grabbed her bag and hurried down the aisle to freshen up. She wanted to get it done and be back in her seat before they descended and heard the "tray tables up and seats in the upright position" announcement prior to landing at Miami.

She returned several minutes later, alert and somewhat rested, and decidedly more presentable. Marplot could tell she had washed her face and put on a small amount of make up, and brushed out her hair so it fell naturally to frame her face. All evidence of stress and exertions from the previous day's events were erased.

Sitting back in her seat she suddenly felt hungry; reconsidered and pressed the button for the flight attendant. Soon she was happily sipping some really good coffee and nibbling her way through a number of fruit filled pastries.

Her flight to the Caymans was scheduled to arrive at 2:55AM; about the same time Marplot would be briefing Chief Justice Nagey from their underground control room, he thought.

Since they had no baggage to claim, Sheila and the Plot hugged and said their good bye's under the board advising flight departures. Sheila found the departure information for her flight to the Caymans and started to that part of the international terminal. The Plot cleared immigration and customs, and traversed the main terminal. The driver for his shuttle met him and drove him to the helicopter courier service which took him to the waiting helicopter.

After an uneventful flight to the Hootch, he dumped his bags, and recovered his notes. Notes in hand he went through the pantry rear door, descended the stairs to the control room and climbed into the "commander's" chair that had all the controls and computer keyboards within arms reach. He activated the camera and large screen TV for video conferencing, then autodialed the Chief Justice's home telephone number. Five rings with no answer meant he was still in his office, so Marplot autodialed that number. Chief Justice Nagey picked up on the second ring with, "Yes?"

After Marplot updated him on events to date, he outlined their plans for the immediate future and the Chief Justice said, "So Brown is permanently out of the picture, we met our primary objective. Good. Now you are going after his contacts and organization as well as his money. Is that right?"

"Yes sir Mr. Chief Justice. The biggest target being the Thai monarchy's chief financial advisor who holds U.S. citizenship. He used to be Chief of Staff to the Sultan of Brunei. We are sure he is a hawaladar and responsible for orchestrating Brown's release from the Thai prison.", the Plot added.

"Hawaladar. Ah yes. Those paperless bastards?", the Chief Justice growled.

"Yes sir. We believe that's how Brown was able to smuggle his morphine base out of Thailand to the U.S., U.K., and Europe and move money under the normal radar. And since his confederate is a U.S. citizen; who is also a hawaladar in the office of the Thai monarchy, and also appears to be a representative of the Bank of Brunei, we think he is another candidate to be exploited and neutralized.", the Plot stated with a note of authority.

"Oh you do, do you? And just what happens when the King of Thailand loses his trusted financial advisor? Obviously, this guy is under royal protection and is therefore nationally sanctioned as a high level official. Don't you think you may create a bit of trouble with this one?", the Chief asked sternly.

"Yes sir. There is no doubt it will be difficult, but I believe if we can find out enough about his activities using the Bank of Brunei for his hawaladar activities we may be able to set him up for a big fall. The kind of fall that will remove him from the favors of the Sultan and the King.", Marplot replied. Then he said, "If it looks like we can't make it work in our favor, I'll shut the operation down immediately. Of course we will keep you informed as the operation progresses."

"Alright Plot. But let me caution you. There will be no international incidents allowed. Then as if an afterthought he asked, " By the way, how's Elmore working out?"

"Couldn't ask for a better man. Can I keep him after this is over?", the Plot enthused.

"No. Goodbye.", the Chief said with a note of finality.

It was almost 3:00AM. Even so, he couldn't help but believe there was something going on between the Chief and Elmore that needed deniability on the Chief's part. Ah well, such is the life of the covert and the nameless.

His last thoughts before falling asleep were that Dyke, Bunny and Chico would be arriving at the Hootch later on in the morning. It would be good to have their company.

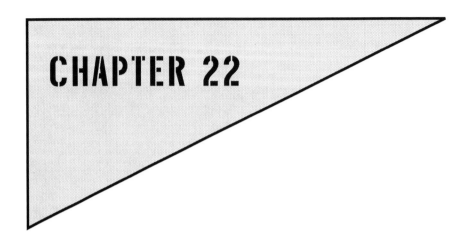

CHAPTER 22

Leopold Farnsworth III , "the turd" as his West Point classmates liked to call him, couldn't figure out what the tapping noise behind his head was. He cracked one eye to find it was almost daylight; false dawn they called it. The tapping came again prompting him to sit up behind the steering wheel to get his bearings. A glance to the left told him immediately that he might be in trouble. It was Sheriff Baugh himself tapping on his window with an enormous black metal flashlight in his hand. He wasn't smiling as he quit tapping and made a "roll your window down" motion with the hand holding the flashlight, his right hand stayed curled around the grip of his holstered pistol.

"You plan on puttin down roots here Mister? Lets see some ID?", he ordered after the window was down. He obviously didn't recognize Farnsworth from the last time he was in his custody, so he simply said, "Ain't got nun sir. I wuz robbed in Miami. Two thugs jumped me in the bus station bathroom. They roughed me up an took my wallet an alla my money while I wuz takin a dump! My name's Jonathan Smith," he added with an ingratiating smile.

"Well Mr. Smith, yer in kind of a pickle then ain't ya? You drivin Murf's truck here? That's drivin without a license ya know.", Sheriff Baugh stated with less of a scowl on his face.

"Yes sir. Murf lent it to me to go see Whitey about his ultra light airplane that's for sale. But since he ain't got no headlights I pulled over an slept in it last night.", Farnsworth said, then pleaded, "I know drivin without a license is illegal, but I hope yall'l fergive me fer that little infraction so I can get Murf his truck back now that it's daylight."

Sheriff Baugh was in his mid sixties now and had been reelected to the Dade Municipal Sheriff's job eight consecutive times. Reelection came primarily because of his knowledge and friendship with key people in business and politics. More than once he had personally hauled the Mayor of Miami out of a "sensitive" situation with a young lady or ladies, and it was also a good thing to know Simon Arpslot who was very powerful in his own subtle fashion. Anyway, he knew his responsibilities were limited to the area outside the city limits of Miami since the merger between Dade county and Miami. He looked closer at Farnsworth, he thought he remembered something about that face, but it quickly faded so he said, "OK Mr. Smith. You crank er up and drive her to the Crossroads Motel 6. I'll be a following ya to see if there's any of Whitey's moonshine doin some of the drivin too; and if'n there is you're comin' with me. Unnerstand?"

"Yes sir.", was all Farnsworth could say as he started up the old truck and waited for Sheriff Baugh to back out so he could do the same and head toward Crossroads. When they arrived, the main entrance to the Motel 6 was locked. Murf hadn't shown up for work yet, so Farnsworth decided to change the relationship and offered, "Buy you a cup of coffee Sheriff?"

"Thought you said you wuz robbed.", he quickly responded.

"Well, I always keep a little money in my socks when I'm traveling Sheriff. Didn't fall off no turnip truck, ya know. Heh, heh.", he laughed.

"Well then, by all means. I'll have some coffee, and probably some scrambled eggs with sausage links and grits too. Don't know how big your socks are, but I'll do the buyin since ya got robbed in my town.

Breakfast is on me. That bus station is givin me heartburn with all that muggin and other shit goes down there.", he complained.

"I really 'preciate that Sheriff; socks ain't all that big.", Farnsworth said quietly as they approached the restaurant's counter. A new waitress he didn't know who cheerily asked, "Hey Sheriff, ya havin the usual this morning? And how about you Mr. John Deere?"

"Yup, the usual Peggy. Ya ought to try it son. They make their own pork sausage here. Make their own biscuits too, none of that frozen or packaged crap. Can't beat it.", Sheriff Baugh exclaimed.

"Sounds good to me; but I'd like my eggs over medium instead of scrambled, OK?", Farnsworth meekly offered.

"No problem. Be right back with two coffee's. You want cream, it's on the counter in the little silver cup.", Peggy announced over her shoulder, already headed to the window with the order slip.

Sheriff Baugh looked over his coffee at Farnsworth's John Deere hat and between appreciative sips asked, "What brings ya to these parts, if'n ya don't mind my askin?"

"Oh, I hope to buy about 20 acres of land from Simon Arpslot at that Range 19 company and start up a commercial shrimp raising and processing facility. He's got a strip of fallow land right next to the highway that has 28 inches of topsoil before you hit the water table, an that's just perfect for a pond with filtering and water transfer. And there'll be enough property to build facilities for harvesting, cleaning, and packaging as well as cold storage. I plan to truck the shrimp to supermarkets and restaurants in the Miami area; maybe even ship em out by air to classy places in the Midwest.", Farnsworth spun his tale.

Sheriff Baugh was stirring his fourth tablespoon of sugar into his coffee cup listening carefully and doubtfully to what Farnsworth was saying because he knew Simon Arpslot wasn't likely to sell any of the Range 19 property. Still he played along and asked, "What do you feed baby shrimp anyway? And where do you get em in the first place?

Sounds like risky business to me. You do know you'll be dealing with brackish water doncha?"

Peggy arrived with their plates of food still steaming and said, "Bony Peeteet" and left.

Farnsworth had done some of his homework and was getting into the game, "There's a few weeks in April when you can buy huge female shrimp with eggs still attached to their underside. Those are the best, but you can also buy baby shrimp from other commercial shrimp farmers who are willing to sell some. Feedin em the right mixture of whey protein mixed with fine-grained corn or soy is the tricky part; ya gotta really baby the little devils until they get big enough to eat real plankton out of the sea. As far as the brackish water is concerned, tha's wher th filterin comes in; ya add salt and keep track of the water's salination. I'll admit. I ain't no genius at it, but I'm willin to put all my savins and pension into makin it work. Never can tell. I jus might be the next Forrest Gump!", Farnsworth threw his head back and startled the Sherrif when he hee hawed at his own joke. Sheriff inhaled sharply and started choking on the big piece of sausage he had just popped into his mouth.

Murf had just entered unnoticed, walked up behind the Sheriff and slapped him on the back rather stiffly and hollered, "No need for a doctor, I've just saved the Sheriff's life performin the Murflick maneuver. I see you two've met an my fav-or-ite pickumup truck is in the lot."

"Thanks fer the Murflich whatever. Next time jus let me see ya comin; that'll be enough to unchoke a rat snake with a possum half way down.", the Sheriff said wiping tears the choking generated from his eyes with a paper napkin.

Before Murf could say anything about Farnsworth's dealings, he thanked the Sheriff for breakfast and headed to his room to catch a few hours sleep in a bed! As he was leaving and offering the Sheriff his thanks, he looked straight at Murf and said, "Ya might wanna look at that engine a yours Murf. It was missin some drivin it here. Comon an I'll crank er up and show ya.".

Murf followed Farnsworth outside to the truck and after he cranked it up and both were looking under the hood he said, "No need to talk any bout the dynamite to the Sheriff is there?" "Nope. All I know is you're here to see about buyin Whitey's lil plane an that's why I loaned you the truck.", Murf replied. "You should also know I got robbed at the bus station in the Miami shithouse and don't have any ID or drivers license; he'll probably eat on you for loanin yer truck to me. Jus tell him ya didn't think to ask an won't let me have it again.", Farnsworth said as he backed up and said, "I think yer carberater needs adjustin.". He shook Murf's hands and saw Sheriff Baugh looking at them through the restaurant window.

"Murph, you ought to know better than to loan out yer truck to somebody without even askin if they got a license to drive.", Sheriff Baugh chastised.

"I swear Sheriff, I didn't even think of it at the time. Won't happen again, I promise.", Murf humbly said.

"What do you know about this guy, anyway?", the Sheriff asked.

Murf carefully thought about it, then said, "Not much. Here to buy Whitey's ultra light airplane he's got for sale cause he always wanted to fly. Lent him my truck on condition he paid the bill to get the transmission fixed and gave it back full of gas; and that's bout it."

"Humph!", was all the Sheriff said. He wondered just how big those socks old Jonathan was wearing really were if he could do all that renting and buying. He'd give Simon a call and see if he knew anything about this guy wanting his land. And there was something familiar about Mr. Smith that he just couldn't put his finger on; but then again he was startin to forget things these days anyway.

Farnsworth had to come up with something to get him out of Crossroads and Sheriff Baugh's "crosshairs" quick. He knew the Sheriff would be checking with Arpslot to see if he'd been contacted about selling the land yet, and that would lead him back to Farnsworth and a Social Security Number check…and Farnsworth. Once he saw the name he would remember everything and he would be coming down hard on him if he got his hands on him. He had to get away nice and quiet like, and soon. Even though it was only 9:15 in the morning he rang the front desk and Murf answered with, "Operator. Oh, it's you. Whatcha need?"

"I need Whitey's number Murf. Can you connect me or do I dial it from my room?", Farnsworth asked.

"I'll ring him up fer ya, but it'll probly take nine er ten rings to get him up off his drunk ass.", Murf said, then dialed the number and stayed on the line. Sure enough, it took nine rings before Whitey answered with a gravel voiced, "What?".

"Whitey, I need ya to call Rob and ask him to bring me out to yur place so's I can pay you the resta what I owe you for the plane. I cain't drive Murf's truck cus the Sheriff's here an knows I ain't got no license cus I got robbed at the Miami bus station cumin here.", Farnsworth pleaded.

"Cain't it wait til after lunchtime? What the hell time is it anyway?", he asked.

"No Whitey. It can't wait. If I'm gonna get the plane it's got to be now. Call Rob and tell him I'll be over in about five minutes if'n ya want yer $3200.", Farnsworth loudly announced. Then he asked in a normal tone after he heard Whitey hang up,

"Murf? You still on the line?"

"Yup. I coulda called Rob ya know.", he said.

Without acknowledging that fact Farnsworth asked, "You got those two sticks of dynamite handy? I'll give ya fifty apiece fer em right now if ya gottem in hand."

"Sure, but I thought……", and he recognized the phone had been hung up. He got up and went over to the closet and opened the door. He reached up on the top shelf in the right rear corner and grabbed the paper bag he knew was there and left the office with the bag under his shirt. He only had to rap once on Farnsworth's door and Farnsworth pulled him inside and closed it shut.

Farnsworth asked, "You got em?"

"Yup, right here.", as Murf handed the paper bag to Farnsworth, who immediately handed Murf a folded one hundred dollar bill. Then Murf said, "What's the big rush, anyway?"

"Murf, my man, what you don't know can't hurt you. I've got an old score to settle an I gotta do it quick since the Sheriff is probably gonna start askin questions I don wanna answer. You've been a big help to me an I don't want you to get in no trouble, so don't ask anymore questions, OK?", Farnsworth said as he put the paper bag inside his duffel bag and left saying, "Maybe I'll see ya around Murf. Thanks for everything.", and headed across the street to Rob's Auto Parts and Repair shop.

Rob was already in his truck looking through the passenger side window at Farnsworth coming toward him carrying a big duffel bag; and he was wondering why Whitey had all but begged him to give this guy a ride out to his place; had to be money or shine, one or the other. Then it struck him. This was the guy that was buying Whitey's ultra light and he was gonna fly it out.

"Howdy. Whitey said you'd be wearin a John Deere hat. Buyin his lil Rotex plane are ya?", Rob asked as Farnsworth threw his duffel bag in the back of the truck and got in the front seat.

"Hey Rob. Really appreciate the lift, and yeah I'm buyin Whitey's plane. Always wanted to learn how to fly an Whitey taught me how to fly his two seater, so the lil one shouldn't be a problem.", Farnsworth said as Rob pulled out onto the highway and turned right at the intersection headed towards Whitey's. Then he said, "Whitey tol me you got shot up pretty bad down in South America on some drug raid while you was flyin helicopters. Said it was some kid with an AK and your door gunner had to waste him."

"Whitey talks too much; especially when he's fulla shine. He tol me you were hit in Desert Storm n' thas why you favor your left foot.", he replied.

"Yeah. You're right. Whitey does talk too much; but yeah I was hit in Desert

Storm. Amazing what a hundred hour war can do to a fella. That's as long as it lasted ya know.", Farnsworth said. His thoughts then turned to what he had really done in that 100 hour war, and how Slaughter had brought him up on charges for rape. That nurse had wanted it. She was a slut and everybody knew it, but Slaughter saw to it that he was thrown out of the Army with a Dishonorable Discharge. Well, he was about to get his Dudley Do Right ass blown off.

"Where ya headed with the lil plane?", Rob asked changing the subject.

"Nowhere til tomorrow or the next day. Guess I'll be sleepin in it till then. Waitin on a phone call at Whitey's that says I can use a fella's field and shed to put it in.", Farnsworth smoothly replied thinking about the extra hundred dollars he'd given Murf to let him know at Whitey's when Simon Arpslot was at the Hootch so he could find out if Slaughter was there by telling Simon an old friend was trying to get in touch with him. Farnsworth had told Murf to tell Simon the guy said to tell him it was "The Polack", and he'd be staying at the Motel 6 for the next two days, then going back to Pennsylvania.

They arrived to find Whitey drinking his coffee right out of the pot while standing at his front door in his long underwear; eyebrows pinched in a huge frown. After they had parked in the yard beside Whitey's truck and gotten out he bellowed, "What in God's name are ya getting me outta my sleep afore lunch fer Chrissake?"

"I tol ya. Came to pay ya an ask a favor. Need to stay here an wait for a phone call telling me it's OK to fly the lil bird to this guy's field where I can keep it. Shouldn't be but a day or two at the most.", Farnsworth asked, knowing Whitey would go along with it to get his money. And he did.

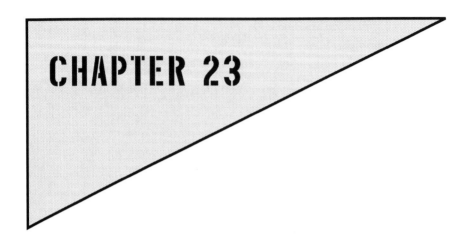

CHAPTER 23

SLAUGHTER, DYKE, BUNNY, AND CHICO USED THE Boston Whaler to transit the water from the dock to the Hootch; and after greetings from Marplot went straight to their beds. They were all dragging ass after the long day's activities and the night flight where slumber is not really sleep.

Earlier, Guido reported that Elmore and Sheila had arrived and were settled in at the Marriott in the Caymans. Guido said he may have a lead, and after some prompting said, "I've been able to establish a contact down here, a lady that knows her way around the financial district and just happens to work for James Julius Enterprises, Inc.; but I don't know the extent of her involvement in any of his illegal activities. I want to find out about that right away before I go into my hard line approach with her. I may need a few days to deal with that part."

"That's good news. You were very lucky to track down his office that fast. Sheila and Elmore need to get some rest and to orient themselves before they get involved, so that should give you time to find out what you can from her.", the Plot agreed

Guido was calling from the beach in front of Tammy's bungalow. Spotting her coming down the steps from her back door he cut the conversation with, "Gotta go, she's coming back. Later." Snapping the phone shut he slipped it into the pocket of his slacks. He had returned to his slacks after their amorous interlude and left his new eye popping swim trunks drying in the shower.

"I hope you like rum,: she announced gaily, "it's all I had in stock. I like it mixed with Coca Cola; very simple, no?", she smiled at him as she placed the already sweating glasses on top of an old wooden barrel bottom stuck in the sand between their lawn chairs.

"Rum and coke is great by me. It could be diesel fuel and I'd drink to your beauty Tammy.", Guido softly said to her.

"You are in love with me now, no? You should not be. Even though we have made good sex it is not enough to make us "in love, yes?", she smiled at his serious grey eyes. Then she continued with, "I do not mean to make you confused; it is the French in me that allows me to tell you that I can love you, but being "in love" is different for me. Does that make sense to you?"

"Sure. I understand completely. I think we can continue seeing each other until one or both of us finds out if we're "in love", yes?, he asked with a smile.

"Of course, my love. Will you stay with me in the bungalow, yes?", she asked.

"Tonight, but tomorrow I must meet the rest of my team to chase down the drug smuggling money trail of our suspect. I'll have to stay in my hotel room to work with them; but, we will surely find time for each other every day, believe me.", he said leaning over to give her a soft kiss on the lips. His soft kiss was reciprocated leading to a more intense exchange. Soon Tammy joined Guido by climbing over to sit on his thighs facing him. Framing his face in both of her hands, she gave him a much longer, deeper searching kiss. She he pulled back to look into his eyes only to see he had his dreamy face on.

For his part he was glad she wasn't sitting directly in his lap. He took in a deep breath, exhaled slowly and said, "Wow. To quote a line in a song, 'You take my breath away'." Momentarily satisfied with their exchange, she lifted to her feet and holding Guido's left hand she returned to her lawn chair. Still holding his hand she settled back into her chair; found her glass and took a sip of her drink, a pensive smile playing around her lips.

Guido gave her a few minutes to relax, then asked, "How much do you know about moving money around?"

"Mon cher, it's part of my job to move money around. I know a bit of the mechanics and the laws we operate under: yes I know something about doing that, and some of the limitations as well.", she stated matter of factly.

"How about hawaladars?", Guido prompted.

"Oh Sure. We do business with them all the time, they perform a definitive service to much of the world. But we don't deal with individual hawalas, only those officially affiliated with a financial institution.

"I sure would like to meet some of those people, if for no other reason than to learn about them; to gain knowledge of their history. You know, how the system started and how it has evolved over the hundreds of years they've been in existence.", he excitedly rambled. Then he asked, "Exactly what happens, what are the mechanics, when your boss, for example, wants a hawala who has his client company's money to send him some? But first, tell me what your role is in this banking business.", he asked carefully. He wanted to find out if this beautiful intriguing woman was in any way a conspirator to Julius Brown's smuggling operation.

"Not much actually, I'm really more of a senior office manager. I am paid well to hold down his office: I make sure his money transfers are completed correctly and performed within the appropriate banking regulations and laws. I also have two clients of my own. I serve as their financial advisor dealing mostly on the international futures market. The company gets 15% of whatever I make from my own endeavors.

It's a very good deal for me, but sometimes Mr. Julius takes care of his own transactions without my involvement at all, and that is OK by me. I have no desire to go to jail for conspiracy. More time for me to cultivate my own clients, no? To answer your question about moving money by Hawaladars. It depends on several things. First it depends on which bank the hawaladar is affiliated with. Second it depends on how much value can be transferred at one time without accompanying paperwork being required. For example, if he is affiliated with the International Bank of Thailand the hawaladar could wire transfer any amount up to ten million U.S. dollars. Any amount above that would require the royal approval, which is usually processed by their financial advisor, Mr. Grey. And, of course, any bank in the Caymans will accept any amount of money without question if it's a new account, or as long as there is a PIN and account number with the transfer. Then on other occasions, the hawaladar must abide by the host government's wire transfer limits or reporting procedures. Does that help any?", she asked like a teacher finishing a review prior to a pop quiz.

"It sure does Tammy.", He said hiding the measure of relief he felt that she was most likely not a collaborator in any of it; then he said. "But I was under the impression that hawaladars often brokered other assets. Stuff like commodities, precious metals and jewels and money with no paper trail whatsoever. That's where the mystery lies; how to track money transfers concerning the opium smuggling business. How do they do it without attracting the attention of the authorities.", he frowned saying it as a statement, leaving the real questions unasked.

Tammy sat back in her chair and took a deep sip of her drink before responding, "Well, I would suspect that a hawaladar would obtain control of a volume of raw opium resin in exchange for some gold coins, rice, tobacco, mules, canned milk…you name it; whatever the poppy growers negotiate for. From there he would pay to have the resin taken to a processing facility to turn it into raw morphine and heroin; again for an exchange of money or commodities. He may even deal through another hawaladar; maybe one holding money for him that can make payment for the drug operations. Once he's got the final product under his command he would pay to have it smuggled to countries with paying customers.", she continued. "But you must also understand that the world's largest poppy growing area is the Southern province of Helmand in Afghanistan. The city of Garmser is the hub for most of the opium resin trading and right now the opium farmers are paying a heavy tax to the Taliban, and so is the Hawalader in the form of safe passage fees.", she said.

"OK. I follow the concept, but how does the Hawaladar get money in hand when its all done?", he asked with raised eyebrows.

"Usually, shell companies are established with the final proceeds deposited in their accounts in a bank in the U.S., U.K. or elsewhere in Europe. The ones that can, wire transfer money to other banks that can operate with less scrutiny by their governments or like the ones in the Channel Islands that operate outside of national controls. Some of these companies present a legitimate appearance and even make money on their own, but most are just fronts. Most of them charge enormous fees to provide fictitious services to other shell companies; or sell products like tobacco at 1000% of the normal cost. Legitimate companies like laundry services can also be used as a front for money laundering, ha ha ha.", she said finishing with that infectious laugh of hers. And then she said, "I bet you are a really good policeman, yes? Then abruptly changing tack she stated, "I'm getting hungry. How about you?", to which he nodded. He was saturated with new information and wanted to make some notes as soon as he could, but he knew that business would have to wait for the moment.

"Lets go then. I know of a terrific seafood place.", she cooed in his ear. That was all it took for him to respond with a light kiss and, "Great. But we'll need to stop by my hotel room first so I can shave and put on a clean shirt…no more than 10 minutes at the most." He would have to talk fast to get it all into his digital voice recorder; he would transcribe it into his computer later when he had more time.

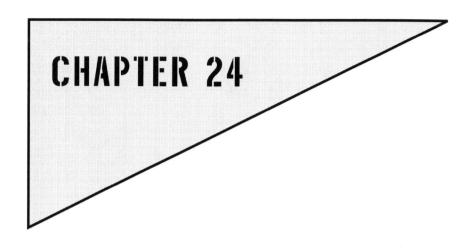

CHAPTER 24

AFTER FARNSWORTH HAD PAID WHITEY HIS MONEY he told him he wanted to fly the plane for an hour or two to get used to it's handling characteristics while Whitey was able to observe, which touched the aging ego of the man who said, "Thas probly a good idea, son. She's fully acrobatic ya know, an kin git away frum ya real easy like. Ya gotta be smooth on the controls since she's much more tuchie; flip ya ina heartbeat."

So Farnsworth flew the little plane through at least a dozen traffic patterns and after the first few when Whitey called him to a stop to tell him something he did wrong, all the rest were "touch and go's" until he finally came in and pushed the little plane back into the shed.. Whitey even went back up to the house before he'd finished to get a canning jar with a peach in it as the sun began to head toward the horizon over the "glades".

After offering Farnsworth a sip when he came up, he said, "Ya done right well, son. I truly believe ya can hanl'er wifout killin yursef." He offered Farnsworth another drink, but Farnsworth declined saying he wanted to go over the little plane for a careful post flight check of the control surfaces, actuator arms, bolt and nut safety wiring, and control cables. Whitey was impressed and said so, then went to the swing at the end of the porch to eyeball the peach some more.

Farnsworth picked up his duffel bag and headed toward the shed where the little plane was parked. On his way he stopped just inside the shed and grabbed two empty one gallon plastic milk cartons from the huge pile sitting there and then went to the opposite corner out of sight in the shadow of both planes. He dropped the duffel bag and began removing the paper bag with the two sticks of dynamite, some of his clothing, duck tape, clothesline rope, twine, and then just left the big bag of fertilizer which was on top of the black plastic trash bags inside. He opened the top of the bag of fertilizer and used his hands to fill each milk carton half way. Then he went over to Whitey's barrel of used motor oil, and by pushing the milk carton down into the oil until it began flowing into the carton, he filled both of them up to about two thirds full. He carefully wiped off the excess oil from the outside of the cartons using some rags Whitey had laying on the floor, then went back to his corner and mixed the oil and fertilizer together into a mush. He then carefully wrapped the dynamite sticks in two layers of duck tape so none of the oil and muck mixture could permeate the wax paper covering of the dynamite. He stuck one stick of dynamite inside the muck in the milk carton so that only about an inch of the top stuck out and taped it into place. He would cut and insert the fuzes just before he took off for his "bombing run" on the Hootch. He carefully took both cartons over to the little plane and set one carton on each side of his seat on the ground. When he got in the seat, he found that he would be able to attach each carton to each side of the landing gear spar that was a main part of the undercarriage structure; and rig them with a quick release knot in the rope in such a way that he could release each of them with one hand allowing them to fall free of the aircraft.

He would cut each fuze enough to allow two wooden kitchen match heads to be glued inside, and a strip of high grit sandpaper tied just tight enough to strike the match heads and lighting them immediately after he pulled the quick release. The match heads would ignite the powder train inside the fuzes without him having to try and light them with a lighter or lit cigar, and then try and cut the duck tape.

He was glad he had thought about how he would rig the duffel bag with the dynamite, fuzes and match heads before; and had managed to snatch a few from Whitey's kitchen when he was there the first time. He hid the rigged milk cartons behind his duffel bag and found himself daydreaming about body parts flying through the air, and that made him wonder just how high he would have to fly so they wouldn't hit him and the little plane.

Satisfied with his work he decided to go up and sit with Whitey and see if the peach had anything left around it. As he ascended the porch steps he said with a smile, "All's in good order. Mind if I sit with ya a spell?" Whitey was sitting on a swing at the end of the porch just barely pushing himself back and forth keeping his feet on the floor and canning jar held in his lap and said, "Naw, come and sit if'n ya don mind a little "to an fro"; and here, have a pull. Ya done good today, in my book at leas."

"Thanks Whitey, for everything. And by the way, I asked Murf to call here when he finds out that Simon Arpslot is back at his place on that island so's I kin talk to him bout the land. Hope you don mind.", Farnsworth said. Whitey didn't mind and retrieved the canning jar for a huge swallow that all but emptied it, then abruptly handed it back to Farnsworth and got up saying, "I'm goin to bed. You can sleep onna couch. Hep yersef to a ham sandwich in the fridge if'n ya want. Gunight."

As Farnsworth was making himself a huge ham sandwich he began to envision just how simple a plan it had turned out to be; but there was just one thing left. He had no escape plan. The little plane wouldn't get him very far, and if he landed in any populated area he would attract too much attention. Whitey had a fairly new truck that he always left the keys in, and Farnsworth still had a little over $5000 in cash left; plus he'd be leaving the little plane as well. Yes, that would work, but he'd only leave Whitey $3000 because he believed that the total was all the truck was really worth. He could make it back into Miami and get lost in the Cuban section; maybe even sell or trade the truck for something the cops wouldn't be looking for. Yes. That's what he would do; and he'd leave Whitey a note suggesting he had to have the truck to get to Sarasota where his little sister was in the hospital as a result of a car accident. That would start the search for him along the Western side of Florida and maybe buy him a few hours time.

He ran through the details in his mind over and over until he finally fell asleep on Whitey's well worn couch and began dreaming of himself making Stukka dive bomb runs over France in WWII.

CHAPTER 25

LTC PICKETT, FEET UP ON HIS DESK in his U.S. Embassy office, the office with Defense Military Attaché painted in black letters on the door. He was trying to figure a way to officially go to Rio to help out Simon Arpslot, the "Plot" with his money problem. It had been almost two days since the call for Pickett's help; and it had been two fruitless days of calling the Military Attaché at the U. S. Embassy in Sao Paulo without an answer. The slot must be vacant, or the guy must be back in Washington at the five sided wind tunnel called the pentagon kissing ass.

Finally, in near desperation he gave up and dialed the Deputy Consul wimp, the one with mother's milk still on his upper lip and when he answered, "Deputy Consul Morganstill, how may I help you?"

Pickett replied, Morganstill I need to go to Rio to check into something for DIA. The military attaché assigned to Sao Paulo is out of pocket. Request just came in by secure phone. I'll be sending you a travel request for three days. I need to leave right away." He knew Morganstill hated being called by his last name rather than his title.

A small man with a huge ego, Morganstill waffled a reply, "I'm not sure I can authorize that without more information. The Ambassador might ask, for example, what exactly does the DIA want you to do?"

Pickett knew Morganstill didn't know squat about military activities or items of equipment beyond a plane, tank, or bullet so he simply said it's a rather sensitive matter and details are quite classified, but if you want to discuss this matter over the phone that's fine. It's..." "No no no. I'll be right down, Morganstill broke in rapidly and rattled the phone in its cradle in his hurry to hang up. It wasn't often that the Embassy got any truly classified stuff, especially from the DIA. Most of it was from the State Department and was either For Official Use Only (FOUO), No Foreign Dissemination (NOFORN), or just Confidential and classified to make the originator feel important.

Within a minute Morganstill was at the door to Pickett's office and nearly jerked his arm out of the socket when he tried to open it and found it locked. (most offices had cipher locks on them). His chagrin mounted as he was forced to buzz for entry expecting to be kept waiting for a minute or so, but Pickett wanted something so he opened it immediately. Once inside, he pulled the coattails of his jacket down and crossed his arms over his chest and assumed what he thought was a stern look of authority on his face. After all, by position he outranked Pickett even though Pickett was the U.S. military intelligence representative in Peru and tied in closely with the Central Intelligence Agency (CIA) Station Chief in Lima. Morganstill's daddy a senior official in the State Department as a Deputy Director in International Law had helped him get this job before he had really earned it, but he acted as if he had. His father had explained about Military

Attaché's and what they really did, so he blurted out, "Well, what is it this time?" as if "it" happened much more frequently than desired.

"Do you know what an Aquila UAV is?", Pickett asked.

"No. What is it? Some kind of SUV, an exotic bird, or some special cocktail we've got to be prepared to make for a visiting VIP?", he squeaked.

Pickett paused and stared at the fatuous posturing imbecile knowing it would unnerve him. When it had its effect he finally said, "No, your excellence. It's not a car, a bird or a fucking cocktail. It's a remotely controlled unmanned aerial vehicle that our neighbors to the North East bought from us years ago and are now using to conduct air strikes on indigenous peoples by mounting 2.75 inch rockets under the wings. At least that's what's being reported by a source in Rio; and, DIA wants me to go there and review and photograph the evidence they have. Can you remember all of that just in case the "boss" wants to know? I can write it all down for you if you'd like," he finished with an innocent look on his face.

"No, no. That won't be necessary," snapped the Deputy Ambassador. "Do you have your travel voucher and passport ready for my signature and the stamp?" "Fine.", he said after Pickett had leaned forward over his desk to shove the documents forward, but leaving his feet comfortably on his desk. As Morganstill turned to leave Pickett calmly said, "Oh by the way your highness, this is strictly for limited distribution. You are the only person here except myself that knows anything about this activity. I'll be attending a friend's wedding if anyone asks; and if you breathe a word of this to anyone I WILL find out and hook your balls up to that wall socket over there and let them fry until they are nice. and crispy, and then feed them to you between your screams of pain." Pickett's dismissal comment of " Have a nice day", was accompanied by the same innocent unreadable expression that unsettled Morganstill every time he faced it.

Morganstill's face turned white as a newly bleached sheet under the cosmetic tan he affected and he hurried out of Pickett's office and back to his own office where he could regain his composure behind his closed door. He sat deep in his specially designed leather chair; a chair that seemed to comfort him in its hugging embrace. It was higher than normal to compensate for his lack of height and the rich leather presented a cool luxurious surface to the touch. Fuming at his treatment, he contemplated calling daddy about the threat. Then memory overcame emotion as he recalled the chastising his father gave him the last time he complained about Pickett. He could remember the exact words, "Son, that man has been through more hell than you can imagine, and he's got more decorations for valor in combat than you can count on all your fingers and toes. As a former member of a highly classified and credible unit at Fort Bragg, you might just want to believe whatever it is that he tells you. You'll get along much better that way."

Pickett's old friend and the senior enlisted member of the DATT office, MSG Doug Bates, had called him to their top floor security vault to listen to the taped conversation with daddy and both had had a good belly laugh.

He had already made flight arrangements to Rio for that evening, so he secured all his paperwork, and set the alarm on his office door and left to go pack what he would need on the trip. He would travel in his Class A green uniform with all of his awards, decorations, and qualification badges. He had learned that traveling in "uniform de gala" in South America made almost everything easier.

He used his personal secure satellite phone to tell the Plot he'd be coming to Rio to handle the money himself. When the plot told him he'd need to dig it up from just inside the front door of a burned out farmhouse at Longitude such and such, and Latitude such and such, his thoughts went to his hand held GPS, then to the folding entrenching tool he kept in his ready bag. Then they shifted to a more complex issue; what to do with the money once he'd dug it up.

The Plot's instructions were for him to meet with the president of the International Bank of Brazil, set up an account number with a personal identification number; and if he asked any questions to just tell him that the money was going to be used as bait for a drug bust that was being coordinated between the U.S, Colombia, and Brazilian authorities; and that for the time being it need not be advertised in any way. The Plot had already met the president of the bank where he presented his diplomatic passport and other documentation validating his position as a Class A financial agent from the U.S. Justice Department. He also provided the names and other vital information of those officials authorized to function on this project, which included Pickett's. While the drug bust operation was being planned, the bank could forgo paying any interest on the money as long as it was kept as a confidential account. The bank president's initially hesitant tone and barely cooperative attitude changed immediately with that bit of information: he instantly understood that he could charge the bank the interest anyway, and quietly slide it into his own pocket.

"Once the cash is on deposit", the Plot continued, "call me secure with the PIN and account number so I can move the money to the account our man in the Caymans is establishing. If the president wants a penalty for not leaving the money in his bank long enough, tell him we are limited to $2,500 in U.S., otherwise his whole bank will be swarming with international and Brazilian authorities."

"OK. You got it.", Pickett said. He walked to an internal phone and told the Marine controlling the entrance to the main building to call for a car and driver to take him to the airport.

As he expected, his uniform, diplomatic passport and Peruvian carnet allowed him to breeze through security at Lima, and through customs at Rio. He caught a taxi and checked in at the most expensive hotel in Rio, the Hyatt on the beach. Before going up to his room he pulled the concierge aside and asked him, "I need a four wheel drive vehicle full of gas, preferably a Land Rover or equivalent, and a map of this area. I want to take some photos and will be using unimproved roads. Oh, make sure they include a D-handled shovel in case I have to dig myself out." During the taxi ride he had slung his camera around his neck looking every bit the tourist, even in his uniform.

The concierge bowed gracefully and said, "Certainly sir. How soon will you need it?"

"Right away.", he replied as he handed the man a crisp $50.00 bill, and then said, "All I have to do is go upstairs, change clothes, and I'll be ready."

The concierge had nodded and all but ran back to his desk to snatch up the phone. Within minutes he had arranged with his cousin to provide one of his dealership demonstration Land Rovers and to stop off on the way over to the hotel and buy a shovel and put it in the back storage compartment. Then he opened a drawer in his desk and extracted several maps of the surrounding area.

The cousin knew he would be paid well for this one, so he drove it to the hotel himself. The vehicle had 58 miles on it, so he would caution the driver to be careful; any scratches or dents would cost extra.

Pickett was standing at the curb of the hotel entrance, glanced at his GMT Rolex and cursed softly . It was too early to go to the farmhouse. He had already plotted the coordinates on his map and punched them into his hand held GPS but he didn't want to get there during daylight. In fact, he would park the Land Rover behind a knoll about a mile from the place and walk the rest of the way in to avoid drawing unnecessary attention. Now he would have to do something to eat up time and also give him a legitimate reason for being wherever he would be. At the knoll he would be there to pray since he had been told it was an ancient prayer mound. At the farmhouse, he would be assessing the damage and estimating the cleanup costs to rebuild on the property at the behest of the Commandante of the militia, or the International Bank of Brazil, the lien holder. "Shit", he said out loud. Anyway you looked at it, his cover stories were pretty lame.

Having heard Pickett's epithet the concierge rushed up and sputtered, "It will only be a moment sir, I assure you."

Pickett didn't say anything; just waved his hand in the air in dismissal. He was really thinking about what to do to kill a couple of hours before heading out to the farmhouse. He finally asked the concierge, "Where is the International Bank of Brazil from here?"

"Ah, it is only a few blocks from here. As you leave the hotel entrance and stop at the sign, turn right. Go down two blocks on the beach road and then turn right again. That is the main thoroughfare through Rio. The bank is on the corner at the next block and it has underground parking for its customers.", he smoothly replied just as his cousin pulled up in a shiny new tan colored Land Rover.

Pickett thanked the concierge, passed another bill when shaking hands, and passed still another bill to the driver and quickly jumped in the idling vehicle. Before anyone could say a word he drove off on squealing tires avoiding any cautions about dents or scratches. He followed the directions to the bank, found it, but continued on the main street careful not to run over anyone or anything. Traffic was a mess, and dealing with it was starting to piss Pickett off so he pulled out of traffic at the first opening at the side of the road and turned the engine off. He sat for a moment surveying his back trail and the different stores, vendors, and other places of business nearby. Finally he decided he'd like a cold beer. He locked the car and walked to the outdoor café close to his parking spot.

Pickett's irritation at the traffic continued in the café. He wasn't counting, but he estimated he had been propositioned at least a dozen times since he had sat down. He was almost sure at least a third of them were men dressed as women. Prostitution was legal in Rio, and there were apparently plenty to go around. He continued to sip at his beer, a $3.00 Corona, expensive for Rio, but he preferred it rather than the local brands; and when the waiter offered him a frosted glass, he declined. The last thing he needed was the shits.

Pickett decided to use his hand held GPS as a backup, and tapped the Long and Lat for the farmhouse into the new Land Rover's dash mounted GPS. A map quickly popped up on the six inch by eight inch screen. It displayed a blinking red dot indicating his present position, and a blinking green dot for the farmhouse. The map also highlighted the route to follow to the destination.. The selected route included instructions for a detour to avoid some construction, the construction site indicated by a blinking pickax. "Wow. This damned thing is loaded.", he said out loud.

The sun had set over an hour before he arrived at the knoll he had selected to leave the car. He stopped the car and put the transmission in park, then sat a few minutes to look the area over. Satisfied he cut the engine, grabbed his gear and locked the Land Rover. Moonrise wasn't for another hour. He brought his rucksack with a few green chemlights and two bottles of distilled water. He carried his hand held GPS and the short D-handled shovel. He wished he had brought his leather flight jacket as well; the night air was rapidly cooling and he had to keep a good pace just to avoid a chill.

Arriving at the burned out farmhouse he quickly discerned where the front entrance had been. He took three steps in from the threshold , turned around and began digging. The digging was easy as the dirt was only lightly packed on top; and about two feet down he discovered a canvas surface. He popped a chemlight so he could see into the hole more clearly, then gently tried brushing the dirt away. He soon found he would have to dig more laterally due to the size of the bundle. When he finally reached one edge and had a better idea of the size of the bundle he changed his plan. "The hell with this digging," he said to himself," I'll just cut the sonofabitch open and transfer the money to my rucksack." He sliced the canvas open and quickly filled his rucksack with U.S. $100 dollar bills in wrapped $5000 packets. As he transferred the money he developed a strong desire to strangle Marplot. There was at least another rucksack load left in the canvas bag. He would have to either wear the ruck and drag the bag, or make two trips. This damn job was going to be an all nighter.

He set the packed rucksack to one side and pulled the rest of the canvas container out of the hole, sliding it alongside the rucksack.

Sweating heavily he stopped and chugged a bottle of water, discarding the empty into the gaping hole. After a few minutes he returned to his shovel and filled in the hole with as much profanity and doubt about Marplot's ancestry as he did dirt. Finally he added some more dirt from the yard to fill the hole then tied the shovel to the back of the rucksack. He shouldered the rucksack; wrapped up the rest of the money in the original canvas bag and began his trek back to the Land Rover. Every twenty yards he imagined another kind of payback that just might be satisfactory. This friendship crap was vastly over rated!

At 1:30PM the phone in his hotel room rang dragging him from a very deep sleep. He was not in as good a shape physically as he thought he was, and by the time he had put out the "Do Not Disturb" sign, stashed the money in the closet, and drank everything in the minibar he was dead to the world. He reached over and fumbled the phone into his hand, and with gravel in his voice answered, "Yeah."

"Well. It sounds like I just woke you up. Did everything go OK last night, or haven't you gone to the site yet?", Marplot asked, some anxiety evident in his voice.

"You sorry sack of shit. The next time I can get my hands on you I'm gonna rip your balls off. Why didn't you tell me what kind of tonnage I'd be dealing with? And I had to make two trips up the elevator at three fucking AM because my rucksack would only hold half at a time. And now you wake me up to tell me what?", an angry Pickett yelled his question into the phone.

"Easy, my friend, easy. A huge mistake on my part; I'm truly sorry, but glad you're in such fine spirits this morning because I have good news for you. I contacted Morganstill and massaged his ego some and made him think he is part of some major intelligence related activity that demands no official paper trail. He agreed, but demanded that if anything goes wrong he will put you on ordinary vacation leave instead of official TDY. That change will be made effective the day you left Lima if necessary. Plausible deniability. He can disavow any knowledge of whatever shit you get into. On a positive note, the banker agreed to our cash handling fee as previously discussed, and I have provided all the documentation he needs. All you have to do is get some drawers on and wait for the banker's men to come and get the money; they should be there within the hour, and then have a good time. You're not due back for three days and I'll cover all your expenses, so enjoy.", the Plot soothed.

"Marplot, it'll take me three days to get over the thoughts of strangling your broke dick ass.", Pickett said and hung up the phone. As soon as his head hit the pillow he began thinking about how he would spend three days floating around Rio. Oh well, he was sure he'd manage somehow. Maybe he'd go back to that outdoor café and watch the pros fight over him. Then he wondered what kind of "expenses" he could expect from the Plot and get away with.

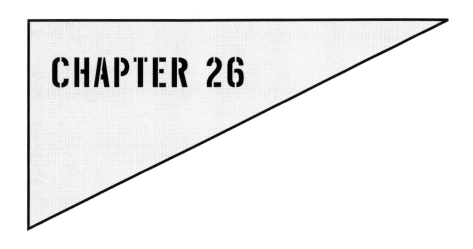

CHAPTER 26

THE PHONE AT WHITEY'S RANG THE NEXT afternoon during Oprah, one of his favorites, and he answered it, hit the mute on his remote and said, "It's Murf, for you."

"Hey Murf. Whacha got?", Farnsworth asked, taking the phone and starting his side of the conversation.

"Is that so. What did he have to say about the land deal?", Farnsworth prompted.

"Hadn't considered selling, huh? Well, maybe if I talk to him about what I want to do with it he'll come around. Did it sound like there were other people there, I wouldn't want to discuss it in front of a crowd ya know.", Farnsworth stated. "Several huh. Oh well; I think I might give him a call anyway. Maybe he'll meet me at his big mailbox and I can show him the parcel I want. I really appreciate yer help Murf.", Farnsworth said and hung up thinking that Slaughter must be there. He and the Plot were rarely separated. He would take off just before sunset so he could find the little island before dark.

"You goin out to Range 19 to see Mr. Arpslot bout the land?", Whitey asked; then continued with, "He ain't gonna sell. Even if'n he did it'd be like stealing yer money. That land ain't good fer nothing cept mud bugs an saw grass. County tax is next to nothing.

"You're probably right Whitey, but I thought there was about a four acre strip next to the highway that looked elevated enough to have a pond. You know what, I think I'll take a look at it from the air tomorrow morning and see what it looks like around there and maybe some other places as well."

When Murf spoke to the Plot he mentioned a Mr. Jonathan Smith wanting to buy four or five acres of the mainland property next to the highway. Marplot was immediately suspicious and asked Murf what the guy looked like, how old he might be, and anything else that was peculiar to the guy. When Murf described this Mr. Smith as kinda short, maybe in his mid forties, and that he limped on his left foot; the alarm sounded in his brain. Farnsworth again.

"Well Murf, I can't believe anyone would want to buy that land, but I'll talk to this stranger if he wants. Thanks for the call.", the Plot said and hung up leaving his options open. Punching his speed dial he soon got a reply and asked the other person, "Would you please patch me through to Sheriff Baugh?"

"Sure nuf Mr. Simon. Howyabeen?", the woman who answered asked.

"Fine Linda Sue. How about you and Big John?", he politely inquired about her unemployed husband, knowing it would lead to a three act tragedy.

"Well, Big John ain't doin so well" she lamented. "He done lopped off his thumb with his big Rambo knife when he was cleanin a catfish whilst he was drunk as a skunk. Lopped the sucker clean off. Least he had sense enough to wrap the thumb in plastic wrap and put it in his beer cooler. Then he wrapped his hand with ice till he got to the hospital. He saw that on TV on the discovery channel. They sewed it back on, but the doc says it's fifty-fifty unless they can get some leeches to suck the dead blood cells outta his thumb and he don't smoke, dip or chew. Ya ever heard a such a thing? An they gotta fly them damn leeches in from England cause that's the only place that grows em fer medicinal purposes; $128.00 apiece they are doncha know. And as far as not smoking, dipping or chewing! Hah! Big John's pissed as a - - - uh, sure Sheriff; he's on the line Mr. Simon. Give you the rest later."

"No. Linda Sue ask Sheriff Baugh to hold on a minute, would you please?", and after she had done that he said to Linda Sue, "I want you to call a Dr. Mossman at the Homestead Surgical Clinic. Tell him I asked you to, and tell him about Big John and the leeches. I believe he has some he's experimenting with. Tell him you won't charge him anything for using Big John as a guinea pig. That'll convince him to help you, ha ha.", the Plot chuckled.

"God bless you Simon." she said. Then, "Here's Terry".

"Hey Terry", he started, " Good to talk to you. I might have a problem; same one we had before. Remember Farnsworth.?", the Plot finished.

"Hmmm," the sheriff mused, adding, "I knew there was something familiar about that guy I found sleeping in Murf's truck last night. He's not changed much. except he fooled me with his short haired local look, John Deere hat and all; plus driving Murf's truck.

"He said he was on his way back to Murf's Motel 6 when he realized he didn't have any headlights, so he pulled over to sleep in the truck till morning. Said he was out at Whitey's looking to buy that little plane he's got for sale. I didn't recognize him, but even if I had, there wasn't nothing I could arrest him for. He wasn't driving and had pulled over on a public road.", Sheriff Baugh said somewhat apologetically.

The Plot listened carefully to what Sheriff Baugh had said, then asked, "Did he say anything about wanting to buy land along the highway?"

"Yep, now that you mention it, he sure did. I reckon I could've picked up on that. Ain't no land along the Tamiami Gulf side worth buyin for 50 miles.", the Sheriff said; then continued with, "I'll run him in and see if I can find out what he's up to Simon."

The plot demurred, "No need for you to be bothered yet Terry. Let me see if I can find out what he's up to. If I need your help I'll give you a call, OK?", the Plot asked.

"OK Simon.", the Sheriff agreed, adding, "But I'm gonna rattle Murf some to see what he knows. I got a suspicion that he's checked out of the Motel 6 and is staying out at Whitey's to avoid any contact with me. I may have to do some arm twisting on that scrawny little fart, but I'll get whatever he knows outta him and let you know."

"Thanks Terry. I owe you another one. Talk to you later", the Plot ended and hung up. Almost simultaneously he punched a little button next to the phone which activated a ringing bell that could be heard only within the confines of the Hootch and little island. Dyke, Bunny, Chico, and Slaughter came from wherever they had been to gather in the kitchen. Dobbin and Lee An Too were absent. The two were out in the boat snorkeling, but Plot didn't need either of them so he didn't use the radio to "buzz" them underwater.

When they were all at the table he asked the assembly, "Guess who's back?"

"Son of a bitch.", Slaughter said softly; then, "It's that fucking Farnsworth, isn't it?"

"I'm afraid so. And this time it appears he might be planning to pull some kind of Jimmy Doolittle on us.", the Plot said while scratching his chin as he mulled the situation, and then continued, "I might be jumping to a conclusion, but it's my bet he's bought Whitey's little red Rotex ultra light airplane and probably plans some kind of attack on us. Maybe he rigged up some homemade bombs to drop on us; and it looks like he might plan to do it by daylight tomorrow. From what the sheriff told me, I think he'll be staying at Whitey's tonight to avoid any attention, and then high tail it out of here as soon as he's done all the damage he can. In any case my friends, we have a mission tonight, so lets get it out on the table now."

"Hell man, by 1000PM Whitey'll be passed out in his bed upstairs. Farnsworth will nap someplace until just before daybreak, so I think we just slip in, snatch him and then dump him so far out in the glades nobody'll ever find him before he's a line of alligator turds.", Dyke offered.

"Why risk thu sposure? Why don't we jus suffocate his sorry ass wherever we find em?", Bunny said.

"How bout we find his little plane an rig it to crash; or, better yet, we sabotage his bombs if that's his choice of weapon, so his bomb blows up under the little plane right after he lets it go?", Chico enthused.

"No dammit. I want the bastard to myself. I'm the one he's after. I'll handle it. You guys don't need to be involved at all. End of discussion.", Slaughter thundered slamming his open hand on the kitchen table. He turned angrily and stomped out of the kitchen.

Unperturbed, Dyke went to the refrigerator and grabbed a Tuborg bottle of beer asking, "Anybody else?", to which all except the Plot said "Yo"

That evening nobody but the Plot saw Slaughter leave in the powerboat. He was standing on the dock in front of the Hootch and watched as the black clad figure faded into the gloom with only a small light in front to mark his progress. He was the only one privy to what Slaughter had planned, and had no doubt he would succeed.

It would take 30 to 40 minutes to navigate the maze of manmade waterways to the one behind Whitey's farm. And since the waterway was about 500 meters from the back of the farmhouse it would take another five to six minutes to get there on foot; perhaps longer depending on the level of saw grass and depth of swamp water he had to slog through. He'd travel light with only his lensatic compass with tritium arrows, a GPS, his Randall knife, duct tape, plastic flex-ties, 100' of 550 parachute cord, modified suppressed Ruger .22 cal pistol , Leatherman tool, night vision goggles, small flashlight, a small can of WD40, and one of Lee An Too's bamboo slivers tipped with his exotic sleeping juice. He didn't expect to use the pistol, but Murphy's law was always a consideration and he did not want to leave anything to chance in this environment.

Even using a handheld GPS and recent satellite imagery, Slaughter made two wrong turns and had to backtrack each time as he tried to use the big city lights of Crossroads to locate the blackwater channel to Whitey's where he cut the outboard and shifted to the electric trolling motor to close on his destination.

It was almost midnight when he finally cut and stowed the engine and beached the boat in the reedy bank. He pulled the boat as far up the bank as he could securing it by planting the anchor further inland.. He tied a green chemlight to the anchor and activated it. He used it just in case his NVGs went South, or Murphy's law took effect.

As soon as he crested the bank he could see a light at the farm. He started out and after a few hundred yards of slipping through the swamp grass and slogging through the mucky surface he saw that the only lights coming from the farmhouse were the yard light out front and the glow from some small light inside; probably the bathroom light. It took him ten minutes to break through the thicker growth near the waterway but soon made the last walk to the back door steps in less than 5 minutes. He had everything in a specific place and had practiced reaching and extracting every item he had; so he reached into the left side cargo pocket of his trousers to extract the small can of WD40 to spray the steps where the boards met and were nailed at the ends. Next he sprayed the hinges on the screen door; opened it slowly, and sprayed the hinges and seams of the door handle on the wooden inner door. He tried the door handle.

Like many doors on farm houses it was unlocked. He slipped inside the screen door and opened the wooden door just far enough to step through. He let the screen door close silently, entered the house fully and pulled the wooden door back until the edge of the door just met the door jamb. He didn't want to have to turn the door knob to open the door while carrying Farnsworth out of the house. Slaughter had only used the NVG to scan on his way to the house but he was wearing them for the entry. Now he had them focused for relatively close range and could see everything clearly through the green hue they produced. He expected Farnsworth would be sleeping inside to avoid the ubiquitous mosquitoes and other flying and crawling critters common to the Florida nights.

He quietly made his way into the living room where he discovered Farnsworth sleeping on his side facing the back of a sagging couch. Lee An Too told him to hold the bamboo sliver a half inch from the sharpened end and to jab it into the side of the neck just under the ear and not pull it out for at least two seconds. They had practiced on a ham with an ear drawn on the side earlier so he knew how to hold the bamboo and what resistance to expect.

The effect would be immediate if he did it right. If not, well he was on his own for not keeping it personal and not letting a "professional" come along to perform the procedure. The unknown was how Farnsworth would react when the sliver penetrated. He would just have to be prepared for anything.

Slaughter crossed the room as quietly as he could. He kept his weight on the rear foot until the lead foot had been lowered softly before shifting he weight forward. Things were moving smoothly with almost complete silence during his movement.

Slaughter started to move toward the couch keeping his weight on the rear foot until he was sure the lead foot was lowered silently. He was within a three feet of the sleeping man when he lowered his foot and as he shifted his weight the board under his foot creaked out a high squeal. Slaughter froze in place, and watched as Farnsworth turned over. Instinctively, Slaughter quickly side stepped to stand in the shadow behind a large hutch. He leaned forward just far enough to look around the hutch and watched as Farnsworth slowly sat up and rubbed his eyes. He just sat there, apparently adjusting himself to where he was and the gloom.

Pulling a small flashlight from his shirt pocket he turned it on and stood up shining it on his watch, then casually working out the kinks in his shoulders and back and walked across the living room and out the front door. Slaughter waited about 30 seconds and followed him out the front door himself. He could see the little flashlight's beam jerking back and forth as Farnsworth walked along the pathway leading to the long storage shed where Whitey kept his planes. He followed at a distance being careful not to kick any empty beer cans or step on any fallen branches.

Slaughter watched Farnsworth enter a door at the far end of the shed noting the metal to metal screech it made when he opened it. That noise made a decision for him; it meant he would have to enter from the front and hope he wouldn't bump into the little fart. It took him a long minute to reach the edge of the long open shed so that he could view the interior. The blue two seater was parked closest to him; the little red one was further back and next to the far wall.

Slaughter could see the light pattern from Farnsworth's little flashlight moving around the front of the landing gear of the little plane. He moved stealthily inside avoiding the debris scattered around the shed as he crept closer. finally he could see that Farnsworth had tied what appeared to be a plastic milk carton on each of the two legs of the landing gear. He was too far away to be sure but they seemed to be secured with a some kind of cord or rope. He could also tell that the milk cartons looked as if they were filled with oil or some other dark fluid. Farnsworth had his back to Slaughter as he removed clothing and other items from a duffel bag set against the far wall. Suddenly he straightened; put the flashlight inside his mouth, and held a white washcloth in the beam of light. Slaughter was about ten feet away, but when Farnsworth unfolded the washcloth he saw what were unmistakably several pieces of jewelry; flashes of light sparkled from the mounted gems. Damn, what'd the little shit do, hold up a pawn shop?

Farnsworth quickly refolded the washcloth and stuffed it in the bottom of his duffel bag, followed by the rest of his junk. He placed all of the bag's metal grommets over the "U" shaped metal clasp; placed a padlock through the "U" bolt and locked it. He had the key to the lock around his neck on a small chain and fingered it gently before tucking it inside his shirt.

Apparently satisfied, Farnsworth took the flashlight from his mouth, turned and went back out the squeaking door. Slaughter hurriedly backtracked to the open end of the shed to watch him return to the farmhouse. He guessed Farnsworth was going back up to make himself a cup of the instant coffee he had noticed set out on the kitchen counter, and to probably take a crap. Regardless, Slaughter had about 5-10 minutes at the most to do what he came to do.

First he retrieved the washcloth full of jewelry by simply slicing a hole in the bottom of the duffel bag with his razor sharp Randall. He cut it just large enough to get his hand in to find the washcloth on the bottom of the bag. He wadded the bundle into his fist, pulled it out, and put it into his front trouser pocket.

Leaving the duffel bag he moved to the starboard landing gear strut and took time to adjust the focus of his NVGs to allow him to see the milk cartons with more definition. Then he knelt so he could carefully inspect the milk carton. He could see it was rigged so that when the slip knot trail line was pulled, the milk carton would fall free. Further investigation showed that when it fell the container would pull the three match heads surrounding the fuze in the middle of the stick of dynamite so that they would ignite from sliding against the rough sand paper taped to the strut. It was a clever rig if he did say so himself. Pulling out his Leatherman he unfolded it so he could use the long nose pliers to carefully pull the fuze out of the dynamite. There was about an inch and a half that had been inside the stick, and about two and a half inches above that to the match sticks, all wrapped in duct tape. He quickly calculated that if he cut two inches off the bottom of the fuze and then repositioned an inch of fuze inside the dynamite, that would only leave an inch of fuze surrounded by match heads; and maybe 3 seconds before it exploded. It should make for an interesting flight.

Slaughter rewrapped the fuze and match head combination and repeated the procedure on the other side since he didn't know which one he would attempt to drop first. Happy in his work, Slaughter cleaned up the area removing all trace of his presence and headed back to the boat. He left keeping to the shadows until he was well into the swamp grass and out of sight of anyone at the house.

Everything was going great until he hit the saw grass and swamp. Negotiating the stuff coming in was not too bad because he was hyped up, but coming back out was mighty rough going. By the time he had made it to the boat he just flopped down on the back seat and collapsed. He had brought water with him; and it was in the cooler in the boat, but he wanted to cool off a little and catch his breath before he could even think about getting up.

"Son of a bitch"., Slaughter said softly. He had immediately looked at his watch and discovered he had dozed off for almost an hour. He figured it was about an hour before daybreak and he had to haul ass.

After pocketing the light stick and stowing the anchor, he fired up one engine and put it in gear at idle until the boat was about a half mile away from where they were, then he fired up the other engine and advanced the throttles half way. Once he was in the calm Gulf waters he advanced the throttles forward and soon the boat was doing about 25 knots. He removed his NVGs since the false dawn was already upon the horizon. His thoughts immediately turned to Farnsworth as he could barely hear the roar of the little plane's engine. He needed to get under some kind of cover before Farnsworth spotted the boat, so he slowed and soon guided the boat around a hammock with large mangroves to the opposite side from Farnsworth's probable route to the Hootch. He sat idling the engines while holding a large branch to steady the boat. Mosquitoes immediately swarmed every piece of exposed skin. He scrambled under the dash for bug juice and splashed it in his hands to wipe it over all of his exposed skin, but it was too late. They had already enjoyed their frenzied feast. He decided he'd better call the Plot on the Radio to let him know he was about to have company.

"Sierra to Papa, over.", he said as he held down the transmit button on the boat's microphone. He waited a full minute and tried again. This time he got a response, "Papa up five by. Send your traffic, over.", the Plot responded mechanically from his days as a young commo specialist on then Captain Slaughter's team at the end of the Vietnam war. When they had been ambushed with mortars and automatic weapons fire, Specialist Fourth class Simon Arpslot had been hit badly by shrapnel in the waist and both legs. Slaughter had used Arpslot's radio to call for gunship cover and medevac from the closest landing zone not quite a kilometer away. He had then scooped up Specialist Arpslot, guts hanging out, both legs with tourniquets, radio, and rucksack along with whatever leaves and branches were attached and carried him all the way to the LZ. It was during this trek that Slaughter gave Simon Arpslot his new nickname of Marplot. "Do you know what a Marplot is asshole? It's an individual that consistently screws up a good plan through his officious meddling. You had no business standing up until I told you we were moving again. You should've crawled over to me.", Slaughter wheezed as he continued his jog toward the incoming helicopters. He could hear the gun ship's 2.75 inch rockets impacting as well as the door mounted M60 machine guns chattering away.

By the time they reached the medivac helicopter the Plot was unconscious and with streaks of sweat and tears streaming down his dirty face Slaughter said out loud, "You better live you son of a bitch or I'll visit your grave every year just to piss on it.". Then his thoughts came back as he heard the little airplane fly over some distance inland from where he was.

"Uh, this is Sierra. Expect a little airborne company in about ten minutes. If it tries to poop on you, the poo poo may hit the fan; you might want to stay inside and maybe in a hardened room, do you copy over?.", Slaughter transmitted.

"Sierra, this is Papa. Understand we may have some fireworks overhead with sudden impact. Is that it? Over."

Slaughter thought about this for a moment, then said, "Roger that. Out.", and for some unknown reason he started whistling "I've been working on the railroad, all the livelong day - - -".

CHAPTER 27

THE FIRST THING ELMORE DID WHEN HE got to his hotel room was put the MP5-SD away. He placed it behind the room's air conditioner mounted against the wall beneath the large window overlooking the ocean. He used a long strip of duct tape to secure it in place out of sight. Getting it through customs had been a breeze since he had called ahead to let his "contact" know his arrival time. His "contact" Charles, just happened to be the MI6 senior agent in the Caymans. Charles was also a very good friend whom he had saved from what would have surely been a very ugly death several years back during an operation in Bulgaria. Needless to say, Charles was glad to see Elmore and gave him the courtesy of not asking why he needed an MP5SD. As a professional intelligence operative he knew Elmore would tell him what he needed to know and nothing else.

"I say, it's jolly good to see you old boy, he said with genuine enjoyment, "and getting a little paunchy are we? Damn watery high calorie Yank beer I wager, eh mate?.

Right! Here's my car, and you can throw your bag in the boot, if you can remember where that is, ha ha.", Charles rattled on in his best English public school accent. He had a dozen accents at his command; spoke nine languages, and could read and write reasonably well in five others.

"Good to see you too; and thanks for the favor at customs. There's no target. I just feel more comfortable with it.", Elmore said.

"You haven't changed a bit, my friend. I suspect we all have our little "druthers" as you might say.", he smiled as he said the last while patting the area over his heart drawing his attention to the slight bulge in his rumpled suit jacket.

"So what brings you to our lovely island? I do need to send in a report on you, you know. Your name still rings a few bells in the home office. Do you want me to develop a shallow cover for you, and if so for how long?", Charles asked.

"No cover necessary Charles. I'm here overt. My task is to find out as much as I can about bank accounts in the name of James Julius aka Julius Brown. Bastard bought his way out of a Thai prison after we went to the trouble of getting his sorry ass convicted of opium smuggling. I was hoping you might cut through some of the red tape with these banks; and that you guys might have already gathered some of the information we need.", Elmore said as he started to roll down his backseat window.

"I wouldn't do that if I were you." he said quickly, continuing to explain, "There are elements in the Caymans that highly resent the wealthy, or the appearance of wealth; and this old Bentley touring car and driver have been targets for mango pits and Molotov cocktails ever since it's been here, about 45 years. That's why the windows have been upgraded to handle 7.62 AK-47 ammunition and are heavily tinted. I've repeatedly asked for more common transport, but the Admiralty insists. Their position is that this car is a visible symbol of our heritage as founding fathers of the islands. I got my lowers gnawed for suggesting the Admiralty should therefore send a founding father to ride around in it if that's what's required.

Anyway, on to another subject though. There's evidence that suggests that some of our banks here might not be as squeaky clean as they're supposed to be; U.K passage of Bank Secrecy Laws of 1934 and so on. Seems they can impose a time limit on dormant accounts of one year. If the account is dormant over that 12 month period the bank can start charging what they call "maintenance fees"; rather significant I might add, until the funds in that account are exhausted. Also, there may be connections to the Island government. It seems the government levies taxes on the fees. Plus these fees require government approval before the bank can begin with drawls. If the government would spend some of that money on dealing with island poverty, perhaps we'd be able to roll the old Bentley's windows down. Nevertheless, as it is, I'm afraid there's very little my office can do to help you penetrate the banking industry itself. However I think we might be of some assistance as pertains to your James Julius. He keeps an office here and employs an office assistant; a totally gorgeous assistant. Don't know how in hell he ever managed to hire her. Anyway, he has an account with the International Bank of the Caymans and seems to have moved a lot of money recently, activity which attracted our attention. Small amounts each time, and lately quite a few have been to financial institutions in Asia and the Bank of Brunei. Unfortunately that's about all we know.", Charles said.

Elmore sank back into the worn but comfortable leather seats of the aged Bentley and suddenly felt more comfortable than he had in quite a while. It was great sitting in this car chatting with his old friend Charley. Of course it didn't hurt to know that Slats would be arriving tonight as well. Somehow things just didn't seem the same without her around. Ah well, he thought, coming back to the present, back to business.

As he shifted his mind to the present he noticed Charley looking at him with a widening smile on his face. Then he said, "Find a bird did you?"

"Yeah, and I don't need a bird dog to find her you lecherous old crankshaft.", Elmore chided him laughingly, then asked, "Where do you recommend we start Charley?"

"From the inside, of course.", he quickly responded over raised eyebrows.

"And how do you suggest we get inside, oh brilliant one?", Elmore asked while tilting his head left and right, behind steepled hands in a supplicating way.

"Through the office worker in James Julius' office of course. We kidnap her and apply a bit of hose on her to make her talk - - - my hose, of course Ha Ha Agh Ha Ha." Charley gagged out.

"With the exception of your hose, I'd agree that she could offer the quickest entry and be the best source of current information about money transfer transactions and account holdings; and guess what, we've already got one of our people working on her. Ex New York City Detective named Guido Lempke.", Elmore said still chuckling at the concept of Charley's proposed "hose treatment".

"Lempke? Lempke Seems like I remember that name from a case that was in the headlines at least ten years ago. Was he the cop that pinned the tail on the guy for murdering his driver, a bodyguard, and his mistress and her boyfriend in New York. What ever happened to the guy that did it anyway? Last I heard he just disappeared skipping out on some serious bail.", Charley asked.

"Apparently you know more about that case than I do. I've never met her.

CHAPTER 28

THE LITTLE RED PLANE HAD PLENTY OF power, but Farnsworth knew better than to try and muscle it into the air with the two milk cartons adding the drag that they did; and he also remembered Whitey's advice about being smooth on the controls. With that in mind, he slowly advanced the power until the tail wheel came off the ground, and then just a bit more until the main landing gear lifted off. He kept it straight and level until he was about 500 feet in the air and then turned to the left towards the mainland and the Crossroads lights.

He could see a few cars coming and going on the Tamiami highway; all of them probably headed to work. Most of them were making better speed than he was, but that was OK. The sun wasn't up yet and he needed the highway traffic to navigate until it was daylight, and that should only be a few more minutes.

As he flew along about a mile to a half of a mile following the string of hammocks and the Gulf, yet maintaining sight of the highway. He decided to once again check that he could keep control of the aircraft and reach the trailing end of the slip knot rope with his left hand. He would launch the left side jug first since he preferred his right hand to use the overhead cyclic control and its twist grip throttle. His feet, of course, would keep the little plane straight and level and in trim. All he had to do was get lined up on the center of the Hootch's roof, and since there was no wind to deal with, he could make a short dive from 500 feet and drop as soon as he flew over the edge of the place.

In another five minutes he saw the big mailbox alongside the highway. He turned to the right and flew over the empty dock. The boat must be at the Hootch, he thought. He would know for sure in about another five minutes.

The dock was empty; no boat. He could see the empty dock and the Hootch clearly now. The boys must be out diving or fishing. He prayed Slaughter wasn't one of them as he maneuvered the plane around the island for a clear approach over the Hootch. He set himself up on a final approach.

He was only about a thousand yards away when he noticed two guys, one black and the other very big, come out of the door to the Hootch. The black guy had a shotgun and was raising it to aim at him. Farnsworth instinctively pulled back on the cyclic and added power to gain altitude while at the same time grabbing the slip knot lanyard.

Realizing his mistake, he went into his dive and when he saw the edge of the Hootch come underneath the nose of his plane, he yanked the lanyard and watched the explosive jug fall away from the plane. At the same instant he turned his head to the right and heard an immediate explosion, the blast of which almost made him lose control of the airplane. He also instantly felt something sting him on the bottom of his legs all the way up to his ass. They had shot him with that damn shotgun. It must've been loaded with buckshot because some pellets went right through his cotton seat, and some hit the seat's frame, but he was still able to fly the plane.

He would make another run; this time he would come in from over the mangroves. As he flew the circular route to line himself up he noticed that the two guys were still standing just outside the door to the Hootch with the shotgun, but something was wrong. From all he could tell there wasn't any damage to the Hootch from his homemade bomb. Something had gone wrong. The jug must've exploded too soon. He certainly felt the blast and its affect on the little airplane.

No matter; he was lined up now and having some trouble keeping the aircraft steady using his left hand to fly it. He again saw the two guys with the big guy now aiming the shotgun straight up at him. He pulled the lanyard for the other jug and watched it fall away. When he looked back up all he saw was a dark cloud and then he felt another kick in the ass. This time the little plane rolled over on its left wing and crashed into the water about 50 feet from the little island; and the last thing Farnsworth remembered was pulling the cyclic stick back with both hands before crashing into the water. The little plane went in tail first, probably saving his life.

"Should we just let'm drown Dyke?", Bunny asked as the Plot emerged from the door to the Hootch saying, "Don't just stand there. Go get him."

They both looked at him as if he were a hog looking at a wristwatch, but started wading into the water grumbling about saving a worthless piece of shit no mother would own. Naturally, the little shit was face up and breathing, but out like a light. They unbuckled his three point harness and man handled him out of the water, whereupon Dyke said, "Let me have him; be easier going for both of us.", as he easily hoisted Farnsworth up into a fireman's carry.

As soon as Dyke reached the hard ground he flopped Farnsworth down face up and went with Chico to get the fresh water hose and get washed down. When they were done, they stripped and hosed down Farnsworth, who groaned and puked up brackish water and choked before passing out again.

"Whatcha catch, a flying turd?", Slaughter hollered from the dock as he tied up the boat.

By this time Lee An Too, Dobbin, and the housekeepers were all up from the basement control room where the Plot had them braced for the bombing. Lee An Too immediately started posturing over Farnsworth's bloody legs and backside and said, "He need my professional medical attention or he die of shrivel. You two take him to wash room down stairs.", he ordered Dyke and Chico, who just looked at each other for a moment, and then to the Plot who just nodded.

Farnsworth found himself strapped to the same stainless steel table he had been confined to over 10 years ago. He looked around and could see that nothing had changed. It was like an operating room with the exception of the overhead lights. They were just common florescent lights in three bulb reflectors. The whole room was painted white, and there was a large, double basin stainless steel sink with a goose neck faucet and hot and cold "elbow" shut off handles like in a real scrub room.

After the quick "once over" Farnsworth realized he was in great pain. They had strapped him on his back with a pillow under him, but that didn't seem to stop the throbbing pain, and without even realizing it, he was groaning out loud.

Lee An Too seemed to appear in front of his face like a demon from hell. He was all dressed in his Peruvian witch doctor's outfit with his face painted like a skull, and he had bones in his nose and earlobes. He had a fan made of feathers and some kind of dust he threw in the air over Farnsworth's face and fanned into smaller clouds which Farnsworth could not help but inhale.

Lee An Too was immune to the powdered snake venom and stuck his face close to Farnsworth's and said, "You go back to sleep now. Shut mouth and think of watermelon, or whatever you like to eat. You very lucky Lee An Too here to save you. Farnsworth's head lolled from side to side and then suddenly stopped so that Lee An Too could unbuckle and examine him. His ass and rear of his upper thighs were covered in buckshot holes, each one oozing blood.

Lee An Too dug in his bag and came up with a set of bamboo tongs and a bamboo scoop the exact size of the buckshot. Before he attempted to remove any of the buckshot, he first jabbed Farnsworth in the right buttock with another bamboo sliver whose tip had some wasp stinger and fire ant venom which had been mashed into a gel that was at least ten times as potent as lidocane. He would do the same to the left buttock once he was done with the right side of Farnsworth's ass and leg.

Lee An Too went to work like he had done this sort of procedure a hundred times. He would probe for the buckshot with the bamboo scooper by first mashing beneath the skin and flesh with his fingers, and then inserting the scooper. Once he felt the buckshot was in the bottom of the scooper, he would insert the bamboo tongs and grasp the buckshot firmly; and then pull all three items out of the wound. The increased bleeding didn't seem to bother Lee An Too's ability to get the job done, and after he had removed the buckshot, he poked a wad of finely woven leafy material into the wound as deeply as he could, and then covered it with a paste he had chewed up in his mouth while working.

When he was all done he rolled Farnsworth back over and strapped him back in the steel gurney, then washed all the blood down the drain in the center of the floor. He collected all of his instruments, washed them thoroughly, put them back in his bag and went upstairs to announce, "He be fine in ten days."

"Sheriff Baugh, what do you think?", the Plot asked.

"Well, obviously he was tryin to blow up the Hootch; an act of mass destruction and possession of illegal explosives. As soon as he comes to I'll read him his rights and arrest him for attempted murder etc. etc.", he said.

"How about grand theft as well?", Slaughter said as he dumped his handful of brilliant jewelry out of the washcloth and onto the kitchen table where they were assembled.

"Well I'll be damned. Your Mr. Farnsworth may also be guilty of murder in the first degree. The whole Miami Dade Metro has been looking for the person who they think strangled a little old lady and stole all of her jewelry on a bus from Orlando. Guess we've got our guy now, huh?", Sheriff beamed as he mentally counted the votes this would get him in the next election. I'll call the paramedics to take him to the hospital and put him under guard, and handcuffed to his bed. Nice work with that shotgun. By the way, I'll need the little plane as evidence along with all the buckshot pellets Lee An Too removed from his ass.", Sheriff Baugh chuckled.

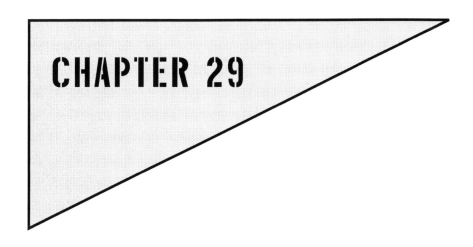

CHAPTER 29

SHEILA HOBGOOD HAD ARRIVED AT THE MARRIOTT in the Cayman Islands at 3:30AM and had stripped as she walked toward the bed, then crashed. The next thing she heard was the "sing song" ringing of the telephone in her ear. She grabbed the thing off of its European style hooks and said, "What"?

"Well, I'm glad you made it safely my dear.", the Plot said with a hint of humor in his voice. Did I wake you? Would you like me to call you back later?"

"Too late.", she snapped. "I'm already awake. Any news out of Guido regarding Julius Brown?", she asked.

"As a matter of fact there is. He's managed to befriend the office manager of his business there, and I got the distinct impression there was some kind of chemical attraction between them. He was able to get the account numbers and PINs we needed, to transfer Brown's money there; and, I suspect he'll be able to find out quite a bit more about his dealings shortly. Also, we had a visitor yesterday evening. Our old friend Farnsworth made a bombing attack on the Hootch with an ultra light airplane. We shot him down with the 12 guage, fished him out of the drink, and Lee An Too had some work to do pulling the pellets out of his legs and ass. We turned him over to Sheriff Baugh. Seems he also murdered a woman on a bus for her jewelry. I had Lee An Too frog juice him into believing he's Charles Manson; can't have him talking about why he's trying to kill us. That'll just lead to more questions.", the Plot told her.

"Good God. What next?", she exclaimed.

"Well, on the positive side, I've booked Slaughter direct to Bangkok, Thailand to run down this financial advisor to the monarchy; and you and Elmore to Islamabad, Pakistan where you will meet up with one of Elmore's contacts, a retired operator named Haynes. He's an intelligence type who speaks Urdu in several tribal dialects fluently. He will escort you across the border into Afghanistan; specifically Garmser in Helmand province.", the Plot smoothly toned.

"What the hell? Are you trying to get me killed. That's Taliban and Al Qaeda country and a long walk.", she loudly protested.

"Sheila, you said you wanted to write about the opium trade and smuggling. Helmand province in Afghanistan is where 90% of the worlds opium is grown. Haynes knows his way around, speaks the language, and is a certified tandem master parachutist, which means the three of you will jump in after a flight of less than an hour. He also knows the Pakistani tribal leaders and he knows how to get you there. All three of you will go dressed in Muslim drag; you in a full black burka, and you will have U.S. Agriculture Identification. The British coalition forces have responsibility for Helmand province and a U.S. agricultural team is already there working with the local farmers on alternative crops to opium poppies, like pomegranates . You can see the opium trading going on for yourself. Do you still want to go?", the Plot asked.

There was a long pause before Sheila yelled, "We're gonna jump from a friggin plane? You're crazy. No, you're not crazy, you're an idiot if you think I'm gonna do that."

The plot also let several seconds go by, then said, "Just think how it will read in your Pulitzer prize winning article."

She gave out a long sigh and said, "I guess it's the only way to get at the bottom of it all, huh? Yes, I want to go, but what about money and passports and all that stuff?", she rattled off.

"Not to worry my dear. I've sent it overnight express to you in care of the hotel. You should have it waiting for you at the desk by the time you get dressed and go down for breakfast.", he said and she could almost see him smiling over the phone line; what a smartass.

"Just out of curiosity, what's Slaughter going to do once he finds that financial advisor?", she asked, changing the subject.

"He's going to tail him and find out all that he can about him until you and Elmore get back to Pakistan. Hopefully you'll find linkage between Brown and his release from prison, the opium smuggling, and this guy so he can be set up with the monarchy to take a fall. Your international media coverage of it all ought to do it.", the Plot said, then continued with, "Your package at the desk also contains open tickets to Islamabad and the account number and PIN at the Grand Cayman Bank in case you need more money. I had Pickett send Brown's money to the International Bank of Grand Cayman Island once we had the PINs and account numbers from his assistant in the Caymans. But don't take out more than $9,000.00 at a time; no need for suspicious activity there. Our Fed's monitor things like that you know.

Always the reporter, her inquisitive mind kicked in with, "How did we get Brown's PIN and account numbers?

The Plot thought for a moment and then said, "I do believe it was a result of romance, my dear."

"Guido. Right?", she asked.

"Yup.", he replied.

"It figures. You know he'll probably want to stay here if that's the case.", she stated.

"Yes. And I think that may be a very good idea to have a resource here; two resources if you count it as a married couple.", the Plot chimed, then continued with, "Now. About your mission in Pakistan and Afghanistan. I believe you should be visibly pregnant, and - - -"

"Once again you've thought of everything but my creature comforts getting from Pakistan to Afghanistan Plot. I am now to become a beast of burden carrying all the secret squirrel stuff over my gut.

"Gee, I thought that was all part of being an investigative reporter my dear.", he laughed.

"Screw you Marplot!", she yelled and hung up.

CHAPTER 30

GUIDO WAS AT ELMORE'S HOTEL ROOM DOOR promptly at 5:00PM. Arriving alone, he initially briefed Elmore on how he had become "acquainted" with Brown's assistant, and only other employee in his Cayman office; and how his account numbers and PINs were made available. He explained that, "Mr. Brown, has a total of over two and a half million in his Cayman account, and about fifty million in each of his accounts at the Bank of Thailand and the one he has with the Bank of Brunei, now that Pickett has transferred his Rio money here. Tammy pulled up the latest figures less than an hour ago." Guido said.

Elmore didn't want to ask about his relationship with Tammy, but was puzzled enough to ask, "What I can't understand is why he would leave any of his money in Thailand after escaping from their palace prison; doesn't make any sense to me".

"Actually, it does if you're dealing opium with a hawalader who happens to be the financial advisor to the Thai monarchy; and of course, the Thai Prime Minister. Old Thaksin Shinawatsa, resigned and skipped the country after corruption charges were filed against him by his fellow parliamentarians, and you can bet two things. First, the corruption charges are true, and second, he's in bed with the same hawalader that acts as a conduit for the monarchy", Guido said with the bland assurance and authority only a NYPD detective with 'stand up in court' evidence could project.

"What's this hawalader's name? Do we know anything about him; name and what he looks like for example?", Elmore asked.

"As it so happens, there was an article in 'Popular Mechanics' magazine about him. He is a dedicated aircraft model maker and they showcased him with his scale model F-16 with real jet engines a few months back. Name's Tom Grey and he's got dual Thai and U.S. citizenship", Guido said softly.

"Why are you whispering?", Elmore asked, then softly said, "You're right, this room hasn't been swept for any critters with ears."

Elmore grabbed the remote to select a Spanish language news program on the TV and increased the volume to near maximum. Then he continued the briefing. He told Guido that Slaughter was in Pakistan and had married up with his contact and Sheila was inbound. He spelled out all of the main details of their plan for Sheila to investigate the opium trade and for Slaughter to set up Mr. Grey for at least incarceration or at best beheading or something by the monarchy.

Guido stayed mute concerning his newfound honey bun, and somehow felt guilty at having such a good time so easily. All he had to do was play it cool and see how things evolved. He might even become a long term resident of this place.

"Huh", interjected Elmore. "It just occurred to me that the PM's corruption charges may involve Grey in other locations and specifically to Brown's money here", Elmore said with some measure of concern in his voice. Then he said, "We'd better close this account and transfer all of the money to the Grand Cayman account under a different name and number as soon as possible, don't you agree?"

"Great minds think alike. The PM could very easily have his money tied up with Mr. Grey and could blackmail him into dipping into

Brown's account, especially if Grey is unable to reach Brown for an extended period of time.", Guido said.

"I'll see if Tammy can make that transfer happen first thing this morning", he continued.

Elmore smiled reading into what had not been stated and said, "I do believe you've established yourself with Brown's assistant very well my friend." Guido didn't blush. As a NYPD detective for so many years he'd learned to control his physiognomy and was pretty good at keeping a poker face. He just smiled back and said, "Yes, I did."

Back at Guido's room Elmore called the Plot and brought him up to date on their plans. The Plot put them on hold and called Slaughter to alert him of the money transfer from Thailand to the Caymans and the possibility that Grey may be linked to the Thai PM's resignation and corruption charges. Slaughter opined that the transfer and possible pending charges might help shake Grey out of his tree and make him easier to find.

The Plot rang off with Slaughter and returned to give Elmore the go ahead to consolidate all of Brown's money into one new account at Grand Cayman island; just over five and a half million dollars; and then get to Islamabad as quickly as possible.

The Plot then called the chief justice to brief him on the events and plans. The chief justice agreed and asked, "OK, but don't forget you've got to do an itemized budget to keep that money. Otherwise, it will have to wind up in the U.S. Treasury coming from the DEA."

"Yes sir, I understand"; knowing it was a bluff since he'd have to account for it. "Meanwhile, would you consider the possibility of Range 19 having it's own G5 aircraft and a YH-60 helicopter? As I review our future target list and our currently assigned mission, I find a number of scenarios that absolutely call for items with those capabilities and it would make our operations much more effective.", the Plot smoothly offered.

"Holy shit Plot! Don't you think that's a bit exorbitant?", the chief justice challenged. I wonder if you're not getting too big for your britches!

"Not considering that I only need half my britches in the first place, what we are expected to accomplish in a timely manner and with adequate `plausible deniability' to protect your office, no sir I don't. think the request is out of line at all", the Plot sternly replied and continued, "You know it's Range 19's total demise not to mention an incredible flap if we are ever compromised. We must move fast using our own assets in order to be mission capable while eliminating a lot of excess paper trails and minimizing any possibility of compromise."

"Alright, alright, already; but give me cost data and an itemized budget along with an operational scenario supporting the need, so I can keep up with your smart ass", the chief justice chuckled and asked, "By the way, who are you going to get to fly it?"

"I think we can persuade Slats to take on that responsibility since she's commercially rated, and all we would need is manufacturer's transition training to the G5 `type and kind', and we would include manufacturer's maintenance in the purchase contract.", the Plot said confidently.

After a long pause, the chief justice of the U.S. just said, "Hmmmpf". and hung up.

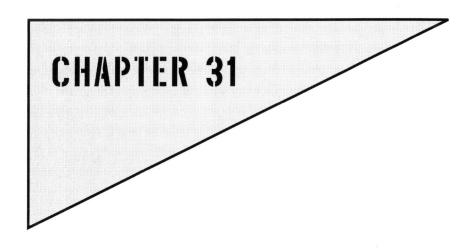

CHAPTER 31

SHEILA MET ELMORE AT THE ISLAMABAD AIRPORT baggage pick up area with her typical shotgun blast of questions, but he just ignored her. Haynes, behind the wheel of their rental car, watched the reunion with bemusement; and Elmore, in his mind was being out of character, but in this case he seemed totally receptive. It was difficult for Haynes to accept this side of the man, since he'd never seen Elmore display other facets of his personality in any similar fashion.

After loading all of her luggage, Sheila and Elmore got in the back; and Haynes couldn't resist with, "Where now Sahib? Hotel room for two?"

"No smartass. See if you can make it through this traffic without killing any innocent Pakistani's, Tribal Chief's, or Taliban nuns.", Sheila barked.

Tom Grey was highly pissed at not being able to reach Brown in Rio. It had been three days now and no contact. He was supposed to check in with him at least three times a week. Then, of all things, the jerk deposits two and half million in his Thai bank account for which he's the only one with access. What the hell is he playing at he wondered. The King had his internal network of "information gatherers" as he liked to call them in every nook and cranny; and the one at the bank just happened to inform his highness of the money transfer from Rio to Brown's account. Grey could account for the two and a half million. They were Brown's residual funds, which, in two months according to Thai banking laws, the bank could start charging rather stiff "no activity" fees which Brown had agreed to in order to keep the money there. But now there had been unanticipated activity that Grey had to explain, and he couldn't. The original money was to pay for an opium shipment that Grey had arranged for Brown. It comprised almost two tons of the shit and he had already spent almost a million dollars of his own money getting it in position in Karachi in a shipping container. It sat ready to be loaded once Brown transferred two million to Grey's account in Brunei, of which the King would get his 12% investment payment. Things were falling behind schedule and as the sweat rolled down the back of his neck as the King asked pleasantly, "Well Thomas, who's money is it?

Grey was as adept at soothing the King as he was at masking his true emotions. "I'm afraid that is not yet determined your majesty, although I expect significant returns in the near future. The money now in Brown's account is a result of Brazilian inquiries into his financial affairs. I spoke with the Brazilian Minister of Finance to encourage a thorough investigation and, in your name, offered him a visit to discuss new trade agreements should his government desire. As you may know, Brazil is leading the world in ethanol advancement as an alternative fuel source, and I believe early trade agreements with them could lead to our mutual benefit. Besides, in two months we will be able to charge a monthly fee on Brown's money for laying dormant.", Grey said, attempting to

divert the King's attention away from Brown's new total account issue. The King was notorious for having a short attention span, but he was still very astute when it came to money.

"But how much is that? And how can we do that if he's doubled his account total?", the King quietly asked.

"No activity means that he isn't doing anything with the money. No investments or purchases. We can levy 2% each month the money is inactive; approximately $110,000.", Grey said evenly.

The King looked at Grey for a moment without saying anything, then said, "That's quite a sum to rent a bank account. Have you spoken to Mr. Brown lately?"

"I'm afraid not. He's been unreachable for three days now. I've asked the Brazilian Minister of Finance to ask his counterpart in Justice to seek him out if at all possible. You do know he has his own jet and has a habit of flying off to vacation spots around the world.", Grey lied.

"Ah well. He does know the penalty for letting his money sit idle does he not?", the King asked.

"Of course, your highness.", Grey lied again.

"And I really like the idea of a trade agreement with Brazil to explore the ethanol alternative for our cars and trucks. The oily smoke cloud choking Krungtep (the King used the old name for the capital) is a disgrace to my kingdom. Once again, you've done well my friend. Please keep me informed of when we can expect money in our till and for the ambassador from Brazil to request a visit to discuss our mutual interests", the King said, essentially dismissing Grey.

Once outside the huge double doors of the Kings palace he began to breath normally, again. It had seemed an eternity before he could escape the palace and the King's inquiries.

CHAPTER 32

Sheila and Elmore made two rehearsal jumps along with Haynes in his role as the guidance controller for the Parapoint load of equipment they would need on the ground. Slats flew the CASA for the drops and they conducted the exercise at an isolated dirt airstrip occasionally used by agricultural aircraft. Currently unused the site was located about 30 miles out of the city and seemed to only draw interest from a few local children.

They made the first tandem jump in the late afternoon to work with the system and determine canopy guidance and stall characteristics and landing as a team. Then they made the second jump in the evening just after sundown so they could practice with the Night Vision Goggles and still have enough ambient light to land safely or take emergency procedures if necessary. Haynes jumped solo on each lift to perfect his technique of simultaneously guiding his own parachute and the cargo package to safe landings. He would use the Parapoint to guide the canopy of the cargo package to a safe site and land immediately next to it. Elmore had Sheila as his cargo package, and only themselves to guide so their mission was to land close to Haynes and the cargo. A few small glitches were identified but both jumps went off well and all systems were a go.

The next day they repacked their parachutes and rigged all their equipment, put in new batteries where needed, recharged or exchanged other batteries, ran their check lists and double checked their equipment and plans, researched weather forecasts and received the most recent imagery and information concerning the entry area that Haynes somehow obtained.

A cold front was due and would push out the low that had been in place for several days but winds were forecast to be light to moderate, and clouds were forecast to be thin cirrus with near zero probability of any form of precipitation.

Slats had the CASA on line for a 10:00PM takeoff from a second isolated airport located outside Islamabad where the prime contractor had ground transportation available, and after the shuttle to the aircraft in the open air "bench truck" they only had a few minutes left at the rear ramp to go over anything someone felt was left out of the planning. At about 10 minutes to engine start, the trio looked at one another, shrugged their shoulders, and climbed aboard and loaded and secured everything while Slats waited for Elmore to come up to the cockpit and perform his second seat duties during start. These duties were just reading off the checklist that Slats could've recited to him since she had it memorized.

The flight would take about an hour and fifteen minutes, and the altitude winds favored a higher opening than normal. They also had thin layers of stratus that allowed the illumination from the three quarter moon which relegated the night vision goggles hanging around their neck to a supporting role. Tonight the M-One eyeball would rule till they got on the ground.

Slats settled in at 12,000 feet above ground and after a few minutes of light choppy turbulence her approach was smooth and level. She mounted an oxygen mask connected to a low pressure oxygen system and trimmed for flat and level flight, although they were still at a relatively low altitude they were taking no chances on anyone loosing mental acuity from lack of oxygen!

They would drop using a GPS coordinate for the release point, backed up with visual confirmation of several physical checkpoints located along their approach. They calculated their desired release point using available data on winds aloft, forward throw, and desired landing site.

Twenty minutes out Elmore hit a switch to bathe the cargo bay in red light, Red light would make it hard to check items based on their color but it would not adversely affect their night vision. The cargo was contained in a wicker basket not unlike a giant picnic basket or the passenger basket used on hot air balloons.

They released the stowing straps on the cargo basket and rolled it along a floor mounted roller conveyer to a new position near the tailgate. There they secured it with a quick release and attached the static line to a cargo ring on the floor. Next, Haynes helped the tandem jumpers into their equipment, then donned his own gear. Elmore and Haynes exchanged jumpmaster checks and Haynes double checked the cargo system. He used his pen light to check settings on the automatic opener set to open the parachute at 3500 feet, 500 feet below that of the jumpers. Then he ran his control system to see if the control servos on the Parapoint were in sync. Everything checked out so he waddled forward to tell Slats all was ready and on schedule. Slats pulled her oxygen mask free and they exchanged a few words, and confirmed that the GPS coordinates on Haynes portable GPS matched the aircraft instruments. He returned to the rear to make himself comfortable and to pass around a low pressure oxygen bottle for everyone to suck on. Even at 12,000 they needed their brains to be clear and alert.

Six minutes out Slats lifted the upper cargo door and lowered the ramp. The jumpers struggled to their feet and stood along the sides, keeping one hand on the plane to steady themselves while passing the oxygen around. Haynes knelt to observe the ground and the skies around them to ensure they had no airborne visitors. As a natural skeptic he never really trusted instruments and wanted to visually confirm they were really where they should be.

The solid layer of thin cloud just above jump altitude indicated some moisture in the air and another layer of scattered cloud below them reflected some changes were underway in local weather, but the moon light shined brightly and the geographic check points were easily identified. They were on track and on time.

Haynes, jumping single, would be jumpmaster. Once they got the signal to go, he would shove the cargo out and follow immediately to keep the chemical lights on the basket in sight. The tandem team would exit a second or so after Haynes and once stable they would track off a short distance to fall off to one side of the cargo and Haynes but still able to keep both in sight. The static line on the cargo rig deployed a drogue chute that would keep the basket from tumbling and minimize lateral movement during free fall.

Slats flipped the toggle switch controlling the red lights in the cargo bay three times to signal they were 1 minute out. Elmore activated the chemical lights on Haynes helmet and container and Haynes did the same to him. Haynes knelt next to the cargo container, released the straps securing the cargo and rolled the basket to the edge of the tailgate. Elmore and Sheila stowed the oxygen bottle and shuffled in lockstep to the edge aware of the crisp ozone smell in the air and the cold starting to penetrate their clothes and gloves.

Just as Haynes spotted the dry river bed 200 meters short of their desired landing zone Slats flipped the green light toggle repeatedly to signal GO!

In an instant the cargo container and Haynes disappeared with the tandem pair tumbling forward to disappear a second later.

Haynes went out stable and never lost view of the basket. Initially he was almost within arms reach and he could see the chemical lights and watch the shape of the basket against lighter colored patches of cloud below them. Then he hit moisture and his goggles and altimeter iced over. From a nice clear simple drop he was blind! He reached up to scrape the ice off his goggles with some success and then looked for his altimeter. Even though their altimeters had a built in light, the face was iced over. Cursing slightly Haynes scraped ice away to see they were still safely high then searched for the bundle. He did not see it.

He did a quick 360 turn looking down and level with no joy. Where in hell was the damn thing? He realized he had tightened up his body while clearing the ice, maybe he was below it? He sat up and there it was, almost directly overhead, clearly visible against the solid cloud above. He did not see the tandem jumpers but they were on their own for now. He slid backwards for a count of two, spread his arms and legs, and got big! A few seconds more and the basket seemed to slide by very slowly 30 feet to his right front. A glance at his altimeter said PULL NOW Idiot, your are going low! As he snatched his ripcord the light on top of the basket disappeared as the canopy deployed. They would open together.

Elmore and Sheila had less drama. Elmore had done a lot of high altitude jumps in Europe where icing was common. For all practical purposes he never lost sight of anyone or lost track of altitude. He just tracked into position while Sheila acted the perfect passenger. She was shocked by the ice at first but Elmore had mentioned it prior to exit. She remembered the comment so she rubbed her goggles to rid herself of the ice and enjoyed the view. They had been falling face down soon after exit when Elmore deployed their own drogue. It made lateral movement slow but kept everyone stable and face to earth during the free fall part of the jump.

Slats would close the tail gate and fly the empty plane back to the primary airfield near Islamabad and record a successful maintenance check ride.

At 4000 feet Elmore spotted where they wanted the cargo to land and where they wanted to execute the landing with Sheila attached . It was a football sized area of nothing but sand, and maybe a few rocks. He hoped she wouldn't hit one. Unfortunately winds aloft had been greater than predicted and they were at least 500 meters away with wind in their faces. He searched for Haynes but did not see him. Then he searched for the cargo and had good news; he spotted it lower than expected but his concern for Haynes evaporated when he saw his rig very close to the cargo in space and altitude. The bad news was that they were farther from the desired DZ than he was.

Haynes considered their location, the winds and altitudes and looked for an alternate landing point. He set the parapoint up flying into the wind and did a measured 360 turn to scan the area. It seemed to be all broken ground between them and the big sandy area they picked earlier. Dark ground filled with shadows and relief. He stabilized the cargo again and did another recon; and when directly opposite the sandy area he spotted an area of even color and few shadows. Well maybe it was level and it was within reach to make chicken salad out of chicken shit! He turned the cargo chute towards the DZ and spun his own with a front riser turn to cut it off to get into position to control the landing.

Elmore was uneasy. He saw the same rough terrain and didn't like what he saw. He might land OK, but Sheila would be at risk hanging down a bit and on a rough surface or uneven surface he might land on her and cause serious injury. He turned as he spotted Haynes' turn and followed. He stopped almost directly over Haynes and did his belated stall check and then just began doing S' turns on half brakes to keep position in the wind and watch Haynes and the cargo chute. As they got lower he could see the area Haynes had selected and felt better. It seemed relatively level and free of obstacles. He watched the cargo chute collapse and a few seconds later Haynes canopy collapsed about ten feet short of it.

Elmore was still about 800 feet but almost on top of the cargo and Haynes in spite of his holding and turns, so he did a smooth 360 degree turn to get some distance and loose some altitude. Coming out of the turn he turned into the wind line and set up for landing. Throughout the entire time both had been silent. Elmore warned Sheila that noise carried at night and noise from above carried even farther. She listened and obeyed. Till now.

As they slid through 500 feet Sheila squirmed and reverted to type. She did not like what she saw and tried to tell him where to steer the parachute. She saw a patch of white and figured it was sand and wanted to land there!

Elmore was focused on fine controls and picking the best possible place to land that he could find. The wind suddenly seemed to be shifting. They were drifting left and below his desired glide path. Her squirming and shifting her weight did not help his fine control measures, so he put the canopy into full flight and released his right hand toggle to slap the back of her helmet and stage whisper, "I'm the driver, don't bother me now"! She obeyed and sulked in silence.

It was an anti climax. Some local farmer had plowed a small patch of ground close to a steam bed. With Sheila stable Elmore got back on the wind line and glide path to produce a standing landing. Haynes was on their short range radio complementing their graceful entry, and that the Parapoint load was in a shallow depression 100 feet North of them. He had made his stand up landing right next to the cargo container and his canopy had collapsed on top of it shielding the site from the jumpers above.

"Show off"., Elmore said as they de-rigged and collected the parachute. They were about to bury about $12,000 worth of parachute equipment in Pakistani terra firma, but it was Brown's money anyway.

Since they were still hyped up after the jump anyway, they decided to head towards some lights not far off; probably a compound or small village of some kind.

Haynes said, "You guys feel like making contact tonight or camping out and waiting until dawn?", while he unfolded the map he carried in his shirt.

"Do you have any idea where we are yet?", Elmore asked.

"Roughly. According to the GPS those lights over there are from a small village I think is Ashinda. Our coordinates are good, but a lot of the maps are not too accurate and villages appear and disappear from a variety of causes. It's about five clicks from the Peshawan area we need to enter to find one of the tribal chiefs I know; and if we're not going to attract unwanted attention, we need to change and bury all this sky god gear.", Haynes said.

The next phase was underway. Sheila smiled to herself. She knew that one day someone would find this stuff and wonder what is was all about! And she actually jumped in. She must make some notes about it as soon as possible. Details.

There was enough moonlight to move safely without using NVGs, and even though they moved slower than normal, they made good time. Soon after dawn a couple of scrawny dogs earned their scraps by announcing the group's entrance to the village looking exactly like weary travelers. Haynes inquired of a young man loading panniers of something onto a donkey and was directed to a mud brick building that took in travelers. It was next to what seemed to be a market, and after knocking on the solid wood door they were allowed into a room where an old woman was serving tea and sludge called coffee. Haynes explained to the man that seemed to be in charge, that they were weary travelers and he and his relatives needed a place to stay. He said they were full but they could sleep on the floor in the back of his storage room as a favor to the woman, who appeared pregnant with her cargo of money and comfort items underneath her robes.

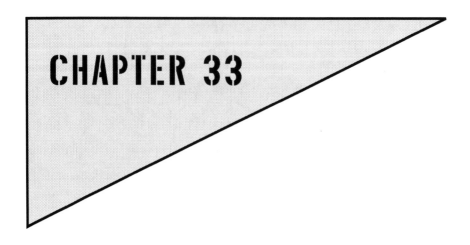

CHAPTER 33

"WELL, WHAT DO YOU WANT TO DO Guido?", the Plot asked irritably.

"I believe Tammy and I should sit tight while all of Brown's money is still here. I also think we need to move it to a different bank in the name of Simon Arpslot Enterprises; or bust it up into several accounts under cover names. We have to erase any audit trail to Brown, otherwise the Federal snoops will catch on sooner or later - probably sooner since it's such a large amount, $556,000,000 to round it off."

"I agree. What are your intentions with Tammy whatshername?" the Plot asked ,abruptly.

"That's a tough one. She's French and has a nonchalance, a je ne sais que pas about sex and relationships. I doubt she's interested in marriage.", Guido stated factually.

"Are you?", the Plot demanded.

"I very well could be with her; but I'd have to quit work all together just to keep up with her, and I'm not sure I want to do that yet. Unless you've got some other ideas for me, I plan to enjoy the hell out of myself making love in the sunshine with a beautiful woman and lots of money to play with, say $100,000 for her cooperation and whatever you think I'm worth.", Guido chuckled.

After the proverbial pregnant pause, the Plot surrendered laughing,

"Guido, you're a dog! I envy you. Do this. Earmark the $100,000 for her into her own account at a different bank and do the same for yourself. Divide the rest in half to be deposited in two other banks there with one in my name and the other in Slaughter's. I don't want my personal company involved in any way whatsoever. Got it?", the Plot asked sharply.

"Absolutely.", Guido said. Then before he could say anything further the Plot said, "Verbal gratitude is unnecessary Guido. You've done us a great service. Goodbye.

When Guido told Tammy about the conversation, especially when he explained her `severance' package, she flew into his arms knocking him back on the couch and asked him to marry her immediately. Guido was as shocked at her proposal as she was at the severance pay she was getting. She started to ask about Mr. Brown, but Guido put his forefinger over his lips and pulled her down for what could be considered a wet consent.

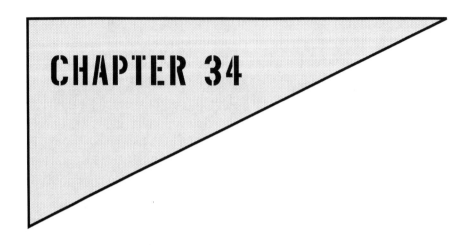

CHAPTER 34

SLAUGHTER MOVED IN CLOSER TO THE PODIUM fronting the concierge and laid his right hand holding the $100.00 dollar bill on the front edge and asked, "I'm looking for a colleague here in the city. His name is Thomas Grey and he ---".

"But of course", interrupted the concierge! "I know him well. He refers all of his friends and business affiliates to this hotel. He's also quite a fan of Cuban cigars that I, Seriba, personally, provide for him. How may I help you?

"Well, I'd like to get his telephone number and address so that I can make contact with him if that's possible.", Slaughter said.

"Oh, I can do better than that. I shall call him myself and make arrangements for you. I insist.", Seriba said while glancing at the hundred dollar bill.

"No. Please don't do that yet," said Slaughter, "I want to surprise him. We are old friends and `competitors' shall I say. We compete with model airplanes", Slaughter said.

"Ah yes, I see," replied Seriba, " I know of his achievements in that sport. Let me write down his phone number and address for you now", which he did, but retained the information until Slaughter left the hundred on the flat surface of his podium while looking directly into his eyes. Then Slaughter inched close to the man's face and said in a whisper,

"If you spoil my surprise, you'll wish you had a different job; like shoveling shit in the worst cesspool in this city. Do you understand?" The man just nodded with eyes much wider than usual.

Tom Grey was suffering a genuine funk. In three days the "no activity fee" would go into effect and he would have to buy time by transferring that money from a personal account in Brunei. Although over 10 million rested in that account from his opium trade, it still bothered him that something had happened to Brown, and that all of Brown's money had been transferred into a Grand Cayman account. Something was happening, it was bad and he couldn't figure it out. If it all went sour the King would flick a finger and one of his minions would toss him to the sharks in his private pool; or put him in the banded krait pit like he had seen happen twice before. A jangling phone interrupted his dismal thoughts. He picked it up answering, "Grey".

"Mr. Grey, I'm sorry to bother you but - - -

"That's alright, what is it Mr. Concierge?", who's voice he recognized immediately.

"There's a gentleman her asking to meet with you. May I send him to your house now, or would you prefer later? He says he is an American entrepreneur with a potentially profitable proposition for you." Grey welcomed the chance for a distraction and replied, "Well, send him over". He mused to himself," I guess I'll find out what this is all about now."

Slaughter discovered that just about everyone he talked to in Bangkok knew of Grey and his relations with the monarchy, as well as his affinity for Cuban cigars and building scale model airplanes for competition. As the taxi driver chattered away in broken English, he was reviewing the cover he would use and the hook he would use to perk Grey's interest. Money was key. He would pretend to represent the absent Brown, explain that Brown had to drop out of sight for undisclosed reasons but had directed him to represent him on the opium activity; the product he and Grey had rotting in a shipping container awaiting transport to the U.S. The raw opium tar had been dropped into melted wax where it was sealed when the wax cooled, then hidden inside Thai dolls and carved teak wood arts and crafts routinely imported to several businesses located in San Diego, Los Angeles, San Francisco, and Chicago. Slaughter would propose subsequent shipments to New York. He would explain that he and Brown had better contacts there and was ready to expand his operation.

Grey was leaning against the ornately carved teak frame of the door to his villa when the taxi arrived. , When the passenger got out and told the driver to wait, his first feeling was apprehension. The man looked like a 50 year old wearing the body of a 20 year old. His brushed hair showed some grey hair over the ears and in the sideburns and shiny black above. The body stood six feet tall with broad shoulders and tight waist but he moved unlike any business man or financier he ever saw before. His dress was Southwest formal, a high quality white dress shirt, neatly pressed and tucked into pressed Levis, and well shined black cowboy boots – but oddly to Grey, he wore no belt.

"Mr. Grey, my name is Tim Michaels. Thank you for meeting me on such short notice and no references.", Slaughter said as he stuck out his right hand; which Grey shook three times firmly and then asked,

"It's good to meet you uh Mr. Michaels. What can I do for you?"

"Call me Tim, please. I represent a client in Brazil whom I believe you know. For reasons I cannot explain, my client is forced to avoid any contact with Brazilian authorities as well as some other organizations, and has moved his residence to an undisclosed location . He sent me to reassure you that funds transferred out of Thailand to the Caymans are intact. He will transfer the balance of your original amount, the monies agreed to for the product currently sitting in the shipping container; eight million dollars I believe. He also wants to expand his business with follow-on shipments to New York and will advance four million each if the quantity and price per kilo remains the same. Another four million to follow once the container has been made ready for shipment. He will arrange and pay for all movement from Pakistan to the destination as usual."

"Well now---Tim. That was a mouthful.", Grey said as he pulled out a cigar and motioned an offer to Slaughter, who declined with a wave of his hand and said, "No thanks. Never developed a taste for tobacco; but go ahead, I like the smell."

"Cuban. I have them shipped in through the Russian embassy in Havana. A good cigar helps me think. I have a problem caused by Brown's actions. Right now I'm in a tight spot with the King as a result of your client's removal of his money from the bank of Thailand. The King will want to know why he did that after leaving it dormant for so long. In three days the King was expecting to withdraw, under Thai banking law, a rather tidy "no activity" fee. Now I've got to explain and convince him everything is OK, before one of his banking informants can poison the well, of what happened and why, and how he is going to reap long term benefits. Perhaps you can help me with that before we discuss your other business.", Grey said spewing cigar smoke off to the side of Slaughter's face.

"Hmm, how much does the King expect for a "no activity fee?", Slaughter asked with no change of expression.

"$253,000", Grey stated. It was a small lie but he felt entitled for the stress he was under. But I need to know why he moved all of that money. I have to give the King a reasonable explanation.", he said as he waved the cigar in the air in a swooping motion. His stress and worry was obvious.

"Tell the King that it was the only way his new country would accept him and grant permanent resident status and allow him to buy his own villa and servants etc. As a gesture of good will, I will transfer $253,000 to the Bank of Thailand in your name in the morning. It will come from an account in another name as my client cannot transfer his own money from his new country to himself in another country at the moment. You can then tell the King the "no activity fee" has been paid as such.", Slaughter said with a smile. Grey looked into Slaughter's unblinking, pale gray eyes and thought what fortuitous genie had brought this man to him; providing him with money and answers for the King. This entire conversation had evolved standing on the top stair of the villa's entrance. He smiled and as a great weight left his shoulders said, "Please, let's go inside. I've forgotten my manners. You must forgive me. What would you care to drink?"

"A cold beer would be great Mr. Grey", Slaughter said.

"Tom. Please call me Tom; and a cold beer is my choice as well. I like the way you do business Tim. I believe all we have to discuss at this point are details and a time table. Agreed?", Grey asked pointedly and watched as Slaughter took a frosty San Miguel from the tray a servant presented and took a long appreciative pull from the bottle. Grey took the other bottle and the two men nodded and clinked a toast to their new relationship. If Tomas Grey only knew what awaited him in his immediate future.

CHAPTER 35

THE PLOT SIGHED AND GLANCED AT HIS watch, 20:35 or 8:35 PM for civilians. It had been a long involved day and for the first time in his life the Plot felt he was losing control of events. He was comfortable with how things with Farnsworth were progressing, but he didn't like the time and information delays that accompanied deployed teams scattered to the corners of the globe. He could communicate with his people, but often there were delays due to time zone differences and ongoing activities. Arrangements were the easy part because he had an intimate friendship with a Miami travel agent named Nora. Nobody knew about it, but it was wonderful for him to have such a relationship at his age and with his involvement in a growing organization, albeit covert. She was just what he needed at this time in his life; and when he felt overwhelmed by events like he did now, and it was a reasonable hour, he called her at her home number.

"Nora my dear, how are you?

"Fine dear, and you are lucky. I just finished sexually exhausting three professional wrestlers on the living room floor. I pinned them all for a three count. But enough on my evening, how are you lover?", she asked.

The Plot laughed as he shed his unease with genuine laughter at the mental image. "You made my day with that. I just wish I could've been there to take advantage of you're depleted energies myself.", the Plot laughingly replied..

"Besides calling to hear your lovely voice again, I was wondering if you knew anyone in the container shipping industry that I could talk to, confidentially of course?", he asked.

"Sure. I know several companies that routinely deal with international container transporting. Problem is the 'confidentiality part'. These people are paid by the tonnage they move and it's highly corrupt unless you're dealing with a company that has its own containers and shipping arrangements. What are you really after; or should we discuss that one on one? I'd like that anyway. Why don't you come on over?", she asked with a sexy whisper.

"Jesus! you can't imagine how much I'd like to do that love; but I'm currently totally tied up keeping track of my offshore businesses and I'm time bound to come up with some solutions", the Plot soothed.

"Don't make it too much later. There's plenty of acrobats, contortionists and professional wrestlers out there you know", she chuckled.

"As soon as I can, my dear. Promise! But in the meantime, could you hook me up with someone in the container shipping business that I can trust to keep our conversation confidential?", he pleaded.

"Sure. Then you'll owe me big time, huh?", she replied.

"I'll always owe you for all the help you've provided Nora; you know that.", then, "Call me when you get me a contact OK? Bye love." and then softly hung up the phone..

Aside from Guido, his relationship with Mr. Brown's assistant on Grand Cayman island, Tammy, and ex-West Point Major Leopold Farnsworth's disposition, he felt awash. He really didn't feel comfortable about events in Pakistan concerning Sheila, Elmore, Haynes, and Slats. He was unsure about exactly where they were and what they were doing. Elmore had a satellite phone, but hadn't called in over 48 hours. He had to accept that no news was good news and assume they had jumped into Northern Pakistan and were on their way to Afghanistan's Helmand province in search of a poppy field. Slaughter had not checked in for over a day either. He's was to set up a meeting with Tom Grey, the financial advisor to the Thai monarchy. The Plot was particularly interested in just how Slaughter was going to set him up for his fall with the King of Thailand. He didn't want anything leading back to the good old U.S. of A. at all. He was impatient for news and activity, like any good operations officer, when everyone was deployed and all he had to do was scratch his ass, pick his nose and drink crummy coffee while fuming impotently. He was generating a decent frustration when Crud Junior came running into the kitchen slipping and sliding with his claws tapping and scraping on the tile. He had a huge blue crab in his mouth. He planted the crab on the floor under the Plot's feet where he proceeded to chomp away at the critter. Shortly, the crunching led to crab guts and pieces of shell scattered everywhere.

Simon Arpslot, the Plot, couldn't resist watching the dog eat the crab meat while slobbering inedible parts all over the floor; and when he was done, he claw tapped his way over to the corner next to the door to spin three times and plop with a deep felt sigh exactly where Crud Sr. (God rest his soul) always laid. The Plot looked at his Submariner Rolex and set the bezel. Sure enough, exactly nine minutes later Crud Jr. rolled his eyes at the Plot, cut the most silent ,deadly, and teeth staining fart imaginable. He lowered his lids and with what seemed to be sly grin on his lips, went to sleep. At least that part of the RANGE 19 complex had its measure of normalcy.

Then as if Plot's chagrin was transmitted telepathically halfway around the world the buzzer went of indicating an incoming secure satellite phone call. He rushed through the false pantry door and half ran downstairs to the control room and to his chair with a phone in the arm rest and picked it up demanding, "Which of you two miscreants is it?"

"It's me Plot.", Elmore said somewhat out of breath and then continued. "I can't talk long so I'll be brief. The insertion went fine.

We spent last night in a tribal village who's chief Haynes knows. He provided guards and passage to the edge of the Afghan border near Helmand province. Haynes gave him six Viagra pills which, with him being over 60 years old with five wives thrilled the shit out of him. When the next caravan comes along, we plan to join them by following along behind as travelers to Lashkar Gah, the provincial capital. We are traveling for the purpose of visiting my uncle Farid and his family and to attend his daughter Fareeza's wedding. We are poor and need to travel under the protection of the caravan and will pay a small fee for the priviledge. So far, so good. How copy, over?"

"Viagra? No money or weapons or anything else?", the Plot asked, amazed at their audacity, but amused at their understanding of what had value and where .

"Yup. Just six little blue pills and the chief lit up like a Christmas tree. The CIA found out about it first. As you know, money and weapons just get turned against us.", Elmore said, finally remembering he was on a telephone and radio procedures weren't necessary; even though it felt odd for him being in an isolated rocky wilderness.

"How's Sheila holding up?", the Plot asked.

"She's doing better than I thought she would. I think the jump generated self confidence in her that she didn't know she had. We've stuffed her burka with our key equipment so she looks like she's pregnant. The chief even threw in a donkey for her to ride based on her condition; and I can tell Haynes is either an active operative or under contract. The man knows his shit.", Elmore stated matter of factly, but with respect and appreciation in his voice.

"You don't think he'll be a problem for us do you?", the Plot asked.

"No. Absolutely not, just the opposite. I also believe he's taking advantage of the opportunity to develop sources in the region and to infiltrate the Taliban network while he is traveling with us. Two of our guards on the way to the edge of the chief's territory along the Afghan border are Taliban, and before long he gained their confidence and he was chatting them up like they were long lost brothers. Of course he listened a lot more than he talked. Good listener. They even offered to hook us up with a vehicle once we get to the main road across the border. It's apparently the historic entrance to the Kyber pass and even has an arch over it. There, our province chief's guide will meet with the Darah province chief to provide an escort the rest of the way. I didn't understand a word, but afterwards Haynes used some kind of key board to write up some traffic. Later he sent a coded burst through his own Sat phone; and when I asked about it he just said it was what put money into his retirement fund", Elmore chuckled.

"OK. If possible, give me a call at least once a day. You know I need to know what is going on so I can be prepared to act if need be. Take care, and good luck."

CHAPTER 36

IMMEDIATELY AFTER THE PLOT HUNG UP WITH Elmore the buzzer went off again, loudly. It was set that way so upstairs it was heard as a faint buzzing like a bumblebee's hum. This time it was Slaughter. His frustration mollified by the first call, the Plot picked up the phone and answered in a polite even tone, "How's it going, my friend?"

"I'll make it brief. I made contact with Grey using my cover as Brown's agent. I explained Brown's absence and delayed money transfer due to relocation problems stemming from his move to a different country and because of unforeseen difficulties with Brazilian and other national authorities. I explained that the conditions of living in his new country required him to transfer his available funds to their National Bank; this requirement was imposed by a bent government official before he could live as a resident. Apparently they have dead ones living there with money in their bank. Nazi holdovers who's money has been confiscated after their death.", Slaughter chuckled, then continued with, "I sweetened the bad news by telling Grey that as a gesture of good will to ensure continued cooperation by the Thai monarchy I was authorized to transfer $253,000 to Grey's account to cover the "no activity fee" coming due in a few days.

"Then I shifted to future activities and worked on his greed. I said

Brown would authorize payment of eight million dollars for a second and subsequent, comparable container shipment of his product from Pakistan to New York, paid on arrival. I added that Brown and I would handle all the transportation arrangements and make any required payments associated with the second shipment.

With this new deal on the table Grey and I are soon beer drinking buddies and he is relieved because now he can explain everything to the King without jeopardizing his relationship. After his third beer, he relaxed into a state of financial relief and opened up to me. He even told me all about his toy factories; one in Bangkok and another in Lashkar Gah where the opium is sealed in waxed and put inside the toys. About that time I decided to use my U.S. Marshal's credentials to inform the monarchy's intelligence chief that the DEA is looking for the toy factory in Bangkok, and that Mr. Grey is a person of interest in the matter.", Slaughter finished with a chuckle..

"Well that ought to get their attention. What about the loaded container ready for shipment to the West Coast., the Plot asked?

"When we hit Brown's mountaintop villa we found some active shipping documents and his rolodex. After a bit of research we confirmed the container number, GPS tracking, and loading and departure date from Karachi, Pakistan. We learned it would be off loaded at San Francisco on or about the middle of the month; which will be a week from now. Maybe you could pick up the ball and track the arrival if I give you the container number, GPS number, and some phone numbers for the shipping company.

You can play with the technical stuff, make an anonymous call using a throw away prepaid cell phone, use one of the new voice modulators to tell the DEA about the activity. If you keep it short and sweet and route the call through enough sites they won't be able to run a trace and you might even be able to make it look like the info originated overseas. What do you think?", Slaughter asked.

"Fax me the information and I'll sleep on it. Just `spit balling' here, but if we want to really nail Grey's ass, we could divert the shipment to Miami where we have contacts like Sheriff Baugh and he has contacts in all the local state and federal agencies there. ; The drug dealers on the West coast would be out for Brown and Grey's heads leaving us out of it; and the authorities would just assume Brown was setting a new breath holding record on the bottom of the Pacific because of the deal gone bad.", the Plot said the last comment as if he were thinking out loud. Slaughter was the only person he ever did that with, he thought. He imagined he was open with Slaughter because he owed his life to him and trusted him implicitly.

"Devious little runt; aren't you", chuckled Slaughter, " I like it. We still need to keep this one clean though, and make all calls anonymous. Hell, the way this one is playing the Thai monarchy's intelligence chief will probably feed him to the crocs before any drug trafficker could get to him anyway.", Slaughter laughed at the poetic justice of such an end, and then explained that to support the con, he had agreed to the transferring of $253,000 the following day. That way he could hold Grey in place pending arrival of the big money and allow him the opportunity to organize the second container shipment. Grey said it would take about a week to put the shipment together . This whole deal may just work out very well. Maybe Sheila, Elmore and Haynes can get into position to locate the sources in Afghanistan. Maybe they will be able to see the opium loaded at the toy factory, to see the toys coming out the other end for delivery to the container, and then we can all come home for a BBQ.", Slaughter suggested.

"Sounds too neat and easy. Don't forget that Sheila will still want to shadow the toys from Miami if we can arrange it without putting her in too much danger.", the Plot said.

"Yeah, I know, cradle to grave to Pulitzer. Shit. What a woman I've got. I'll have to go with her, and she's not going to like that.", Slaughter mused.

"You're right, we will have to cover her. You may have trail her as best you can, and maybe consider using Elmore and Dyke as well.", the Plot suggested. "I wish we had some more assets that she does not know, but if we are discreet, use good disguises, and plant a beacon on her we should be able to pull it off.

"Yeah, and maybe I'll ram a five cell flashlight up your ass so you can lead the way. I'll work something out. Goodbye runt.", Slaughter ended resignedly, hanging up without waiting for a reply. This bloody obsession for a Pulitzer was his biggest pain in the ass. He knew she'd never be happy until she got the damn thing. As far as he was concerned she was already a tremendous success as a journalist, especially after becoming syndicated and not working exclusively for Housekeeper magazine. She was a household name now and had a room full of awards including Journalist of the year for her coverage of the Bailey scandal , a case which was ultimately proven to have directly caused the deaths of over 47 US servicemen. Every death had been linked directly to Bailey's faulty microchip; a modified Nientendo microchip that aunt and nephew Brain proved to be unreliable.

Bailey banked a fortune, but somehow the guy came up missing. Today his hollow bleached skull resided at the Hootch in a soft leather bag in the possession of Lee An Too thanks to his uncle Doc Leigh. Doc had returned from Peru's jungle temporarily to train his nephew in several advanced techniques, and the skull was kept as a training aid. He used the skull to help teach Lee An Too how to deal with certain head injuries and severe pains when scraping a small hole in the top of the skull, a very tricky procedure, was the prescribed treatment. Of course Sheila confined her story to cover Bailey's greed and corrupt practices which resulted in the unconscionable deaths of at least 47 American servicemen who used equipment and munitions depending on the microchip's reliability. Journalist of the Year, he thought, should be enough. But, he sighed internally, it wasn't enough, and never would be.

CHAPTER 37

Two days after Tom Grey had been promised the $253,000 "no activity fee" money from Mr. Michaels, he was summoned to the King's palace without explanation. None was necessary. He knew the King wanted an accounting of the money, but when Grey called his bank in Brunei to have the money transferred, he learned his account had been frozen at the request of the Thai ambassador. Also, the drugs had somehow been loaded and were headed to Miami, Florida, not California. He had no idea how that happened, but he'd already been paid for his part in that smuggling operation, he had no control over a shipment once it was on the way. The only way it could come back to haunt him was if somebody figured out the money trail or the toy trail.

His toymakers in Lashkar Gah were well paid to glue the raw, waxed opium inside the dolls and wooden curios he shipped them from Thailand. All they had to do was pack stuff and shut up. He was confident of their discretion. But now he was faced with explaining to the King - - - something. He didn't have a clue what the King did or did not know.

"Good evening your highness. What service can I provide for you?", Grey bowed and asked innocently.

"You can tell me the truth for a change Mr. Grey. That might help.", the King said icily as he dismissed all his attendants except his two personal body guards. He usually kept key staff members present whenever he talked politics or money; but Grey knew immediately by their absence that he was in deep trouble.

"If this is about the fee Brown owes your highness, he still has one more day under the original agreement.", Grey began, trying feebly to gain some initiative.

"No!" the King interjected, silencing him. "That has nothing to do with why you are here; although my bankers keep me well informed about movement of funds. This concerns a container that left Pakistan yesterday morning full of toys filled with wax covered raw opium. Toys that originated at your little factory here, and traveled to Afghanistan. What can you tell me about that?", the King roared, the veins in his neck stood out as he leaned forward literally quivering with rage. Grey knew enough to remain silent, no reply was expected or would be accepted.

After a short silence the King regained his composure. He spoke again only this time he spoke in a rough whisper, as if his earlier speech had rendered him hoarse. In this whispering voice, so low that Grey and the bodyguards could barely hear them, "You imbecile. You dolt! Your stupid machinations have led international drug investigators to my door. You have cost me a great loss of face and opened my reign to scandal and base accusations. I am forced to clean up after your stupidity. I find my only alternative is to get rid of you." Expressionless and with a dismissive wave of his right hand, he rose and left the room to Grey and the two bowing bodyguards.

The King was replaced by his burly Chief of Staff. The stern Army Officer filling that position appeared immediately after the King's departure. He entered from a side door and stood just to the rear of a disbelieving Grey. Grey could not believe he had heard the King right. While standing frozen the Chief of Staff came up even with Grey and nodded at the two body guards.

The bodyguards sprang forward to grab Tom Grey by his arms and began dragging him out of the King's audience room and down the long deserted, and ominously silent hallway to a landing at the rear of the palace. They continued dragging a now struggling and crying Tom Grey down three levels of stairs into a large chamber dominated by a huge hole in the ceiling that let sunlight in to illuminate two pits, the larger with spring fed water flowing into it. The expressionless guards ignored Grey's screams begging for mercy, they would have ignored him even if they understood what he was saying as neither understood any language but Thai.

They drug the struggling but weakening man to the edge of the smaller pit. The one containing a number of banded kraits. Standing out to the man's sides they held his arms into a cross and then as if practiced, they smoothly kicked his feet out into the air over the pit and then dropped the fellow into the pit. His struggling and renewed screams only served to alert the snakes in the small pit. The screams echoed off the ceiling of the chamber and excited the other reptiles and crocodiles inhabiting the large pit, .

He fell initially into a vacant corner of the small pit where he could have been safe for a bit, but in his panic he tried to climb out only to fall into a cluster of the reptiles. Assuming they were under attack the venomous creatures bit him repeatedly, each bite injecting approximately .2-.3 milliliters of venom.

The venom is designed by nature to race through the blood stream to the brain, and with the number of bites he had taken there was enough venom in him to kill a herd of elephants. The venom is a neurotoxin that attacks the nervous system and paralyzes the victim. The victim is fully awake and while unable to help themselves, they feel their body die part by part, organ by organ. In seconds, too soon and too mercifully in the mind of the bodyguards, he died foaming at the mouth as all of his life support organs shut down. Shortly after he died, the body guards gaffed the corpse with long poles like the ones used by Marlin and shark fishermen. They drug the limp form across the floor to the large pit that housed a number of enormous crocodiles for final disposal a la Idi Amin style. The two men stayed to watch, faces impassive, to make sure the body was serviced properly. They watched as the beasts tore the corpse apart, dismembered the body and gobbled chunks of flesh torn from the limbs and torso. One smaller crocodile snatched the intestines and ran to a corner of the pit with them trailing behind like a grey rope. If the bodyguards had understood the match with the man's name and the color of his body they might have smiled at the irony. As it was they showed no expression, it was just their job to stay there till all traces were gone. The wait was not long as the savage beasts fought and chewed over the body as if they hadn't been fed for months. Ten minutes later they two men left to have lunch. Today, lunch was shrimp curry. They walked faster so they would get to the table before all the bigger shrimp were gone.

Few knew it, but the two bodyguards to the King of Thailand had volunteered to have their tongues surgically removed at an early age and then go through a rigorous steroid body building program and martial arts regimen to become personal bodyguards to the king. They endured these acts and programs, were deprived any education or the ability to read or write, for the sole purpose of protecting the King. Their reward was that their families were well cared for and they themselves were provided the finest food and drink available, their pick of women, girls or boys that could be provided. All carnal appetites that did not affect their ability to protect the King were satisfied. They just were kept in a state where they were unable to convey what they saw, heard, or did in the Kings service. Grey's disposition was just another job. They didn't care about the reasons, they were brought up in a brutal way and the disposal methods didn't affect them in the least.

Two days later, the local Bangkok paper announced the death of one Thomas Grey, financial advisor to the monarchy. The death was listed as due to natural causes. At the request of the family, who were not identified in the obituary, his remains were cremated and sent to his survivors for private interment. Obituary releases and other arrangements would be announced at a later date. His passing faded from memory and public record quickly, but the event did not go unnoticed by Slaughter. He knew an Army Intelligence Officer in the Defense Attache's Office at the US Embassy. He inquired unofficially and was able to confirm that all information reported concerning the demise of Mr. Tom Grey had originated with the monarchy and no one knew anything else. His property, money, and even the kaytoys the man had cavorted with in his villa, had been placed under monarchy control. Plus, no one knew anything about a tall farang man who dressed in a white shirt, Wrangler Jeans, and shiny black cowboy boots.

Slaughter called the Plot to bring him up to date as he was boarding an airplane for Miami. He would stay at the Sheraton on Miami Beach until Sheila and Elmore returned from Afghanistan; or until other requirements popped up.

Something always popped up, things always changed. Just like any plan after the first shot is fired, we are soon back into the fog of war, he mused. Slaughter had misgivings about the Plot's plan to alert authorities in Miami about the toy shipment of opium, regardless of his relationship with Sheriff Baugh. The contents of the shipment were integral ingredients to Sheila's "cradle to grave" article on the entire production and smuggling operation. She'd be pissed, but she'd just have to either get what she needed from the assembly site in Helmand province or include it as prose about Grey's participation. He would arrive in Miami before the container ship arrived so he could help Plot and the RANGE 19 crew stay out of the picture.

Sheriff Baugh received an anonymous letter about the ships arrival and the container number. He immediately called the Plot to fill him in on the letter's content and asking if he thought should make the bust himself or just feed the info to customs. The good Sheriff appreciated the information the boys at the Hootch provided from time, but he was no fool. He understood that they did so because it served their purposes. He also understood that these guys had resources and assets far beyond anything even the federal agencies in Miami could provide. In this case he intuitively thought the Plot was the author of the letter, this time he decided to probe a little and try to feel him out. The tips the Plot had provided in the past all panned out. He thought some other tips also originated with him or one of his team members; but he was not demanding in his efforts to feel the man out. He enjoyed arresting assholes, he enjoyed winning government grants for his department based on successful operations, and most of all, he enjoyed being reelected.

The Plot said he heard the Sheriff might be planning on retirement. When Sheriff Baugh admitted he might be thinking that way. The Plot told him he'd be a shoo-in for reelection if he and his deputies made the bust themselves. However, he told him that after the arrest, the DEA, FBI, CIA, and Customs would be all over him about the letter. They would demand to know about his informant even if it was a confidential informant. The Feds would want to gain that informant for themselves. So, he should try and find out quickly where the letter came from, so he could find an informant to satisfy them.

"I assume you've screened it for finger prints and only found your own, right?", the Plot asked and Sheriff Baugh replied, "Yeah. Lab boys did that first thing."

"Well then, why don't you start by going to a print plant where they know about type of lettering, ink, and printing. They may be able to help you determine whether or not you're looking for an old typewriter or a particular word processing and printer combination?", the Plot asked.

"Great idea Simon; and I think you're right about turning anything over to the other agencies. After all, it may just be a hoax, right? We don't want to look like we over reacted or are a bunch of country bumpkins who will fall for anything. I'll keep you up to date. Thanks again for your help.", he said and hung up wondering where he should start with the hundreds of printing companies listed in the Yellow pages.

As it turned out, he went alphabetical and AARDVAK Printing and Advertising was able to tell him the letter was not done by a typewriter. It was done by any computer that could use a word processing program; that it was printed on plain bond paper and probably by a Hewlett Packard Deskjet 4100 or other model Deskjet, However it could also be printed on another model printer sold in the thousands all over the world. The letter was virtually impossible to trace. Sheriff Baugh was as happy as a clam at high tide. Before he left he asked the printer if he had read what the letter said and the man said, "Yes. It was a note about the arrival of a container ship and had a container number.", he replied. Then sheriff Baugh asked him, "Do you remember the time and date of arrival and the container number?"

"Uh, no. I wasn't really paying attention to that. Why, should I have?", the man sheepishly asked.

"Well, if you had, I would have to make you a guest of the Dade Metro facilities for a couple of nights.", he said as he stared at the man's eyes sternly.

"No no no. I don't remember any times, dates, or numbers at all. I swear I don't", the man assured the intimidating law man with a nervous voice.

Sheriff Baugh chuckled and patted the nervous clerk on the shoulder reassuringly saying, "Doesn't matter son. I was just pulling your chain."

CHAPTER 38

ELMORE AND SHEILA FOLLOWED HAYNES IN A Land Rover driven by one of his Taliban buddies. Haynes was rode a moped stacked with his bundle of gear behind him. The vehicles had been provided by the Pushtun Chief Haynes knew, along with the Chief's permission slip allowing safe passage to Helmand province in Afghanistan. Translation, any Taliban warriors that mess with them did so at their peril from the Chief.

The trip was proving dirty, very dusty and tiresome . They were stopped frequently by groups of armed fighters that were either local tribesmen or Taliban scouts; and all of them demanded some sort of payment to be allowed to continue. Haynes seemed to know exactly how many rupees or cigarettes were required in each case, and it seemed to correlate to the number of individuals blocking the road. Again, Haynes somehow knew more than Elmore had expected and he was now convinced Haynes was a CIA agent operating under nonofficial cover. When they made the next pit stop, Elmore decided to feel him out about it by asking directly, "Fess up Haynes, are you a company man?"

Haynes laughed and said, "You know I'm just doing my little thing, even if I was you know I would not discuss it with somebody along side the road." The reply was ambiguous but good enough to satisfy Elmore

"Then why are you helping us?", Elmore asked, acting as if the reply had answered all his questions.

"Because your reporter friend is a good cover for me to get to where I need to go; and no, I don't know who you people are really working for either. You don't know it, but I left the same unit two years before you were assigned and I know how to keep my mouth shut. I expect you can too or you would not be doing this. I'm under contract for Homeland Security; a very healthy contract I might add. I've been in the area for over seven years now; mostly tax free.", he added and smiled.

Elmore nodded and after a second look at him, the dark skin might have been chemically helped, full beard with a streak of gray down each side he also noticed his eyes were very dark brown and he rubbed them a lot. He had to ask, "Contacts?"

Haynes nodded and said, "They are really hard to deal with considering all the dust flying around."

When they arrived in Lashkar Gah, the provincial capital of Helmand province, Haynes gave his Taliban buddy a wad of cash and he scurried off on the moped retracing his steps back the way they had come. He left them the Land Rover. Now Elmore turned to Haynes to be their interpreter in their search for the toy factory. Sheila had already obtained three digital photo cards of poppy fields in various stages of opium growth and harvest and had them safely taped away on her upper thighs. None of the locals seemed to mind when they stopped and walked into the fields to relieve themselves, especially since they were driving an expensive vehicle and the two men were carrying AK-47s. What wasn't visible was the 10 inch lettering "U.S.A" on the top of the vehicle. They hoped it was good enough to catch the eye of anyone monitoring a satellite down load or driving a missile armed Predator around looking for a likely target.

Inside the city Haynes seemed to be having trouble getting information. Either no one understood what he wanted or they just did not want to provide local information to strangers. No one he spoke to was able to help them find the toy factory. He kept being referred to the common market place which was, essentially, the mile long main street with vendors on both sides selling every kind of merchandise imaginable. He finally decided that the wealthiest and most powerful vendor would be one selling gold jewelry, and there were several. He decided to pick the oldest one, and after some chatter and chai, a purchase of a gold bauble and an exchange of three blue pills he finally came back smiling. The toy assembly plant was right behind them on the next street and the jeweler would walk them over for a visit.

Sheila walked far enough behind the men so that the noise of her hidden low light digital camera could not be heard. She had two cameras, each loaded with a 36 photo chip and placed in each hand behind a sheer layer of her black burka so she could walk by an object, slightly tilt the camera downward and see the image before she snapped the photo. She was careful to make a rehearsed comment to the woman making the toy just as she tripped the shutter. Most of the women making the toys were chattering loudly amongst themselves anyway, but she didn't want to take any chances.

The men stopped and Haynes was waving his arms in the air like he was disturbed by something the jeweler had said. She noticed that the men were at the end of the assembly line and two huge carpets were suspended from the ceiling to screen the operations underway beyond that point of the long room. Finally, Haynes explained that the jeweler would not allow Elmore or the woman to pass the carpets into the other area, and he wanted 5000 Afganis to escort Haynes for a brief visit. He would do it only for Haynes as he was Taliban. He wanted a fee for his service and was in a hurry as he would earn a healthy 'protection' fee for safely moving the latest collection of toys through Afghanistan and Pakistan to the port of Karachi for shipment. When Haynes explained this to Elmore and Sheila he could tell she was starting to get up tight, so he said, "I've got it covered. Don't sweat the small stuff.", as he showed her the end of a video 'pencil cam' in his sleeve. He saw her posture change with relief and she turned to walk outside with Elmore following.

The older man drew the carpets apart and held one aside to allow Haynes to enter. He actually seemed proud of the project and bragged a bit about how his operation was a holy one. It was a blessed action to send narcotics to poison and afflict the decadent non-believers and to weaken their souls and societies. Then he winked and added that it was not a bad thing for the local farmers to make a decent living again. Finally he smiled describing the toys and how well the opium was concealed "It is very good craftsmanship.

Showing keen interest and agreeing with the old guide who was also proving to be either the manager or owner Haynes asked nonchalantly, "How much raw opium can be put inside each doll or toy?"

"We have three sizes, as you may have noticed. The small ones carry one third of a kilo; the next larger contains two thirds of a kilo and the large ones contain a whole kilo. Each is then given a light coat of wax; all that is needed to keep the dogs away. We have our own dogs to test the shipment before loading.", the jeweler replied.

"And then how do you seal the two halves of the doll together?", Haynes asked.

"Superglue. Its American and we get it shipped in from Iran. I must get back to my shop now so you can select a suitable gift for your pregnant woman.", he said as two men with Kalashnikovs appeared in front of them. The jeweler gave them a cursory wave and put his arm around Haynes' shoulder as he spoke.

After they met Elmore and Shiela in the street, the jeweler led the way back to his shop. The gold shop looked more like a jail than any place of business. It had double steel gates that closed with a two inch solid metal bar that interlocked at the middle, and sported double modern padlocks at each end.

The shop owner noticed the looks Haynes and Elmore gave the

locks and laughed, "This may be country controlled by the Taliban, but thieves existed everywhere." The jeweler called out a name and soon a man wearing western dress but sporting a full beard appeared. The shop owner introduced him as Faraz, his oldest son. The man showed bad teeth and gave a slight bow to these important people commanding his father's attention.

"I have a magnificent selection of hand crafted necklaces to show you over here; very reasonably priced I might add.", the jeweler said as he led them further back into the room. And his wares were magnificent indeed; as were the prices Haynes found out. Jewelry in this part of the world is sold mostly by weight and little value goes with workmanship. A many of the items the old man displayed on a piece of blue velvet showed imagination and skill. Several were exquisite, old an of museum quality.

Haynes quietly asked Elmore if he had $500 in green U.S. dollars. When his chin went north and south he started to reach into his pocket but Haynes, shifted and reached to arrest his movement. Without looking at Elmore, Haynes leaned forward to the jeweler and whispered something in his ear.

The beaming face on the jeweler said it all. He was gratified that his esteemed customer was also a shrewd man who appreciated true beauty but demanded quality for his money. He was a man due respect for his culture and discernment, and the jeweler was making a nice profit for an hours time. He placed the bejeweled intricately worked gold necklace into a kid skin pouch and exchanged it for a sheaf of folded U.S. bills.

The group left with a light step. They had accomplished the hardest part of the mission, they were about to leave the region and Sheila was thrilled to her core thinking about the bejeweled gold necklace she would wear when they left Burka country!

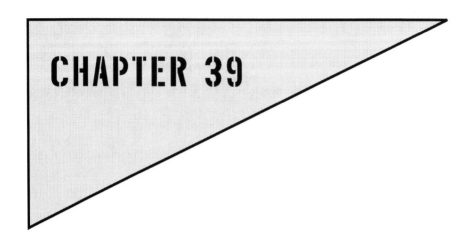

CHAPTER 39

HAYNES APPEARED AT THE LODGING SITE IN Lashkar Gah in two days just as he said he would, but he came with a through and through gunshot wound on his left side. The left side of his inner wrap around was saturated with dried blood, but it had not soaked through his outer sheepskin coat. Sheila immediately wanted to clean his wound and apply a sterile bandage but he refused saying, "I've already taken care of it, see.", as he pulled back his inner wrap to reveal clean white bandages front and rear.

"I'm won't ask what happened. We're ready to leave, will you be able to travel?", Elmore asked.

"Looking forward to it. By the way Sheila, here, I brought you something.", Haynes said smiling crookedly. It was one of the small dolls from the factory. She took it from him and asked, "Does it have opium in it?", she asked. He shook his head and handed her a small, marble sized ball of wax and said, "But this does. It's just an amount someone on the streets of America might buy from a dealer. If you don't want to carry it back with you, take a picture of it alongside a ruler or other known sized object like a pack of cigarettes."

She started to hug him, but looked down at his side and lightly kissed him on the side of his ear with a, "Thank you."

They didn't have much to collect, and while they were packing what they had Haynes hovered over his little keyboard tapping away for a few minutes. Then he adjusted the folding satellite antenna, listened a few seconds and then pushed the "send "button shooting his encrypted message via a "W" relay back to his handlers in the US in less than a second. He quickly folded everything up, tucked it away in his pack and said, "I'm ready. Let's go."

It didn't seem to take as long on the return drive to Islamabad. The Land Rover seemed more comfortable too. It seemed the roadblocks were only interested in traffic coming from the other direction, but cared little for those leaving.

Arriving in Islamabad, they got a hotel room where Elmore and Haynes had to wait over 30 minutes for Sheila to take a shower and wash her hair. While they waited, Elmore asked, "Did you have anything to do with all the fireworks at the high ground across the valley from Lashkar Gar?"

"Yup. Had some luck. I spotted the fat faced number two guy in the Taliban named Mahsud go into a cave and called a buddy of mine in the Air Force at Nellis who happened to be flying a Predator with a thermobaric, laser guided bomb in the area. I used my little laser designator to paint the entrance; and I hope it flew up his ass.", Haynes said grinning mirthlessly. Then, "I got a little too close to the cave to assess the damage and a patrol spotted me. That's when I took the hit. Lucky for me it was a shallow wound and did not even crack a rib. Come on. We need to get moving before the sun goes down."

After that, it was a scramble to dump excess gear that Elmore and Sheila would not need to take with them or that they could explain to customs. During the dumping project Haynes made reservations for their flight to Miami via Los Angeles. Haynes would move to another hotel as soon as they checked out. Once they were safely out of the country and he did not think he was under surveillance or any form of suspicion he would contact his case officer and conduct a debrief. After that, if his trail was cold he would move back into his safe house and let his wound heal. He had been lucky - - - again.

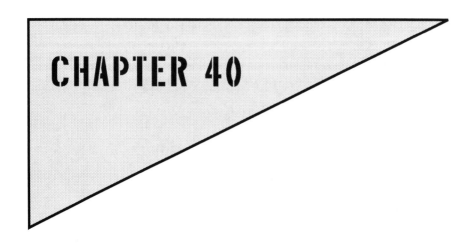

CHAPTER 40

ONCE ELMORE AND SHEILA WERE AIRBORNE ON their way to Los Angeles Elmore used the phone buried in the back of the seat in front of him to call the Plot and let him know they were on their way to Miami.

"Good. Everyone else is here except you two. Guido is staying on Grand Cayman and getting married to Brown's executive secretary, Tammy. They're starting up their own wealth management company which will handle some of the RANGE 19 assets. Now, is Sheila happy with what she got so far?", the Plot asked.

"Can't really tell. You want to talk to her?", he asked.

"Is she writing on her laptop?", the Plot asked.

"Yup. Fast and furious. Does that tell you anything?", Elmore chuckled.

"Yes it does. Let's leave her alone. By the way, Slats is here setting up ASE LLC Aviation. She's already going through the process of negotiating with Lear and Sikorsky for a G5 and YH-60; fully equipped with stuff I've never heard of. She's also got a line on some military ancillary equipment like anti missile warning, chaff, flares and a system called PROPHET that does all kinds of electronic eavesdropping and stuff. Aside from that, it will be an air charter business operating out of what was Homestead AFB.", the Plot excitedly told him.

"Brown's money? No, don't answer that. I think I know what's happening.", Elmore said.

"I kind of suspected you did. How about this guy Haynes? Do you think he knows who we are?", the Plot asked.

"No, but if he wanted to find out I don't think he'd have any problem. He came from the same place Slaughter and I did; he just left two years earlier. Right now he's got his hands full of Taliban. He's been working out of Islamabad for over seven years if that tells you anything.", Elmore said, then continued with, "I believe we should compensate him for helping us the way he did, and put him on our contact list."

"No compensation; he's making plenty of money. He used us as much as helped us according to my intelligence reports and satellite photos of a cave being blown up. But I agree we should keep track of him for anything in the future. If you don't have anything more I'm hanging up.", the Plot said, and after a silent pause he hung up.

Elmore was somewhat surprised at what the Plot knew; but just somewhat.

Sheila Hobgood, freelance reporter, adjusted the focus of her long lens camera as the DEA hauled out the boxes of toys and dolls from the shipping container they had raided based on Sheriff Baugh's anonymous tip. As they tore open the first box and took out a large carved monkey, she watched them pass it under the drug dog's nose without any reaction from the highly trained animal. After a few moments one of the younger DEA agents who was obviously frustrated and had the monkey in his hands smashed it on the ground; whereupon it split open like a ripe melon and one half had a sticky waxed package inside. Sheila zoomed in on it before all the agents surrounded it. She had what she wanted; and since she was in jeopardy of being caught with her camera in a place she shouldn't be, she scurried back to her car and left.

As excited as she was, she was tired.

All she wanted now was a candle light dinner with Slaughter in their little cabana at the Hootch; watch the sun go down with him, and then make love and sleep for two days. At that moment, she had decided to wind up her article, which had turned into a book, by just doing a little legwork with the Miami Dade County Sheriff's department on the opium's "end of the line", including hospitals as well as jails.

That night, Slaughter was surprised when she told him she'd had enough of the roughing it, and would first write an article for publication in newspapers and magazines, and then a book about it all. Over dinner he just kept smiling at her and agreeing with everything she said. He'd been here before and knew what was coming. A little praise of her toughing it out in a foreign land with no creature comforts would go a long way to helping her 'decompress'; which she did as soon as dinner was down. Her eyelids shut before she even left the table, so he undressed her and put her to bed. He grabbed a beer, called for Crud, and went outside to pet his dog and drink the beer.

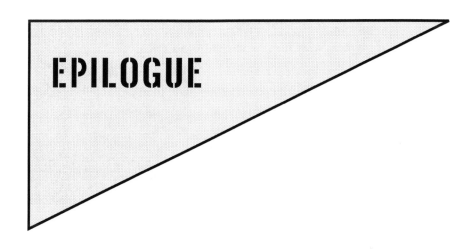

EPILOGUE

CHIEF JUSTICE NAGY WAS 78 YEARS OLD and, although appointed for life, he was ready to retire. He knew who would replace him and had gotten him to agree to keeping the RANGE 19 executive order active with "plausible deniability since they didn't need anything from him and they made their own money. Besides that, he had something for them to do about CEOs of large corporations who were moving their assets offshore as well as conducting price fixing and insider trading using high tech encryption through computer routers which the FBI couldn't seem to do anything about. He'd give this guy Arpslot a call next week.

Slats and Elmore married and moved into a sprawling bungalow near Homestead, FL where they managed ASE Aviation LLC to their convenience and still made money.

Guido and Tammy did the same thing on Grand Cayman island.

Farnsworth was treated for several weeks by Lee An Too. His buckshot wounds healed rapidly, and twice each day Lee An Too would waft the dried concoction of snake and spider venom powder over Farnsworth's nose and mouth while chanting "My name is Elvis. I am the king. Thank you --- very much!" When he was finally turned over to Sheriff Baugh he chanted it over and over. Sheriff Baugh asked the Plot, "What's wrong with him; where should I take him?"

"I'd recommend he be taken to court so the judge can see for himself he needs to be confined to a psychiatric facility for a long time. He's certainly in no condition to assist in his self defense.", the Plot said evenly with Lee An Too at his side nodding.

Crud the dog was now the spitting image of Crud Senior. And he had all the mannerisms and habits as well. Slaughter was reminded of his old friend every time Crud Jr. ballooned a huge fart that would clear any bowling alley in America.

While Dyke, Chico, Dobbin Brain, Slaughter, Sheila, and Crud Jr. were all out on the lanai having cold drinks and watching the sun go down the call came. The Plot came up and got her saying it's some newspaper guy. When she came back outside she ran to Slaughter and threw her arms around him hollering, "My article has been nominated!"

Her article didn't get the Pulitzer; but her book did.